The Cursed Witch

Thomas Ian Doyle

**LOUR
HOUSE**
PUBLISHING

ISBN: 978-1-7642170-0-2
Published by Lour House Publishing

Cover title typography and map design by Benjamin Brooker.
Cover design by the author.

A catalogue record for this
book is available from the
National Library of Australia

For Benjamin,
who asked me how spells were created

NALDY
The Cursed Witch
Thomas Ian Doyle

Book One

Chapter One

CURSES AND EGGSHELLS

The ear-piercing scream belonged to a wrinkled witch named Naldy. She wasn't usually wrinkled, as she was only eighteen, but her face often crinkled when angered.

'What have you just done?' she asked anxiously, meeting his piercing moss-green eyes with her hazel stare.

Although there was no sign that Oak's spell had any disastrous effect, she felt unnerved.

The first golden shafts of morning light rippled through Oak's branches, and a soft breeze fluttered around her black cloak. A small lizard scurried across the leaf-strewn ground. There didn't seem to be any change caused by his incantation.

'There will come a day,' said the oak tree in his drum-like voice, scratching his grey bark, 'when, if you ask me to give you this book, I shall do so gladly. But until that day, your ancestors have entrusted me with it. There is magic in this book that has been forgotten, Naldy, and some would argue it should remain forgotten.'

Naldy searched the clearing for her broomstick, impatiently flicking her long black hair away from her angular face. She found it lying on the forest floor a few metres away. She picked up the old broom and turned her back on the tree.

Oak—the only talking tree Naldy knew of—stood curiously in a small clearing in the pine forest, as if the non-speaking trees were afraid to grow too close to him. He lifted an arm-like bough, holding the red book in his finger-like twigs, far out of Naldy's reach.

'If you won't help me, Oak,' she said, half under her breath, 'then I will deal with this carpet-flying intruder myself.'

Naldy's mother had once told her the tree had the ability to perform magic, but she had never seen him cast a spell in all the years she had known him. She was glad his reading from her family's spellbook hadn't produced any result.

'I have threatened this young man with *Prosterno* spells,' she continued, 'but even they do not deter him. He arrives on that flying carpet every morning, sketching with his feather quill from the pine trees. I'll fly home and come back with an axe—then you'll give me the spell I need.'

Naldy leapt onto the broom, but instead of rising as she'd expected, she fell to the ground with an unpleasant thump. She lifted her head, leaves sticking to her black cloak.

'If you are to one day possess this book,' remarked Oak, raising a mossy eyebrow, 'you will need to learn a few lessons first.'

'What lessons are you talking about?' asked Naldy, gingerly lifting herself from the ground to slowly face him.

'You've been on your own for too long, Naldy,' said Oak tenderly.

She felt tears catching on her bottom eyelids. The tree was right; she had been on her own for almost six years. Naldy had been twelve the day she woke to find her parents gone. There had been no note or explanation, and since that day, she had been alone at the Witch House with nothing but her cat Smookers for company. She only made a few irregular excursions to see the old tree—mainly in hopes of collecting a new spell for her repertoire. The tree had sworn he didn't know where her parents had gone, but Naldy had never truly believed him, always suspecting Oak knew more than he let on.

'There is only one way to undo the curse,' said Oak.

'I am not a child,' said Naldy. 'I don't need to be parented by you. You can keep your lessons to yourself. Wait... did you say curse?'

'When you learn to truly care about others,' he said calmly, 'the curse will be broken.'

'Curse,' repeated Naldy, laughing coldly. 'Such things don't exist.'

'Oh, they do! There are spells, Naldy, that are beyond your knowledge. Now, listen carefully. You can only perform magic when the sun disappears. The curse will break when you learn to truly care for others, but until then, you will not be able to cast magic during daylight.'

'I'll show you magic.' Sneering at the tree, Naldy raised both palms. '*Comburite.*'

Naldy expected a ball of roaring fire, but not even a spark emerged. The oak tree blinked, unperturbed.

'Undo it,' whispered Naldy, barely audible.

'I cannot,' replied the tree.

'Cannot?'

'As I have already mentioned, you must be the one to break the curse, Naldy.'

'I already care about things: the Witch House, Smookers, and finding my parents...'

Naldy hesitated. She couldn't think of any more examples on the spot.

'It is a curse, and I cannot reverse it,' said the tree, unmoved by her list. 'Spells cannot break curses. The cursed one must be the one to break it.'

'You're lying,' said Naldy, lifting a leg over her broomstick. 'These curses are nothing but children's tales. I'll fly home and return with an axe—mark my words. Then you'll undo it. How does that sound?'

Naldy jumped high into the air, bending her knees. To her surprise, gravity pulled her back to the ground, and she ended up with a mouthful of dirt.

The tree let a small laugh escape before trying to conceal his amusement.

'You find this funny, do you? How am I meant to get home, Oak?'

'The sun is up,' he said, regaining his composure and scanning the blue sky. 'It's a fine morning for a walk.'

The tree's eyes fell shut, and he could have been

mistaken for an ordinary tree if it weren't for his snoring. Naldy refused to believe she was cursed. She picked up her broomstick and marched away.

As Naldy navigated the dense thicket of the pine forest, she convinced herself she could produce magic if she put some distance between herself and the oak tree. She thought perhaps he had cast an enchantment similar to those used in prisons, which prevented magical folk from accessing their power while locked away.

'Nonsense,' muttered Naldy to herself as nearby birds chirped loudly. 'Not produce magic until the sun sets? I just need to get far enough away.'

Naldy stopped, realising she had no idea which direction she was going. She had always been accustomed to flying over the tops of the Kirkwood Forest's trees, and everything looked the same amongst their tall, grey-brown trunks.

As she spun to get her bearings, something heavy unexpectedly collided with her, sending her to the ground once more. Naldy leapt to her feet, palms outstretched, scanning the forest for whatever had knocked her down. A large bundle of thick blue fabric lay nearby—something was moving beneath it.

'Come out!' demanded Naldy, raising her body to her full height. 'I'll set you on fire if you don't.'

'I'm trying to come out,' squeaked a man's voice. A strawberry-blonde-haired man, similar in age to Naldy, eventually emerged from beneath the bundle. Naldy recognised the blue fabric he had been trapped under—a familiar magical carpet.

'You,' said Naldy in a strained voice. She immediately identified his annoyingly handsome face, though she had never seen him up this close. 'Yes, I know you. Are you following me? Tell me quickly, or I'll set you on fire.'

'You can't,' replied the pale-faced man, smugly folding his carpet. 'You've been cursed.'

He casually stuffed the blue material into his cloak pocket. Naldy noticed it was the same colour as his glimmering eyes. She assumed it must be enchanted so it could be neatly tucked away.

'You can't use magic,' repeated the man. 'I heard what the old tree said.'

'Shouldn't you be at the Witch House,' said Naldy sourly, 'sketching the turrets. Why have you followed me here?'

'Sketching?' he said, bemused.

'You'll leave me and the Witch House alone,' she said sternly. 'I know you have been drawing my house in your little book—don't deny it because I've seen you. I'll be going now, and I don't want to ever see you again.'

'I wasn't sketching that old building of yours.'

'What have you been doing then? Hiding amongst the trees and always bent over that sketchbook? Are you a witch or wizard? What are you?'

'I'm a scholar.'

'Books?'

The man straightened his green cloak proudly.

'The name is Ralph. Nice to meet you,' said the man, stretching out a hand. Naldy briefly glanced at it but decided to ignore it.

'What sort of scholar are you?' she asked, displeased to see the smile return to his face.

'I study witches.'

'Witchcraft?'

'Not witchcraft, no. I don't have any magical abilities myself. But I study witches.'

He appeared overly excited to be newly acquainted with one—even if Naldy was a witch unable to perform magic at present. The thought crossed her mind that maybe the man had deliberately crashed into her.

'I don't want you writing about me,' she said sharply. 'Is that why you've been following me?'

'No,' replied Ralph, his voice cracking.

'I don't want you walking with me either. Shoo! Go the other way.'

'But I'm going this way, too.'

'Do you know why I was visiting Oak?'

'You wanted a blood-freezing spell.'

'To be rid of you,' said Naldy casually. 'I'd like never to see you again. Is that clear?'

'It's intriguing. I've never seen a blood-freezing spell. I've seen *Prosterno* spells—the ones you sent flying at me, and I've heard they can knock you unconscious. But I've not heard of blood-freezing ones. What exactly do they do?'

Naldy responded through gritted teeth, 'It... freezes... your... blood.'

'I'd like to see that. It sounds frightfully modern.'

'It's an old spell. I glimpsed it in Oak's spellbook'—Naldy coughed before correcting herself—'in *my* spellbook. Give me your carpet.'

'What? No.'

'Give it to me. We should be far enough from Oak's enchantment, and I'll mend it for you so you can be on your way.'

'But,' he said sceptically, 'you can't do magic during the daytime. The curse.'

'Oak is a tree. I wouldn't believe everything trees tell you,' said Naldy, impatiently holding her hand out. 'Enchantments only work if you are within their field, or on objects like your carpet. It's a small tear. I should be able to mend it for you, and then you can fly away.'

Ralph excitedly retrieved the carpet from his cloak pocket, where he had stuffed it. He passed it to her, and Naldy shook the carpet, unravelling it. The gorgeous blue hue of the fabric was mesmerising. She laid it on the forest floor and held a palm over the ripped corner.

'You're a collector of magical items, are you?'

'A little.'

'I'll make you a deal,' said Naldy, a smirk on her lips. 'I'll fix your travelling carpet. But you have to promise to leave me alone. I don't want to be mentioned in your scribblings or sketches. And... I don't ever want to see you again.'

'And if you can't fix it?' questioned Ralph. 'Can I walk with you to the nearest town?'

'I'm a witch,' said Naldy, glaring at him. 'Of course I can fix it. Stand aside.'

Ralph eagerly settled underneath the nearest tree. Naldy rolled back the sleeves of her long black cloak. Then, she muttered a spell under her breath while moving her palms expertly through the air. Ralph watched with enthusiasm.

'You're putting me off, staring at me like that. Turn around.'

Ralph reluctantly obeyed, swivelling to face the tree's trunk. Naldy tried the spell again, this time focusing even harder. '*Restituo!*'

But still, nothing happened.

'How extraordinary! Curses do exist,' remarked Ralph, twisting to face her, his eyes wide in wonderment.

To add to Naldy's irritation, he pulled a small leather book and quill from his cloak pocket and set about scrawling fervently.

'You better put that book away.'

'It's an easy curse to break,' said Ralph, reluctantly returning the book and quill to his pocket. 'The oak tree said that to break it, all you must do is care for others.'

'How do I know your rug even flies?' questioned Naldy. 'You could have simply jumped out at me from a tree.'

'I didn't. I snagged it on a branch. Besides, you've seen it fly before when I dodged your *Prosterno* spells. The nearest town is this way.'

Ralph sauntered through the pines, and Naldy

hurried to keep up with him, conceding that she'd have better luck finding the town with Ralph's guidance.

The sun was high in the sky when they reached Greenswood. To Naldy, the many towns scattered throughout the Kirkwood Forest all seemed alike —quaint, quiet, cute, and charming—radiating a cheerfulness that she detested. She preferred the solitary life on the edge of the forest.

'Well,' she said, stopping on the cobblestone road, 'I've let you walk with me, as promised, and I expect you to leave me alone henceforth. If you don't, I'll make certain you regret it.'

'Shall we find a dwelling to rest our feet?' asked Ralph, happily walking down the road. 'If you buy me a drink, maybe your curse will break.'

Naldy grudgingly admitted to herself that Ralph's plan might just be a good one and went with him to the town's dwelling called *Spitswater.* The dwellingtend, a robust, broad-shouldered woman, informed them several times that the brews bubbling in the nearby cauldrons were concocted locally. Although the brews were appealing, they decided on a pint of cold apple cider each to refresh themselves after their long walk. Naldy resentfully paid.

'Take a seat,' said the dwellingtend, 'and I'll bring it over to yer.'

They settled at a grubby table by the window. Its dusty glass overlooked the town's prized landmark: a large town square where a few townspeople were busy erecting impressive, colourful pavilion tents.

'I appreciate today,' said Ralph as they waited.

'What do you appreciate?'

'You, letting me observe you.'

Naldy turned to the window, trying to stifle another argument with Ralph. She hadn't wanted to walk with him—she had wanted to fly home on her broomstick. She bit her tongue, hoping her kindness might break Oak's curse.

'Are ya 'ere fer the town fair?' asked the large dwellingtend, cheerily delivering their honey-coloured cider.

'The what?' asked Naldy agitatedly.

'It's our annual town fair,' repeated the dwellingtend, pointing a chubby finger at the window. 'Comes once a year—our busiest time 'ere at the dwelling. It's a wonderful experience.'

Naldy returned a weak smile, but she noticed Ralph beaming.

Within a couple of hours, the town square and dwelling were crowded with visitors. Naldy was still unable to perform the simplest of spells, so she decided it was best to accompany Ralph outside to the main festivities, hoping this gesture would sufficiently demonstrate her selflessness.

'It's bustling,' said Naldy as they squeezed between the throng. 'I'll be glad when I'm back on the edge of Kirkwood, back inside the quiet of the Witch House.'

'Oh, look!' cried Ralph, pointing at a small stage where a dozen musicians were making themselves comfortable. They tuned their musical contraptions made from rough, welded metal that caught the afternoon sun. Some instruments were larger than the musicians themselves.

'What are they waiting for?' asked Naldy, staring at the entertainers. Her question was soon answered when a spindly man of about forty made his way onto the stage. He had greased-back black hair and pasty skin, and he carried a black cane to match his long cloak—an accessory he didn't use for support.

The crowd erupted into applause, and after a moment of ear-splitting acclamation, the man raised a long finger to silence them.

'It is a great pleasure to be here again,' he said loudly. 'I see many familiar faces, but also a few new ones. We welcome you to our lovely little town. Welcome to Greenswood!'

The onlookers whistled and cheered, and the man patiently scanned the crowd with his dark eyes until they settled.

'For those who I have not had the pleasure of meeting, my name is Maverick Gadswell, and I am the proud mayor of Greenswood.'

A few more pattering claps broke out.

'Thank you, yes, thank you. I am also the mayor of Valingfield, Gatengar and Merrydale, and I am on the board of the Bleckdale Witchery Museum'— he paused as more pockets of cheering erupted at the mention of each town—'but today, citizens and visitors of Greenswood, we gather here for the annual celebration of this great town. The

Establishment has asked me to pass on its good wishes from The Great City. Now, let us not keep you waiting any longer. I wish you all happiness in your celebrations and declare the Greenswood Town Fair officially open!'

The band started playing, and the metal instruments clanged and dinged with jolliness, making Naldy's stomach queasy. She wasn't sure how much more of this selflessness she could endure. The townspeople nearby began bopping along gaily, while others dispersed to explore the insides of the many colourful pavilions.

Ralph led Naldy inside the nearest tent. She was surprised to see many magical items for sale: the latest woollen elven knits, enchanted dust, and various crystals promising to bring their owners different blessings depending on the type.

'Did you buy your carpet from one of these stalls?' asked Naldy, picking up a jar filled with something slimy and glittery.

Ralph beckoned Naldy over to a table with little jumping rocks.

'Oh, aren't these fun,' said Ralph, beaming.

Naldy was horrified to see so many magical items for sale, yet none of the merchants appeared to be witches or wizards. She could tell, as the stallkeepers had to rely on step ladders to reach the higher shelves and hurried about their tents to assist patrons without the aid of magic.

'It's perverse,' she said, selecting one of the jumping rocks. It tried to bounce out of her hand.

'Oh, come on,' said Ralph, taking the rock from her and placing it back with the others. 'It's for people to enjoy. A little bit of fun.'

'Fun?' repeated Naldy, offended. 'Have you not heard of The Great Witch Hunt?'

'That was a long time ago, Naldy—well before we were born.'

'Townsfolk were the ones who burnt our spellbooks! They've limited our magic, and now look —they're profiting from it.'

'Things have changed since then,' he said as they exited the tent. They strolled through the fair, the afternoon sun casting a lazy yellow glow over the festivities. Naldy's magic would return soon. Ralph smiled as he continued, 'A witch has not been burnt for centuries, and just because townspeople can't perform magic doesn't mean they should be excluded from all its wonderful uses.'

'I don't see any other witch here,' said Naldy. She'd had enough of tolerating Ralph's company and wished her magic were restored so she could hex him. Tears threatened to spill from her eyes. Pushing past a small group, she ducked into the quietest tent, not wanting Ralph to see her emotions.

'Naldy?' called Ralph, going after her. 'Come back. I didn't mean to offend you.'

The inside of the pavilion tent was much smaller and shabbier than the others. No one else was inside, not even a shop assistant. The shelves were strangely bare, except for one wooden stand in the centre bearing four large, grey, ceramic-looking eggs.

'I'm sorry, Naldy,' said Ralph. 'I shouldn't have been so insensitive. It seems I still have much to learn about witches.'

'The effects of The Great Witch Hunt are still felt today,' replied Naldy. 'Some townspeople still treat us like outcasts—using our magic for entertainment but pushing us to the fringes.'

'I thought you enjoyed living on the edge of the forest?'

'I do,' said Naldy, picking up one of the large eggs. 'It's just difficult knowing we used to have many more spells and greater influence before The Great Witch Hunt. These are surprisingly light.'

'Careful, they're expensive,' said Ralph, pointing to a hand-scribbled sign indicating each egg cost two thousand currents.

'They're overpriced,' said Naldy, passing the egg to Ralph.

'Not if they're real,' he replied.

'Real?'

Ralph pointed to the sign again, where black ink read: *Dragon Eggs.*

'They can't be real,' said Naldy. 'Dragons are extinct, and all that's left of them are their bones in museums.'

'Oh,' said a shabby elderly woman, appearing through a slit in the pavilion tent. Her face was heavily lined and weathered. 'That would be a great shame if they were all extinct. Would you like to buy one, my dears?'

'Oh, no, thank you,' said Ralph, passing Naldy the large egg. 'We are just browsing.'

Ralph scanned the empty shelves, unable to find anything else to focus on.

'That egg you are holding,' said the old stallkeeper. 'It is real.'

'It's too light to be real,' said Naldy, setting the egg back on its shelf. The woman tottered over to the stand and picked up the egg.

'Come here. Have a feel of the shell. That's not ceramic, no. You can tell a real dragon egg by its rough texture.'

'It feels empty to me,' said Naldy, as the woman forced the egg into her hands.

'They are not empty,' said the old woman, running her wrinkled hand delicately over the egg's coarse shell, as if she were petting it. 'But you are quite right. There is no dragon inside. That is why the price is so low.'

'Low,' repeated Naldy, chortling.

'I should hope there is no dragon inside,' said Ralph with a strained laugh. 'Imagine! Living dragons!'

'Unborn dragons can survive inside their eggs for thousands of years,' croaked the woman. 'All they require is their mother dragon for incubation to encourage the hatching.'

Naldy moved to put the egg back on its shelf, but the older woman firmly reached out and clasped Naldy's hands around the cold shell.

'These eggs once had baby dragons inside,' continued the stallkeeper tensely, tears welling as she spoke. 'But something else is inside them now.'

'What's inside them?' asked Ralph curiously.

'Each egg has a message,' said the woman. 'The unborn dragons have been transformed into little scrolls. The scroll's message is for the one who cracks the egg. Powerful magic.'

The older woman glanced around nervously, as though afraid someone might overhear.

'Expensive magic,' said Naldy, staring at the woman in disbelief. She tried to wriggle free, but the stallkeeper tightened her grip on Naldy's hands, desperation etched across her face.

'They are real eggs,' said the woman. 'You must believe me. I have come all the way from the Edengar Mountains. Please, you must believe me.'

'Thank you, but we don't want any dragon eggs,' said Ralph, reaching to take the egg from between their hands. 'Whether they contain dragons, scrolls, or just air.'

The stallkeeper let go, as did Naldy, and the egg fell towards the cobblestone floor.

Crack!

—Chapter Two—

THIEVES AND FORTUNES

'Thieves!'

Naldy ruthlessly forced a path through the flabbergasted crowd as the shabby older woman's shrieks echoed across the town square. Ralph was close behind her.

'You wanted to hex her,' said Ralph crossly. 'You could have tried to mend her dragon egg instead.'

It was true that when the egg had smashed on the cobblestones, Naldy had instinctively raised her palms and tried to stun the stallkeeper with a *Prosterno* spell. She had hoped that her efforts to show kindness to Ralph—by tolerating his company—would have broken the curse. But the old woman had remained in control of her movements, and with the sun not yet fully set, they'd had no choice but to dart out of the tent.

'The thieves,' cried the stallkeeper's voice in the distance.

They stopped to catch their breath. All around, townsfolk stared with suspicion.

'We're not thieves,' said Naldy firmly to Ralph. 'We didn't steal anything, and it was the stallkeeper's fault the egg slipped from my fingers and smashed.'

Ralph sheepishly removed a little curled scroll from his cloak pocket. She noticed the parchment was embossed with a decorative pattern of baby dragons.

'You pinched her scroll!' exclaimed Naldy in outrage.

'The secret message is for the one who cracked the egg. I believe it may have been my fault the egg cracked, so the message inside is for me. It's just a bit of paper. You tried to stun her!'

'Thieves!' cried the woman, her voice getting closer.

'Yes, but you didn't pay for it,' said Naldy, glancing around for somewhere to hide. 'Quickly, we'd better take cover in one of these tents. Everybody keeps staring at us.'

They entered the nearest red and black tent. Over its entrance, a tattered sign read: *Enter One Who Seeks Answers.*

Once inside, they could no longer hear the bustling crowd. It was eerily quiet.

'We should be safe in here,' she said, glancing around the tent. The interior was heavily decorated with red and black fabric drapes hanging from ceiling to floor.

'Should we follow it?' asked Ralph, gesturing at a gap in the fabric where a maze-like path led to the depths of the pavilion tent.

'I don't know,' said Naldy, but Ralph ignored her

and had already begun snaking his way through the maze.

The only light came from a few dimly lit candles along the way. Their metal candle holders were attached to the fabric, but surprisingly, their flames didn't set it alight. The air was thick with the smell of thyme and rosemary.

'It's much larger in here than it looks,' said Ralph.

The path led them to an intimate room where the same fabric covered the walls and floor. In the centre stood a low wooden table positioned close to the ground, atop which rested a large glass ball.

'I am a predictor of fortunes,' announced an eccentric middle-aged woman from the corner of the room. She was dressed in jet black and almost blended in with the draping fabric.

'We didn't mean to intrude,' said Ralph as the woman approached.

'Take a seat,' responded the frizzy-haired woman. Her big brown eyes flickered towards the low table. 'The session is now in progress.'

She roamed the room, lighting more candles, though their blue flames added little light to the small space.

'We're not here to—'

'Sit down! You have entered because you seek answers, and answers you shall receive.'

They sat on the uncomfortable, drab cushions strewn across the floor around the table.

'Don't worry,' said the woman, sitting opposite them. 'There is nothing to be frightened of here.

Now put your hands on the table, please.'

Ralph and Naldy glanced at each other before doing as instructed.

'Not you, boy. Her, please.'

'Me?' said Naldy, removing her hands from the table. 'I think Ralph would rather…'

The woman mumbled something inaudible before smiling airily. 'Keep your hands still, and close those eyes of yours.'

Naldy shut them reluctantly.

'My name is Diamone, and I'd like to welcome you. Could you please keep your hands still, sir? Or I will not hesitate to have you shown out.'

Naldy lifted her eyelid slightly and saw Ralph drumming his fingers on his leg.

'Keep them shut. I am not obligated to make any predictions. You will still be charged should nothing come to the glass ball. Crystal clear?'

Naldy and Ralph nodded.

'Open your eyes, yes-yes-yes, and put twenty currents onto the table. Please.'

'Twenty currents!' repeated Naldy, astounded.

Ralph cleared his throat, reminding Naldy that twenty currents were inexpensive compared to the two thousand current cracked egg. She begrudgingly reached into her pocket, retrieved a flat silver twenty current coin, and slid it across the table.

'Look into the glass ball,' continued Diamone, pocketing the coin.

'I don't see anything except my reflection in the

glass.'

'No speaking. Only peering. Peer deep into the soul of the crystal.'

Naldy didn't believe in the art of fortune-telling and thought they were wasting their time waiting for Diamone to conjure some silly predictions. Still, she knew they were far better off remaining inside the pavilion tent than outside.

'Do you see anything?' asked Ralph impatiently, leaning over Naldy to try and glimpse into the ball himself.

'Sure,' said Naldy flatly. 'My reflection.'

'Twenty currents for this codswallop,' groaned Ralph crankily.

'Smoke,' said Naldy, as the glass ball began to cloud over. 'I can see smoke.'

'A fire that will change the course of history,' said Diamone, flourishing a hand dramatically. 'It will destroy something great.'

'Nonsense, there is no fire,' said Naldy, suddenly irritated by the fortune teller. 'I don't see any fire. All I see is smoke.'

Naldy lifted her head and saw dancing flames reflected in the woman's watery brown eyes.

'A tree will burn.'

'You can stop it now,' insisted Naldy. 'We don't want any more of your fortunes. We just need a place to hide for a few minutes.'

'Is it an oak tree?' asked Ralph curiously.

'An oak tree, yes, boy. It is an oak tree.'

'She's making it up,' said Naldy.

'I can almost see when—'

'*Suffoco!*' cried Naldy, raising her palms.

Diamone was lifted from her floor cushion as if an invisible hook had hoisted her towards the ceiling.

'You made it up, admit it,' demanded Naldy testily, raising Diamone higher.

'Naldy, stop!' shouted Ralph. 'She can't talk!'

'I need to know if she is telling the truth, Ralph.'

'I saw a large oak tree,'—but it was not Diamone speaking. Diamone was still floating near the ceiling, desperately trying to get air. It was Ralph's voice that had spoken.

Naldy dropped her palms in shock, and Diamone plunged to the floor with a heavy thud, gasping for breath and clutching her throat.

'An oak tree will burn,' said Ralph monotonously. His eyes had changed from their brilliant blue to a faded grey. 'One of the last defences will fall.'

'Ralph?' called Naldy, trying to snap him out of his trance.

'It has begun,' he said flatly. 'The race to keep magic alive starts now. You must not delay. You must stand in the way of its destruction, or all will suffer. Only you can save magic.'

Ralph's eyes snapped back to their original blue.

'What was all that about?' asked Naldy, but the pavilion tent around them collapsed before Ralph could answer. The roof tore down the middle, and yards of red and black fabric fluttered around them as the material crumpled softly to the ground. The three of them were left standing, surrounded by mounds of cloth. Townsfolk peered at them from all sides. Someone had brought the tent to the ground.

'Diamone,' said a smooth voice. The mayor of Greenswood leant casually on his ornate black cane. 'I expected more of you. Harbouring these criminals.'

The scandalised crowd whispered amongst themselves. Diamone was still on the floor, trying to catch her breath.

'Yes, that's them,' said the wrinkled stallkeeper, whose egg they had smashed.

Naldy momentarily forgot she could perform magic. Before she could raise her palms, the mayor tapped his cane. Two green lights shot out—one colliding with Naldy and the other with Ralph—binding their hands to their sides.

'There'll be no running,' said Maverick, smiling. 'I'll have your feet bound too if you attempt it.'

'You're a wizard?' remarked Naldy, focusing on the black cane.

Ralph flinched as the mayor stepped closer. Naldy had seen that same panicked stare from townsfolk before at the mention of a wizard. Unlike witches, who inherited their magic at birth from a parent who was also a witch, wizards were unique. They were born without any magical abilities, starting out as simple townsfolk. A wizard learnt to wield a magically charged object, like the mayor's cane, which required immense skill and training. They were rare to come by.

Maverick turned to face the crowd, who were eagerly enjoying the drama.

'Let us not allow these thieves to ruin our evening. We do not tolerate criminals here. Take them to the birdcages!'

The crowd applauded as Naldy felt a hand take hold of her arm from behind.

'Greenswood is a safe place once again,' declared the mayor, lifting his cane into the air. 'Come now, let us continue our enjoyment of the festivities! There is still much fun to be had.'

The band launched into their jolliest tune yet.

Less than an hour later, Naldy found herself sitting in a human-sized iron birdcage. It hung from an enormous tree with huge, twisted branches.

Above and to her left, Ralph stood in his own square-shaped prison, pointlessly shaking the iron bars and causing it to sway slightly.

'It's not going to open for you,' sighed Naldy heavily.

They weren't the only ones locked up. About a dozen birdcages, all of varying sizes and shapes, were suspended from the tree's branches. Each one was occupied by a prisoner.

'Try magic again,' said Ralph, calling down to her. 'It's night-time, and it should be working.'

'It won't,' said a man with a thin, rugged face—he could have been a crossbreed between a goblin and a man. He had called up from a cage slightly below Naldy's. 'If he keeps going on like that, he'll wake up the wood fairy.'

'Ralph,' called Naldy in a low voice. 'Ralph, stop it! There's a wood fairy in one of the cages.'

'Oh heavens,' said Ralph, ceasing to rattle on the bars of his cage. 'There must be a spell you can think of. I can't be trapped for eternity in the company of a fairy.'

'It's useless,' said the thin-faced man. He was dressed in shapeless, brown, moth-eaten overalls. 'The cages are enchanted. You'll only be able to perform magic on the outside, and let me tell you this: none of us will ever be on the outside again.'

'You mean they really do leave us here forever?' asked Ralph, slumping to the floor of his cage. He leant his head back, a forlorn expression on his face as he stared up at the twinkling stars.

'My name's Bargen,' said the rugged man in his brassy voice. He smiled, exposing his rotting teeth. 'You'll have plenty of time to get to know everyone here when the sun rises—but the others like a routine, so quiet down.'

'It's cold,' said Ralph, pulling out his blue carpet from his pocket and wrapping it around himself.

Naldy surveyed the other enclosures. All the occupants were curled up and sleeping soundly. Most of them appeared to be townsfolk, apart from Bargen and the fairy. Each sleeping prisoner had a dishevelled and weary appearance, weathered from exposure to the elements.

'Ralph?' whispered Naldy, holding the cage bars.

'Hmm?'

'Do you think Diamone's prediction was

accurate? I mean about magic being threatened. I have an awful feeling it will come true.'

'I wouldn't worry about it. She seemed as mad as they make them.'

'She might have been talking about my family's spellbook being destroyed. Oak always said it contained ancient magic.'

'Trees are lonely creatures,' said Ralph, yawning. 'They'll say anything to convince you to return to them, and they crave company.'

'What is that supposed to mean?'

'Ancient magic doesn't exist anymore,' said Ralph sleepily. 'All the great spellbooks perished during The Great Witch Hunt. And Naldy, magic isn't at risk of being destroyed—so don't worry.'

'Keep it down, you two,' grumbled Bargen.

The two said no more, and Naldy tried to find a comfortable sleeping position. Her mind was racing. Was her family's spellbook at risk of being destroyed? Was she the only person who could save it?

Diamone's words echoed in her mind: *Only you can save magic.* But save it from what?

Chapter Three

THE CAGED CHOIR

Naldy awoke to the smell of warm gruel. She'd hoped it had all been a bad dream, wanting desperately to find herself in her comfortable bed in the Witch House. But instead, there was a bowl of gluggy oats beside her face.

A few rays of the early morning sun cast stripy shadows through the bars of her iron birdcage.

'You should eat it while it's hot,' said Bargen, tucking eagerly into his own gruel.

Naldy looked around, noticing everyone—including Ralph—enjoying their lumpy breakfast.

'They've put a little sugar in it,' said Bargen happily. Then, clocking Naldy's unenthusiastic expression, he added, 'They do that when we get newcomers. Gives it a nice sweetness.'

Naldy took the tiniest bite of her congealed oats but found the sweet tang nauseating.

'Bargen?' asked Naldy, plopping her spoon back into her breakfast. 'Does anybody come by here?'

'Come by? Young lady,' he said, grinning. 'Nobody comes by here.'

'But what about the oats? Who brings the oats?'

'The children,' said Bargen uneasily. He stuck his

own wooden spoon into his bowl of gooey oats. 'They send them from the town. They bring us the gruel. They're sent here as a punishment.'

Naldy's heart skipped with hope.

'You think you can convince them to help us?' said Bargen, staring up at Naldy with his big eyes. 'Well, you can stuff those thoughts right back into your noggin. They don't give the children any keys.'

'But then how do they get the oats into the cages?'

'They pass the gruel up in a little basket on a long stick,' he said, taking a massive mouthful of oats. 'But you shouldn't talk to the children. Their eyes well up in fear if you do that.'

Naldy spent the remainder of the morning thinking of how they might escape. Prisons like this one were designed to hold even powerful witches, and the more she tried to think of an escape plan, the more dispirited she became.

'They've hung us on this side of the forest as a warning,' said Bargen, pushing his potato-like face against the rusting bars of his cage.

'A warning?' remarked Ralph, staring down uneasily.

'This side of the forest'—Bargen pointed at the untamed tangle of trees surrounding them—'is the wild side. There are no known respectable towns on this side of Kirkwood. Savages roam those parts out there. That's why they've hung us here. We are a living warning to anyone who dares venture this close to the respectable town of Greenswood.'

'Do you see many'—Ralph gulped—'savages?'

'I've been living here for many years now,' said Bargen, 'and have seen nothing but the occasional wild boar. Thank goodness for that. Nobody ever comes here, and nothing ever changes.'

Naldy did not want to spend her life decaying in an iron cage.

Bargen rapped his warty fists on his enclosure, and all the prisoners stood to attention. Some of them hoarsely cleared their throats.

'Our *Welcome Song*,' said Bargen, his eyes glimmering with pride.

Naldy forced a smile, noticing Ralph tapping his foot with anticipation. Then, out of tune, all of the prisoners began to sing:

Oh! We welcome you to your cage with no feathers,
Now, please don't fret, as we are all trapped together,
Oh! We welcome you to this beautiful dead-end,
Yes, you are indeed our new treasured best friends,
Oh! Oh! Oh! Together, we are here for bloody ever—

'RALPH!' burst Naldy over the singing, causing it to come to a petering finish.

'We're not done yet,' said Bargen, grimacing at Naldy's rude interruption. 'We have many verses still to go. We can start from the beginning.'

'No more singing,' said Naldy dismissively. 'Ralph, you've got the scroll. From the dragon egg. The one you stole.'

'Dragon eggs?' said Bargen curiously. 'No. Dragons are long gone. You'll never find any dragon eggs. Extinct. The foul things.'

Ralph reached into his cloak pocket and retrieved the little scroll.

'Yes, even if the egg wasn't real,' he said, staring at the rolled parchment, 'the scroll still might be magical.'

Bargen insistently knocked at his cage's bars, but all the prisoners ignored him, their eyes curiously turning towards Ralph. It appeared to be the most exciting thing the inmates had witnessed in a long while.

Ralph slowly unrolled the scroll, his fingers shaking as he did so. But his face changed instantly from glimmering hope to absolute disappointment.

'There's nothing on it,' said Ralph sadly, throwing the scroll out of the cage. It fluttered to the forest floor. 'No message at all—just the imprint of baby dragons. Expensive junk!'

'Can we begin our song again now, please?' Bargen seemed glad the distraction had ended. He refocused the choir as Naldy and Ralph sank into irritable moods.

Unperturbed by their disinterest, the singers soldiered merrily through one hundred and fifty verses. The choir even continued singing when a little girl, no older than six, came by to collect their empty bowls. The child slid a wicker basket attached to a long pole through a small gap in each cage, far too small for a person to climb through—though this didn't stop Naldy and Ralph from trying. Naldy attempted to engage the girl in conversation, but it prompted her to leave without collecting the dirty dishes.

When the song finally concluded, the afternoon sun was casting a golden haze. Neither Naldy nor Ralph clapped—they were relieved it was over. Their lack of enthusiasm didn't deter the prisoners from self-congratulating with vigorous applause.

'Naldy,' said Ralph, scrunching his nose in thought. 'What if I couldn't see any message on the scroll because it was meant for you? Perhaps you were the last one touching it. The woman did say it revealed a message to the one who broke the egg.'

'The old woman could have also been the last one holding it,' said Naldy, peering at the leafy forest floor where Ralph had tossed the parchment. 'She might also have been making it all up to make a profit. Either way, I don't see how we'll check as you've thrown it to the ground.'

A freckled boy came by before sunset to deliver their dinner. Quivering, he attached his basket to the long wooden stick.

'What's your name?' asked Naldy—causing the boy's basket to tremble more violently.

'Don't talk to them,' whispered Bargen sternly. 'They'll leave the basket on the floor and won't feed us.'

'I only want him to pass up that scroll,' said Naldy.

The boy peered up at her warily.

'I'm a mighty witch,' said Naldy, waving her arms in a showy demonstration, trying to appear powerful. 'I can give you whatever your heart desires. What about enough candy to last your entire lifetime?'

'But, but,' mumbled the boy nervously. 'You can't do magic from inside the birdcages. The other children told me you couldn't.'

'All I need,' said Naldy, thrilled the boy was engaging with her, 'is for you to pass me that scroll there.'

'And you'll give me all the candy I want?'

Bargen had begun muttering to himself. Ralph rolled his eyes, knowing no such spell existed. The young boy picked up the scroll and unravelled it.

'There's nothing on it,' said the boy, frowning. 'The baby dragon pattern is nice—but I don't get why you want a blank scroll so much.'

'If you pass it up in your little basket,' instructed Naldy, leaning on the rusty bars, 'I'll give you all the candy you'll ever need.'

The freckled boy stared up at her suspiciously. He shifted nervously, taking in the forest that surrounded them. Night would fall at any moment, and he seemed eager to leave.

'You're lying,' he said firmly, turning to depart. 'I know you can't do magic from inside the birdcage.'

'Wait! What if we make a *Pactum Pactorum?*' suggested Naldy. The idea had suddenly struck her. 'Do you know what a *Pactum Pactorum* is?'

'Yes,' replied the boy, frightened by the proposal. 'It's a contract that witches and wizards make. It forces you to keep your word.'

'All you need to do is pass me that parchment, and I'll give you more candy than you could ever stomach.'

The little boy screwed up his face in thought. Bargen's grumbling was becoming more intense, and he seemed unsettled by it.

'I've never made a *Pactum Pactorum*,' said the boy.

'It's easy,' said Naldy. 'What's your name?'

'Buckley.'

'First, you have to stare into my eyes, Buckley.'

'I know how it works,' said the boy boldly. 'We're not allowed to blink, and we both say *Pactum Pactorum*.'

'Alright,' replied Naldy, fixing her eyes on his. 'I commit to giving you, Buckley, all the candy you could ever eat if you pass me up that scroll. *Pactum Pactorum*.'

'*Pactum Pactorum*,' repeated Buckley, his forehead creased in concentration.

Nothing happened. Naldy noticed Ralph excitedly scribbling in his notebook as he observed them, despite knowing she couldn't perform spells.

'I don't feel anything,' said Buckley, touching his chest. 'I thought I was supposed to feel all warm and tingly?'

'You will,' lied Naldy. 'After you fulfil your end of the *Pactum Pactorum*. Pass me up that parchment.'

Buckley placed the scroll in his basket and lifted it towards Naldy's cage. He seemed excited at the promise of soon receiving mountains of candy. When the basket reached her height, Naldy grabbed and unrolled the scroll.

'It's blank,' said Naldy, her hopes crushed.

'I told you it was blank,' said Buckley, as the sun dipped below the trees. It would soon be night.

'The stallkeeper must have been the last one to touch it,' remarked Ralph, slumping onto the birdcage floor.

'Or she lied about it having a message,' said Naldy.

'When do I get my candy?' called Buckley, losing his patience.

'You don't,' said Naldy bitterly. 'Because for a *Pactum Pactorum* to work, one member partaking must be a witch or a wizard.'

'But you are a witch,' said the little boy, confused.

'Not during the day,' she said, leaning defeatedly against the iron bars. 'I'm a cursed witch until the sun fully sets.'

As she spoke, the last gleam of light disappeared, and night surrounded them. Then, black ink bled across the page.

'Wait, something is appearing,' she said.

Ralph and the other prisoners craned their necks to get a better look at Naldy. Bargen, however, turned away miserably.

'It's not words,' declared Naldy. 'It's a drawing of something. It's slowly forming—it's a picture of a key!'

'Great, it tells us what we already know we need,' said Ralph sarcastically, slumping further onto the floor of his cage. 'Except we don't need a drawing— we need an *actual* key.'

The scroll burst into flame, disintegrating in her hand just as the door of her birdcage swung open. Buckley stumbled backwards in panic, then bolted away, crying as he went.

Ralph stared in astonishment at the open cage door. Naldy jumped, but the distance was greater than she'd anticipated. She was lucky the forest leaves cushioned her fall.

'You've done it! You're free!' called Ralph.

Over his shoulder, Bargen eyed Naldy's newfound freedom, his nose creased with distaste.

'*Aperio*,' said Naldy, holding her palms towards Ralph's cage. But nothing happened. 'That usually works on locks, and the sun has set—my magic should have returned.'

'Your spells won't work on these birdcages,' Bargen grumbled, lowering his eyes spitefully. The other prisoners watched in awe.

'What do you mean?'

'The mayor of Greenswood himself—Maverick —cast the enchantments to protect these locks. Nobody gets in, and nobody gets out.'

'I need to get to Oak,' said Naldy, ignoring Bargen. 'I need to warn him about Diamone's prediction. He might have a spell to help get you out. If the scroll worked, there's bound to be some other spell that can help.'

'You can fly there,' said Ralph.

'My broomstick is all the way in town.'

'Here,' said Ralph, throwing his blue carpet out of his cage. 'You promised me you'd fix it, remember?'

Naldy picked up the carpet.

'*Restituo*,' she uttered. The torn corner was instantly mended—she was relieved to have proof that her magic had returned. She laid out the carpet and settled on top. It lifted from the leafy ground, hovering mid-air.

Ralph was busy scribbling in his notebook again.

'I'll be back soon with a spell, Ralph.'

Naldy had never flown a magic carpet before, and she found the steering temperamental. A single wrong tap on the corner sent her hurtling in the wrong direction.

As she soared above the moonlit treetops, she was surprised to see Ralph's carpet slowly shifting from brilliant blue to a light brown.

The wind rushed past her face, and Naldy realised she was in a prime position. She had regained control of her magic and could sneak up on the oak tree, forcing him to surrender her family's spellbook. She could also leave Ralph sitting in his birdcage, ensuring he would never stalk her at the Witch House again. She would be free of both of them. But was that what she truly wanted?

She finally approached the clearing where Oak was situated, but panic filled her chest—billowing white puffs of smoke filled the sky. Could it be that Diamone's prediction was materialising?

'The book!'

The horrible sight sent shivers down her spine —the tree was waving its hefty, arm-like branches, ablaze with hot flames. With each wave, the fire was accompanied by a whooshing sound.

'Oak,' cried Naldy in distress as she hastily landed the carpet.

The flames were quickly consuming the tree. Naldy strained to think of a suitable spell, knowing she couldn't conjure water from thin air—a spell lost during The Great Witch Hunt. The tree attempted to cast his own magic, but the hot air prevented him from completing his incantations.

'*Turba... Turbatu...,*' the tree began, but he was reduced to coughing before he could finish.

'*Turbatus Venti,*' cried Naldy as a flurry of dirt and dry debris lifted from the ground, whirling around at incredible speed. With her palms outstretched, she directed the small, violent tornado towards the tree. It instantly extinguished the fire, leaving streams of jet-black smoke swirling upwards from the tree's charred branches.

'Oh, Naldy,' said Oak, catching his breath as the wind ceased and the dirt and leaves settled on the forest floor. 'Oh, my dear, Naldy.'

'You're lucky the sun is not up, or you'd be little more than firewood.'

'The worst has happened,' confessed Oak, his wooden eyelids widening in shock.

'The book was burnt,' she said, recalling Diamone's prediction. 'Oak?'

'No, Naldy. The book was not burnt.'

'Well, where is it, then?' asked Naldy, raising her voice. There was no sign of it amongst his singed branches. 'Where is my family's spellbook, Oak?'

'I haven't been completely honest with you, Naldy.'

'Honest?'

The oak tree fell into another coughing fit, expelling black smoke and dirt from his birds-hollow shaped mouth.

'Oak, tell me, where is my book?'

'I fear my honesty might now be too late.'

'Who did this to you? Did they take the book from you? Has it been stolen?'

The tree was still struggling to catch his breath, holding up a long, finger-like twig that was still smoking slightly. Naldy allowed a brief moment to pass—but her patience didn't last.

'Tell me, Oak!'

'Sit down, Naldy, and I will tell you everything.'

—Chapter Four—

THE TALE OF HANNAH HALE

Naldy didn't sit—she couldn't, for she was entirely restless.

'Have you heard of the great witch Hannah Hale?' asked Oak.

'If you drag this out, I'll set you on fire myself.'

The oak tree returned a look of exasperation before continuing.

'Hannah Hale and her team of studious witches created something called the Devante.'

'I don't care about this Devante. I care about what you've done with my book.'

'Creating a new spell,' said Oak, his voice still hoarse from the smoke and swallowed debris, 'was once a possibility, although rather complex. Where do you think the spells that we have today come from?'

The oak tree paused and raised a singed, mossy eyebrow. He waited for Naldy to answer, but she was too busy suppressing a snowballing urge to scream. The tree continued on calmly.

'The Method—that is, the ability to create a new spell—was once passed down from generation to generation of witches. It was a complicated practice. Young witches used to study it for several years before being adequately equipped to invent even the simplest of spells, and—'

'The point, please, Oak.'

'The Establishment,' he said, ignoring Naldy's interruption, 'decided it was far too dangerous for witches to continue designing new magic at their own will.'

Another coughing fit interrupted the Oak tree's speech. Naldy could feel the pressure in her head expanding from pent-up frustration and impatience. She was desperate to know where her family's spellbook was. The tree must have noticed her pinch-faced expression, for once he recovered from coughing, his tone shifted and became sombre.

'Naldy, dear, I know you might think what I'm telling you is unrelated to your family's spellbook.'

'Tell me where it is. Please.'

'But what I am telling you is likely to be the most important thing I will ever share with you.'

Naldy forced a smile, waiting restlessly for Oak to continue.

'The Establishment began the great war on magic. The Great Witch Hunt as it has come to be known, but nothing was great about it. The Great Slaughter is what it should have been called. Books were ordered to be burnt, and witches, too, if they didn't comply. An order of Establishment-approved spells was sent out. Anyone found practising, harbouring, or even documenting spells, other than those on The Establishment's approved list, were to be burnt at the stake.'

'Yes, I know all of this, Oak.'

'But what you mightn't know,' he said gently, 'is that a few witches refused to forget The Method. They refused to accept The Establishment's approved list as a definitive one. Hannah Hale and her team of witches forged spellbooks in secret.'

'Unless this witch Hannah Hale stole my book,' said Naldy, kicking the leaves up from the forest floor, 'I don't want to know any more about her.'

'The books they created in secret were not any old spellbooks, Naldy. They could be used to invent any spell, even without prior knowledge or training in The Method. These books came to be known as the Devante.'

'I'm going home, Oak.'

'Hannah Hale and her team created your family's spellbook. Your spellbook, Naldy, is a Devante.'

'Oh, so what!' barked Naldy. She'd had quite enough of the oak tree's prattling. 'I've always known the book contained forgotten magic. You've used it to curse me, and I know it contains a blood-freezing spell.'

'I don't think you fully grasp the book's importance,' he replied wearily. 'Naldy, it doesn't just contain forgotten magic. The Devante can be used to invent *new* magic.'

'It's no good to us now, is it!'

'I fear it is too late, yes,' sighed Oak. 'Perhaps you were right, and I should have given you the book sooner. I thought you were too young to be responsible for it.'

'But old enough to be cursed,' said Naldy. The revelation that her book was one of these Devante no longer mattered, as she wouldn't reap the benefits of the book's magic. 'If it was as powerful as you say, why didn't you use it to save yourself from the fire?'

'I was unprepared,' he said, lifting a blackened branch to scratch a loose bit of tree bark on his face. 'It was stolen by someone with powerful magic. I have not seen magic that powerful since The Great Witch Hunt.'

'So, Diamone was right,' said Naldy, thinking out loud. 'Someone came along and started a fire to steal it.'

'Diamone?'

'Never mind, Oak,' she said, laying Ralph's carpet on the forest floor. 'It doesn't matter anymore. Not now that it's been stolen. I'm going home to the Witch House.'

Naldy climbed onto the carpet, crossing her legs. She felt worn out, and her heart ached. The spellbook might have helped her find her missing parents. She forced this thought out of her mind, deciding it was best to fly away before her anger returned or before tears could conquer her. Just as she was about to instruct Ralph's magic carpet to take to the night sky, Oak interrupted with another question.

'Naldy, forgive me for the intrusion, but have you

spoken to anybody about the book or its location?'

'No, never!' exclaimed Naldy, offended that he had asked. Her parents had always told her how important it was that Oak and the family spellbook remain a secret. 'Why would I tell anybody where my family's spellbook was hidden?'

It then dawned on her that Ralph had been following her for weeks. He knew about Oak and the spellbook.

'Naldy?'

'I met a man on my walk,' she said quietly. 'He took an interest in me being a witch and said he was a scholar. Maybe, but... he couldn't have taken it. He's locked up in the Greenswood prison as we speak. He doesn't do magic. It couldn't have been him. You said it was someone powerful.'

The oak tree scanned her curiously with his green eyes—he wasn't persuaded that Ralph was blameless. Truthfully, Naldy wasn't wholly convinced of his innocence either. She had found it strange the scholar had taken such a keen interest in her.

'Naldy, do you think this man could be working alongside someone?'

Naldy's fury was beginning to simmer again. Had Ralph been sent as a distraction? Had it been his job to get Naldy out of the way—to land them both in prison, perhaps—so Ralph's accomplice could steal the book unhindered?

'I need to go back and find out if it was him,' she said, as the oak tree mumbled something to himself.

'Oak, I need you to lift the curse. If you want me to retrieve the spellbook, I need you to help me.'

'But there isn't a thing I can do,' said Oak. 'You must be the one to break the—'

'Curse you! Yes, alright. You've spent years carrying that blooming book, and you didn't ever think to invent a counter-curse?'

'Yes, I suppose I could do that. If we had the Devante.'

Irritated, she tightly gripped the corner of Ralph's carpet, which was still brown in colour. She was about to instruct the carpet to fly upwards, but one last question entered her mind. She took a deep breath of the forest air to calm herself. The air still smelt strongly of smoke.

'How many of these spell-inventing books did Hannah and her team create?'

'Devante,' the oak tree corrected her. 'I don't know how many exactly. But it is rumoured that you can tell a magical spellbook is a Devante because it will be branded. Hannah Hale pressed the letter 'H' into the inside of each Devante's cover, or so some people say.'

'Thank you,' said Naldy, and she pulled the front of the carpet. It lifted from the ground, climbing high above the pine trees.

As she soared over the tops of the forest's branches, she tried to ignore the nagging thought that Ralph might have helped orchestrate the theft of her spellbook. She did not want to believe he had betrayed her.

A bitter wind brought dark clouds, obscuring the moon and making navigation difficult. When Naldy glided down to land beneath the large twisted tree hosting the prisoners, she was happy to dismount Ralph's unpredictable carpet.

'You came back for us,' said Bargen, sounding oddly sour about it.

Naldy peered up at the birdcages, her stomach doing a queasy somersault as she saw Ralph's cage hanging empty.

'Where is he?' asked Naldy as Bargen pushed his potato-like face against the bars of his cage. 'How did Ralph get out?'

'The mayor came by,' said Bargen with a strained expression. 'Took him away, see.'

'The mayor?' Naldy repeated in confusion. Had Ralph been acting on instructions from the mayor of Greenswood?

'They both went into town,' continued Bargen, pointing a crooked finger towards the dense trees.

'Please,' begged one of the dishevelled prisoners, 'set us free, would you?'

Naldy picked up Ralph's carpet and stuffed it in her pocket, where it magically folded itself away neatly. She marched off in the direction Bargen had pointed.

'Calm yourselves,' Naldy could hear Bargen telling the prisoners. 'Nobody escapes. They'll be back home soon because nobody escapes. The wizard will bring them back to us.'

Naldy decided not to fly; she didn't want to draw

unwanted attention to herself this close to the town, and she was rubbish at steering Ralph's carpet.

Walking through the towering pines, Naldy realised she had no solid plan to find Ralph or the mayor. Despite the slim odds of finding them, she knew she had to try. She was determined to make them answer for stealing her family's spellbook. It was night-time, and her magic had been restored.

'I should have known better,' mumbled Naldy, striding towards the soft twinkling lights of Greenswood. 'He's been flying around the Witch House for months on his blooming carpet! They have several nasty spells coming their way when I do find them.'

When she reached the edge of town, she noticed the streets were eerily quiet. Wandering down a cobblestone road, she arrived at the familiar town square. It appeared ghostly at this late hour and seemed larger than she remembered, perhaps because the colourful tents and stage had been packed away. The festivities had long since ended, and the surge of visitors had returned to their neighbouring towns.

A small rat darted across the square, giving Naldy a fright. She watched as it stopped, lifted its pointed nose, and sniffed the air. The rat retreated beneath a door she recognised—the entrance to the dwelling *Spitswater.*

The lanterns in the windows were still burning brightly, and as Naldy got closer, she could hear the faint sound of festive music. Upon entering the dwelling, she found a small band playing merrily. A few red-faced townsfolk cheerfully jigged away, with dribbles of apple cider occasionally spilling over the tops of their pints as they twisted and twirled. She wondered if they were locals or stragglers who had yet to return to their own towns.

'What can I do fer yer, love?' called the dwellingtend from behind the bar, her cheeks redder than those of the merry dancers.

'Oh... um,' replied Naldy, approaching the bar and glancing around in search of the mayor or Ralph, neither of whom was in sight. 'I'm... well... I'm looking for the mayor.'

'Of Greenswood?' the dwellingtend asked.

Feeling anxious and half-expecting to be arrested again, Naldy gave a faint nod.

'Oh, Lovey,' said the dwellingtend, 'the mayor will likely be sleepin', if he ain't already returned back to The Great City. Never stays 'ere long.'

'Right, of course,' said Naldy disappointedly.

'Do yer need a room to stay in fer the night?'

'Oh, no,' said Naldy, deciding not to linger. 'I best be going—oh, wait—I checked in my broomstick before the fair.'

'Yes, I've been wonderin' whose stick it was,' said the dwellingtend, taking a swig of her own pint. 'My three little ones wanted to 'ave a go flyin' it, can yer imagine! I had ta tell 'em, brooms are fer witches only. We see little of your lot 'round 'ere.'

Naldy offered the plump dwellingtend a forced smile.

'I'll go and get it fer yer, love.'

The dwellingtend disappeared through a door with a pint of apple cider in hand. Naldy couldn't help but wonder if she had gone to inform someone about the witch who had escaped the birdcages. However, her worry was short-lived, as the pudgy woman soon returned, carrying Naldy's broomstick. She felt a rush of happiness upon seeing it again.

'Can I ask yer a question?' asked the dwellingtend, passing Naldy the broom.

'Yes, okay.'

'Is it the witch 'at's magic or the broomstick?'

'It's both,' she replied, slightly surprised by the question.

The dwellingtend nodded thoughtfully, her flushed face close to Naldy's and her breath smelling of cider. Naldy got the impression that the woman was waiting for her to elaborate.

'The rider has to be a witch or a wizard,' continued Naldy, placing a few currents onto the bar to pay for the cloakroom service. 'But the broomstick also has to be enchanted.'

'Sounds awfully confusing.'

'Your little ones could ride a carpet or a bewitched armchair. The enchantments on those don't require the rider to be magical. Although they're extremely rare and expensive, the magic to create new ones no longer exists.'

The dwellingtend laughed heartily.

'Oh, yer funny. One more thing,' she said, leaning closer as if afraid of being overheard. 'Why are broomsticks always so old and ugly, eh? Why doesn't someone make nicer-lookin' ones?'

'I don't know,' said Naldy, lying as she hastily picked up her broom and exited the dwelling. She didn't want to discuss broomsticks any longer.

Naldy stood outside the dwelling, taking in the dark, empty square. The air had turned cold, and moisture lingered as she breathed deeply. The dwellingtend's question had brought a memory of her six-year-old self to mind. She recalled clinging to her mother's waist during her first broom ride over Kirkwood Forest and asking the same question: *why were broomsticks so old and ugly?* Her mother had explained that the magic to bewitch new broomsticks no longer existed and that they needed to take care not to break the ones they had.

But now, Naldy knew better. She had learnt her family's red spellbook could produce new spells and bewitch new broomsticks. She just had to find it.

Pattering rain began to fall on the cobblestones, jolting Naldy from her thoughts and pulling her back to the present. She stood under the dwelling's wooden awning, but it was doing a poor job of shielding her from the intensifying downpour.

She strained to see through the curtain of rain. Across the town square stood a large building with two enormous columns at its entrance.

She leapt onto her broomstick and glided across the square, landing under a stone column that offered ample protection from the rain. The building had ornate wooden double doors nearly twice her size. Etched into the stone walls were the words *Town Committee Hall.*

'Seems like the sort of place to find a mayor,' she said to herself, 'or at least to find some better shelter.'

She was relieved to find the doors unlocked as she pushed them open. Inside, it was quiet and dark— the grand chandeliers in the large, empty chamber were unlit. At the far end, a grand marble staircase led up to a second landing. Naldy decided to find somewhere warm to wait until the rain stopped before continuing her search for Ralph and the mayor.

At the top of the staircase, two corridors branched off: one to the left and the other to the right. Both were dark, lit only by pale bars of moonlight filtering through clouds and spilling through the windows lining the corridors.

As a precaution, Naldy mounted her broomstick, not wanting anyone to hear her wet footsteps echoing off the marble floor. She flew close to the ceiling, remaining hidden in the shadows, and decided to circle the entire passage at least once to ensure the building was empty. The corridor looped, and she found herself back at the main staircase.

Just as Naldy was about to descend from the ceiling, the double doors at the entrance opened, and the mayor himself came pit-patting up the steps, rain dripping from his cloak.

This was her moment to strike while she was safely atop her broomstick, high in the shadows, while the mayor was unaware of her presence. Naldy searched her brain for a suitable spell that could be cast from her advantageous position. She held out her palms, ready to release a *Prosterno* spell. But as the incantation tingled the tip of her tongue, the entrance doors opened, and another figure walked in.

At first, Naldy thought the second person was Ralph, but as the man stepped into a beam of dull moonlight shining through the high window, she could see he was too round to be Ralph.

'Maverick,' said the short, bald man, as he lumbered up the steps in pursuit of the mayor.

Naldy gripped her broomstick's wooden handle, her palms sweating. She was lucky she hadn't been seen or heard.

'Sallandra is not impressed,' said the plump man as he finally reached the mayor. The two men were directly below her. 'She's talking about an internal inquiry, Maverick.'

Naldy would have taken on the mayor alone—in fact, she would have taken on both the mayor *and* Ralph—but she didn't know if the round stranger below her was magical or not. She couldn't win a fight against the men if they both had powers.

'She won't inquire inward,' said the mayor, leaning on his black cane. 'The museum is looking out, not in. I have the situation under control. Let us walk.'

'I've risked everything for this,' said the stout man, adjusting his floral waistcoat, which appeared on the verge of shedding its buttons. 'If they decide to make an internal inquiry...'

'Getergrin,' said the mayor, tapping his black cane against the round man's chest. 'Let us not waste time on hypothetical inquiries. We have other, more important business to attend to tonight.'

Maverick strode along the left corridor, the man in the floral waistcoat close behind. They both vanished behind one of the wooden doors leading from the passage.

Naldy waited silently in the shadows near the ceiling, struggling to exercise patience. It didn't help that she couldn't hear anything coming from the room the mayor and the large man had entered. Was Ralph behind the door, too? Was her spellbook being kept behind this very door? Was there an entire team who'd helped steal her family's spellbook assembled in this room?

Naldy resisted the urge to descend and enter the room. She was outnumbered and didn't want to end up imprisoned in a birdcage again. After ten excruciating minutes, Maverick and his companion emerged, but there was no sign of her red book or Ralph.

'Would it not be better for us to wait,' suggested the man in the waistcoat, closing the door behind him. 'It could be wise to collect them all first.'

'Getergrin, we must demonstrate our seriousness,' said the mayor, unaware of Naldy floating near the ceiling. 'Waiting would be foolish. Need I remind you that I am in charge of the operation?'

'Yes, yes, of course, Maverick,' replied Getergrin uneasily as he walked behind the mayor down the stone steps. 'I am not questioning your intelligence. It's just a shame it must be done.'

The entrance doors creaked open, and the echo of heavy rain drifted in as Maverick and Getergrin exited the building.

Naldy landed outside the room the mayor and Getergrin had previously entered, her palms held out and her broom tucked under an arm. When she tried the handle, she found the door locked.

'*Aperio*,' whispered Naldy, and after hearing a click from the lock, she entered the room.

In the centre of the circular chamber was a wooden reading table piled high with books. Ralph sat at the table, poring over a book.

'You!' exclaimed Naldy, her palms facing threateningly towards him. 'Step away from the book, Ralph, or you won't like what's coming next.'

Chapter Five

CARPET CHASE

'**D**on't close the door!' exclaimed Ralph in alarm, but it was too late—the door had already clicked shut.

'Step out from behind the table, Ralph.'

'You can't open it from this side,' he said, flipping a page of the book he was bent over. 'Even with magic.'

The circular room had a high ceiling and walls lined entirely with bookshelves. Naldy had never seen so many books crammed into one space. There were no windows, but an elaborate metal chandelier, suspended low from a long, ornate silver chain, cast a warm yellow glow over the room.

'Is that my book?'

'Your book?' asked Ralph, puzzled. He held up the small volume he was reading, its old black cover worn with age.

'Where did you take *my* spellbook, Ralph?'

'Calm your magical fingers. I didn't take your blooming book.'

'Yes, you did,' snapped Naldy bitterly. 'Don't deny it! You're helping them, I know it! You've been stalking me to gather information.'

'Helping them?' remarked Ralph, a confused expression on his face. 'I'm locked in this room, Naldy. Why would I be helping them?'

'Locked?' repeated Naldy. She kept one palm directed at him and tried to open the door with her free hand.

'It won't open,' said Ralph, anxiously turning back to the small black book.

'But if you didn't help steal it,' said Naldy, 'then who did?'

'The mayor came to collect us both from the birdcages,' said Ralph distractedly. 'He was furious you'd escaped and said I wouldn't be harmed if I cooperated.'

'Cooperated? With what?'

'Look here,' he said, passing Naldy a grotty piece of parchment. She took it and examined it:

H,
Corium
Aurum
Lignum
Metallum
Rubrum
Caeruleum
Aurantiaco
Rosea

'I can't read Olde Witchery,' said Naldy, tossing the page to the floor.

'Neither can I,' said Ralph, bending to collect the list before holding up the book he'd been poring over. On its worn cover, slanted gold lettering read *Translating Olde Witchery.*

'Witches once wrote in this language,' said Ralph, flipping a few pages of his pocket-sized book. 'Before The Great Witch Hunt.'

'Yes,' said Naldy in a huff. She knew Olde Witchery was an ancient language once widely used by witches hundreds of years ago, now scarcely used or learnt except for spellcasting. 'What I don't understand, Ralph, is why you are translating a page of it. What are these words, old spells?'

Ralph glanced across the room at Naldy. For the first time, she realised how stressed he appeared. His face was strained, and his eyes glistened as if he were on the verge of tears.

'They gave me this list,' he said. 'The mayor wanted me to write down where Devante is hiding, and I said I didn't know Devante.'

'Devante?'

'Yes, and he said the list should jog my memory. I found this book, and I've been trying to translate it. But it doesn't make any sense to me, and there's yet to be a mention of Devante. The first word means *leather,* and the second translates to *gold.* But I don't know what the 'H' at the top means.'

'It might stand for Hannah Hale.'

'Hannah-who?'

Naldy instantly regretted mentioning Hannah. She was still deciding if she could trust Ralph.

'Naldy,' he said gently. 'I'm on your side. You can help me translate this page and work out who Devante is, or we can wait for the mayor to return and lock us back up in birdcages.'

She hesitated. Was Ralph really being honest with her? Did he truly not assist Maverick? Was the mayor even the thief who stole her family's spellbook? She turned to face the door.

'*Aperio,*' said Naldy. She tugged on the handle, but it wouldn't budge.

'The third word translates to *wood.*'

'The 'H' might be the indent that Hannah Hale placed on the inside cover of her Devante.'

Ralph stared at her, perplexed. From his troubled state, Naldy surmised he was probably telling the truth. She decided to trust him. Over the next five minutes, she hurriedly explained her recent encounter with Oak. When she finished, Ralph blinked at her in disbelief before returning to his translations.

'But, no, they can't be real! Books that invent new spells?'

'They are real, Ralph,' said Naldy, annoyed by his doubt. 'My family's spellbook is one of these Devante, and it's been stolen.'

'I mean, *maybe* your book might contain some lost spells at best. But really, Naldy, a book that invents new magic?'

Naldy turned away from him in frustration. She cast another ineffective spell at the door.

'I told you,' said Ralph, shaking his head. 'You

can only open it from the outside. Unless you are Maverick.'

'We have to find a way out of here,' said Naldy.

'The fourth word,' he said, scribbling on the grubby parchment, 'translates to mean *metal.*'

'Ralph, maybe they have given you a list of... but why would they do that?'

'Do what? You think this is a page of these Devante?'

'Surviving Devante, yes,' said Naldy, desperately scanning the room for a way out. 'I think they believe you know where these Devante are hiding.'

'But I don't know. Do you know?' asked Ralph pryingly.

'No, I've told you everything I know. I wasn't aware of what a Devante was until less than an hour ago.'

Naldy took in the room once more before pulling books from one of the shelves and hurling them haphazardly onto the floor.

'What are you doing?' asked Ralph.

'Maybe there's a secret passage.'

'They're not going to have locked me in a room with a secret passage I can escape through.'

'Well,' she said, continuing to pull more books from the shelf, 'they locked you in a room with an old list of Devante and a book on how to translate it. Why have they done that?'

'They didn't give me the book with the translations. I had to climb up some shelves to fetch it. I'm not sure this actually refers to the Devante you mention—it seems like a pointless page of items.'

She ignored him, reaching into the bookshelf and feeling along the back, searching for a secret door. There was nothing more than a few tiny cracks in the wood.

'The fifth one isn't even an item, it's a colour: *red.* The sixth one is *blue.*'

'Red?' said Naldy, surprised. 'That must be my Devante. My family's spellbook is red.'

'If these Devante are even real,' said Ralph, closing the book on Olde Witchery. 'I have an idea. You have your broomstick. We could surprise them when they return and fly over their heads, although there's no knowing when that will be.'

Naldy ceased searching the bookshelves and removed Ralph's carpet from her cloak pocket.

'Okay, but I'm not sharing,' she said, draping Ralph's carpet over his shoulders. 'Thanks for lending it to me. Don't ask me what happened to its gorgeous blue tone; it just turned brown while I was flying it. But it's mended, as promised.'

'It takes on the eye colour of the person riding it,' he said, smirking. Ralph stood to lay his carpet on the floor. 'You think my eyes are a gorgeous blue tone?'

Naldy ignored his question. Ralph sat cross-legged on the magic carpet, gave it a little tap, and it rose off the ground, hovering placidly.

'I don't understand it,' remarked Naldy, mounting her broomstick and readying herself for take-off. 'If you didn't help the mayor, how did he find my spellbook?'

'Maybe they overheard that awful fortune teller,' suggested Ralph, as his carpet slowly returned to its bright shade of blue.

'Her prediction didn't say anything about Oak's location or about a book. She said a tree would catch fire and that magic would be lost.'

'Disaster and all that nonsense.'

'Hardly nonsense now that it's come true,' said Naldy, glaring at him. 'I've never told anyone where Oak and the book are hiding. How did Maverick find him?'

'Maybe the mayor isn't the person who took it,' suggested Ralph, opening the book on Olde Witchery in his lap.

Naldy fell silent, staring fixedly at the door and willing it to open. She wondered if confiding in Ralph had been a mistake.

'There, I've finished translating,' said Ralph, pleased with himself. 'The seventh is *orange,* and the eighth is *pink.* It doesn't tell us where any of them are, though, and there's no proof they are a list of these Devante things that Oak told you about. A worthless page of four items and four colours.'

'Maybe the mayor wants to collect them all. Pass it to me,' said Naldy, holding out her hand and clicking her fingers. Before Ralph could pass Naldy the parchment, he shouted, 'It's gone!'

'What's gone, Ralph?'

Ralph thrust the list into Naldy's hands, and her

heart panged as she glanced at it. The fifth word, 'Rubrum', had disappeared, leaving only the untidy English translation Ralph had scribbled beside it:

H,

Corium	*Leather*
Aurum	*Gold*
Lignum	*Wood*
Metallum	*Metal*
	Red
Caeruleum	*Blue*
Aurantiaco	*Orange*
Rosea	*Pink*

'You don't think...' began Ralph, but he didn't have the heart to finish his sentence. Naldy felt like her heart had split—one half in her stomach and the other half lodged in her throat.

'Ralph, do you think they've... but surely not... why would the mayor destroy it if it can invent new spells?'

Ralph gave her a pitying look, taking the parchment from Naldy and returning it to his pocket.

'But they wouldn't,' she said, feeling as if a weight was pressing down on her.

Before Ralph could console her, the reading room door swung open. Naldy shot instinctively towards it. Maverick and Getergrin stood dumbfounded in the doorway as Naldy flew over their heads and out into the darkened corridor. She glanced back to see Ralph whizzing wildly around the reading room, narrowly dodging balls of electric light shooting out of Maverick's black cane.

For a split moment, she thought about leaving Ralph in the reading room—but then she remembered he had the list of Devante. Perhaps helping Ralph escape might even help break her curse.

Pivoting her broomstick, she skimmed over Getergrin, who was now cowering on the floor, his chubby hands protecting his bald head.

'Over here,' shouted Naldy, distracting the infuriated mayor.

She swerved her broomstick so sharply that she nearly tumbled off as Maverick's erratic jets of light narrowly missed her.

Ralph seized the opportunity and made for the open door, but Getergrin threw up his hands and took hold of the carpet's corner, sending Ralph catapulting onto the corridor's marble floor. The carpet fell on top of Getergrin, trapping him beneath its shimmering blue material.

Naldy dashed over the top and out into the passage, landing next to Ralph. There was just enough time for him to clamber onto the back of her broomstick before a white light whizzed narrowly past their heads.

'Get up, you fool,' the mayor shouted.

Naldy kicked off the ground, the broomstick flying at a dangerous speed along the corridor. With a quick glance over her shoulder, she caught sight of Maverick helping Getergrin out from beneath the carpet.

'Lucky escape,' said Ralph, his hands gripping tightly around her waist.

As they soared down the marble staircase towards the wooden double doors, another electric flash whirred past.

'We're being pursued,' said Naldy. 'Hold tight.'

She glimpsed Getergrin and Maverick sitting atop Ralph's magic carpet, now turned charcoal black.

'We're going to crash!' cried Ralph as they hurtled towards the closed double doors.

'*Aperta,*' said Naldy, raising her palm. The doors flung open, and they shot out into the pelting rain.

Naldy yanked the broomstick's tip, directing it skyward. They shot upwards at almost a 90-degree angle. The old slanted tiled roofs of the town's buildings grew smaller as they climbed higher, the unrelenting rain drumming against their faces.

'I feel sick,' muttered Ralph, gripping her waist tightly.

A clap of thunder rang out as they climbed higher until they could no longer see the town of Greenswood—only dark clouds and curtains of rain surrounded them.

'I think we're safe,' said Naldy, stopping and hovering mid-air.

'I've never flown at this height before,' said Ralph, peering down nervously. 'Are you sure it's safe to be all the way up here?'

Before Naldy could answer him, a bright

flash streaked past them with a metallic-sounding whoosh. At first, Naldy thought it was a lightning strike, but Maverick and Getergrin soon emerged from the curtain of rain.

The wizard's face was twisted in intense concentration as he endeavoured to control Ralph's carpet. Getergrin's complexion had turned greenish, as if he might vomit—or perhaps already had.

Naldy sped forward, with the carpet close on their tail. The rain was falling thick and fast, and she could barely see a few metres in front of her.

'Can't you simply turn them into toads?' asked Ralph, shivering behind her. 'It's night, and the curse shouldn't be in effect.'

Naldy didn't answer, staying focused. She struggled to keep both hands firmly on the broomstick and couldn't distinguish whether the white flashes were Mother Nature's doing or Maverick's spells.

A night heron flew past, and Naldy watched as a ball of light collided with it. Upon impact, the light formed an air bubble around the bird. The heron flapped its wings desperately, trying to escape the bubble, but it was trapped. Naldy had never seen anything like it.

She leant forward, willing the broom to fly faster. After a good ten minutes of speeding, Naldy finally slowed the broomstick.

'I think we lost them,' she said, peering through the rain.

'We lost my carpet too,' squeaked Ralph. 'Why

didn't you fight back? Did you forget you can use your magic?'

'I didn't want to give away our location with a ball of light,' lied Naldy, steering the broomstick towards the forest. The ground was a muddy mess, and they skidded across it on landing, almost colliding with a large pine tree.

'We should find somewhere warm,' she said, wiping mud from her face.

The real reason she hadn't fought back was her fear of Maverick's advanced level of magic—something she was reluctant to admit to Ralph.

Cold and thoroughly drenched, Naldy and Ralph trudged through the slippery mud in search of the nearest town. They didn't dare risk flying again, preferring to stay under the cover of the pine trees for protection. Despite their sodden state, Ralph seemed content to have his feet on solid ground again.

The nearest town was old, its only dwelling a dilapidated structure in desperate need of repairs. Inside, the reception room was dingy, but at least warm, thanks to a crackling fireplace. The creaking floorboards were covered with tattered rugs—a poor attempt to disguise the rotting wood.

'Our queen suite is available,' said the grey-haired dwellingtend, wheezing as she retrieved a rusty room key from the wall.

'Perfect,' replied Naldy, her wet clothes dripping and forming a small puddle around her feet.

The woman led them up an old wooden staircase

to a long, dark hallway lined with cobweb-covered portraits of long-dead townspeople in ceremonial cloaks.

'Room three, just here,' she wheezed, handing Naldy the key before plodding back down the treacherous stairs.

The room was spacious, though its furnishings had clearly seen better days, with many chips and scuffs. The roof leaked in several places, and metal buckets were strategically placed around the room to catch the trickling water.

'Do you think any of these might be Devante?' asked Ralph, pointing at a stack of books being used as one of the missing legs of the queen bed.

Naldy edged closer to the room's sole luxury —a great fireplace emitting a comforting blaze. They changed into the complimentary dressing gowns, which were comfortable despite their slight muskiness, and hung their wet clothes by the fire to dry.

The dwellingtend soon brought them a fresh pot of warm brew and bid them goodnight. Naldy poured the liquid into cracked cups and handed one to Ralph before sitting on the room's sagging brown sofa.

'Can I see the list again?' said Naldy softly. Ralph stood by the fire, holding his cup and warming his backside.

'Thank you for coming back to save me,' said Ralph, sipping from his cracked cup before passing Naldy the parchment. 'There was a moment when I thought you wouldn't return. I'm sorry about your book, Naldy.'

'We don't know for certain it's gone,' she said tetchily. 'Just because it's vanished from your list doesn't mean it's... you know.'

Ralph awkwardly bit his lip, and Naldy lowered her face, afraid he might see the tears beginning to trickle down her cheeks. She felt the salty liquid catch in her mouth. Ralph gave her an empathetic glance before turning to warm his hands. She knew he was giving her a moment of privacy.

'The thing is,' said Naldy, wiping her wet eyes and pocketing the parchment, 'the book has been in my family for so long. My mother always told me how precious our family spellbook was.'

'Maybe, come morning,' said Ralph, turning to face her again, 'your curse will finally break. You came back to save me. That should have proven you care for others.'

Naldy returned a half-smile. She didn't want to admit that she'd only come back for the parchment.

'It's that foolish tree's fault,' continued Ralph in a consoling tone. 'It was his job to protect the spellbook, not yours. At least we're both safe, and I have you to thank for that.'

'Safe?' said Naldy, raising an eyebrow in dispute. 'Ralph, if the mayor thinks we know the location of the rest of these blooming Devante, I don't think he's going to let us quietly disappear.'

'Do you think they're going to come after us? Do you think they'll try and kill us?'

'Kill us? No,' said Naldy assuredly. 'The mayor was casting a spell to capture us. One collided with a poor night heron. He wasn't aiming to kill us. I think he wanted us alive.'

'Because they think we know where the remainder of these books are?'

'I don't understand why Maverick thinks we know where they are,' she replied, holding her hands out to the fire. 'Though, given his efforts tonight, he'll probably keep hunting us.'

'We should get some sleep,' said Ralph, clearly not wanting to discuss the possibility of a wizard hunting them. 'I'll take the ugly sofa. It'll be an improvement from the birdcages.'

Naldy left the sofa for Ralph to set up his makeshift bed. He walked over to a rickety old cupboard and retrieved a moth-eaten blanket along with a miserable-looking pillow.

'Maverick is a wizard, isn't he?' asked Ralph, laying out the bedding on the sofa.

'Yes, he uses the cane,' Naldy said, noticing Ralph's face crinkle into a worried expression. 'You don't need to be frightened of wizards.'

He returned a pout, clearly unconvinced.

'Wizards can only perform the same spells witches can,' added Naldy, watching him tuck himself under the moth-eaten blanket. 'One is no more powerful than the other.'

Although this was generally true, Naldy knew it wasn't the case with Maverick. She had never seen such powerful magic from any witch or wizard. She decided not to mention this to Ralph.

'I've never met a wizard before,' said Ralph anxiously, 'and I don't like the idea of one of them coming after us.'

In truth, Naldy had never met a wizard either. They were as rare as the magically charged objects they possessed. However, she knew that, like her own magic, a wizard's power was limited to what could be found in spellbooks.

'I don't get it, Naldy. Why would the mayor want to destroy something that could help him invent new spells?'

'We don't know he destroyed it,' she said irritably, going over to the room's wretched bed. She climbed under the threadbare sheets, tucking herself in.

The fire cast a soft, flickering glow over the room, crackling faintly. A silence settled between them, and as Naldy lay staring at the water-damaged ceiling, a painful feeling stirred within her. The truth began to eclipse her stubborn disbelief—her family spellbook was gone.

Since learning that Rubrum could create any spell, Naldy had hoped to recover it and use it to find her parents.

'I'm going to find the other Devante,' said Naldy softly. 'I need to know what happened to my parents.'

'Where would you begin?' mumbled Ralph, in a voice indicating he was already half-asleep. 'There are lots of books in the world'—he yawned—'you and I could spend every day and night searching and still probably never find a single Devante.'

Naldy listened to the drips of leaking water catching in the metal buckets while she took in the reflection of the firelight dancing across the old walls. With each passing minute, she felt more and more compelled to go in search of these Devante.

'I'll come with you,' said Ralph softly—surprising Naldy, who thought he'd fallen asleep. 'I'd like very much to write about you in my scholarly paper about witches.'

'Good night, Ralph.'

The next sound she heard was Ralph's snoring.

—*Chapter Six*—

THE TRAVELLING COUSIN

W hen Naldy awoke the next day, Ralph was gone. His shabby pillow and blanket had been neatly folded at the end of the sofa. She initially felt a little sad at his absence, until she found him downstairs in the dwelling's main bar, clutching a copy of the local newspaper, the *Heatherton Herald.* He was gripping it so tightly the sides had crumpled.

'Help yourself,' he said, gesturing to the wooden board on the table laden with duck eggs, sourdough toast, and a selection of fruit chutneys.

Naldy took a seat opposite him. She was pleased to see a bright sun penetrating the dust-covered window.

'You look angry,' said Naldy, taking a bite of a thick slice of toast. 'Ralph, if it's about what I said last night.'

'It's not.'

'I want you to know I was just upset. I know going in search of these Devante is a ridiculous idea.'

'Naldy, it's not that,' said Ralph, passing her the copy of the *Heatherton Herald* and pointing to a headline. 'There.'

'The Dangers of Mixing Magic, by Barbra Hexogg,' read Naldy aloud. Next to the headline, she noticed a black-and-white photograph of a wrinkled witch with short, choppy white hair.

'She's a controversial journalist,' said Ralph, picking up a slice of toast and one of the duck eggs. 'She's well known amongst scholars. Read on.'

Naldy gave him a curious look, wondering what relevance the article had.

'Magic is a dangerous commodity and is not fit for trade,' read Naldy. 'In recent years, we have seen standards being dangerously lowered as magic has disgracefully wound up in the common marketplace. Let's suppose magical items continue to be sold to ordinary townsfolk at markets and fairs —'

Naldy stopped reading and raised her head with a puzzled expression.

'What does this'—she glanced at the journalist's name—'Barbra Hexogg have to do with you being grumpy this morning?'

'Keep reading,' urged Ralph.

'Witches will soon be forced to face the possibility that their futures may be reduced to little more than producing goods for the non-magical. Mayor Maverick Gadswell,' Naldy paused, glancing briefly at Ralph before continuing, 'has said, "Miss Hexogg is quite right. It is of the utmost importance that magic be protected. It is my new mission as mayor to ensure magic is preserved."'

Naldy silently skimmed the rest of the article.

'I'm inclined to agree with her,' said Naldy.

'I knew you would,' said Ralph as Naldy folded the newspaper. 'Obviously, the mayor is spinning a yarn, and judging by his behaviour last night, he clearly has no intention of protecting magic.'

'Ralph.'

'What I'm trying to say, Naldy, is that you were right. We need to find and protect these Devante-book things, and I want to help you.'

Naldy continued to chew her toast. Last night, while she had lain awake, she'd felt a surge of responsibility. But the morning light had brought a sobering effect, and Naldy could no longer see the point of wasting her time searching for books.

'What do you think, Naldy?'

'I'm happy for you, Ralph,' she said, avoiding his eyes. 'But the best thing for me is to accept my family's spellbook is gone. I have to focus on breaking this blooming curse.'

'But if we go in search—'

'We will never find them, Ralph. And we should take comfort in knowing the mayor will have little chance in finding them either.'

'But you said they'll come after us,' said Ralph, shifting uncomfortably. 'We can't run forever.'

Naldy knew Ralph was probably right. The mayor would not only search for the Devante but might well continue to hunt for them, believing they knew where the Devante were. She took comfort in knowing the Witch House lay on the edge of the Kirkwood Forest, far away from any of the towns that Maverick oversaw.

'I have a cousin,' said Ralph, who seemed determined not to give up on the quest before it had even begun. 'He travels a lot and might know something about these books. I think it's worth asking him.'

'Once night falls, I'm returning home, Ralph.'

'Last night, you wanted to save them,' said Ralph, leaning forward keenly. 'My cousin has travelled as far as the east coast. He might know a suitable place for us to start.'

'I'm not starting anything with you,' said Naldy, putting her half-eaten toast back on the wooden board and leaving the table.

'Naldy,' called Ralph.

She didn't look back as she stomped up the rickety staircase to their room. Naldy flung herself onto the musky-smelling bed. She felt emotionally exhausted. She knew searching for these Devante would not replace her family's spellbook.

A short while later, Ralph returned to the room carrying a tray of freshly stewed brew.

'I'm sorry,' said Ralph, placing the tray on the bed and sitting on its edge. 'I feel responsible because I caused the dragon egg to break, and if we hadn't been locked up in those birdcages, then...'

'Don't be silly, Ralph,' said Naldy. 'The truth is we don't know that Maverick was even the one who stole my family's book.'

'But, Naldy—'

'I'll admit it's likely been destroyed,' said Naldy,

'now that it's vanished from the list. But maybe the mayor was telling the truth when he was interviewed for that article and wants to protect magic. Maybe he thinks we were the ones who destroyed it.'

'Naldy,' said Ralph, shaking his head, 'we were locked up in the reading room when it disappeared from the list, thanks to the mayor. He wants them destroyed, and you know it, and he thinks we know where the rest of them are.'

She shifted uncomfortably, knowing Ralph was right. Everything pointed to Maverick having destroyed Rubrum. His vague words from the article now felt like little more than a smokescreen.

'I don't want to go chasing ancient spellbooks,' said Naldy, taking a cup of brew from the tray. 'I've had enough adventure to last me a long time.'

'Well, you're not obliged to help,' said Ralph. 'But my cousin will be arriving this evening, and I think he could prove useful.'

'You've asked him here?' said Naldy.

'I paid the town's Tebellos a visit early this morning,' said Ralph, fiddling with his hands.

Naldy knew most townships had a Tebellos, where one could send messages via candles. The sender would light a magical candle, called a lucurn candle, and speak their message into its flames. Naldy resented this form of communication, which was used mainly by the non-magical.

'Well, if this cousin of yours isn't here by dinnertime, I'm not waiting around,' said Naldy, pursing her lips.

'Have you checked if you've received any messages? I've got a lucurn candle here,' said Ralph, reaching into his cloak.

'I don't get messages nor send them,' replied Naldy.

Ralph lit the small white pillar candle he'd fished from his inner pocket, its blue flame crackling as it melted the wax. He blew the lucurn candle out, and the drifting smoke shaped itself into words.

'It's The Academy,' said Ralph fretfully, scanning over the words of the curling smoke. 'I'm behind on my paper.'

'Well, don't think you can write about me,' said Naldy sourly before marching from the room.

She was upset that Ralph was making decisions without consulting her—it was her family's prized spellbook that had been destroyed, after all. She ordered another brew at the dwelling's bar but felt too anxious to enjoy it. Later, when Naldy returned to the room, Ralph was busy scribbling in one of his books.

Her irritation grew as she attempted to use her magic for small tasks, like opening the curtains. She would raise her palms and mumble a spell to no effect, then be forced to stand and do it without the aid of magic.

'This darned curse,' said Naldy, standing to fetch a blanket. 'I think I've proven my selflessness. I'll be forever cursed at this rate.'

'It's rather entertaining,' said Ralph, lying on the

sofa and scribbling in his journal. 'Watching you struggle to do ordinary things without the help of your magic. Oh, it's brilliant!'

'Magic isn't effortless, you know. It's simply more efficient.'

When the sun finally set, Naldy abandoned any restraint and used her magic for every conceivable minuscule task.

'Show off,' said Ralph as Naldy instructed a cup— well within arm's reach—to float up to her mouth so she could take a sip.

'What are you writing in that book of yours, anyway? Better not be about me.'

'Witches'—he read from his little book—'I've observed are a stubborn bunch of show-offs.'

Naldy tried to stifle her laugh.

She didn't want to get her hopes up, but the expectation that Ralph's cousin might be able to help them had grown inside her as the day wore on— perhaps he could help them find a Devante. Maybe she could use it to invent a spell to discover where her missing parents were.

'We better go down to the dwellings bar,' said Ralph, closing his book and lifting himself from the sofa. 'Rupert will be arriving soon. Are you coming then?'

Naldy let a smile slip, and together, they made their way downstairs. Ralph ordered each of them a pint of apple cider, and they settled by the fireplace.

'Is that him?' asked Naldy, pointing to an old male witch with a particularly scabby cheek—the only other patron. 'What does your cousin look like, anyway?'

No sooner had she asked the question than the brass bell on the dwelling's door tinkled, and a tall, handsome, athletic man walked in. Ralph and his cousin were similar. The two could have easily been mistaken for brothers. Rupert shared Ralph's strawberry-blonde hair and big blue eyes, but he stood several inches taller, with a more muscular build and a more noticeable jawline.

Rupert broke into a warm, contagious smile when he saw them and strode over to lock Ralph in an embrace.

'Cousin Ralph, I was thrilled when I received your message,' said Rupert, his eyes twinkling. His rough voice had a slightly sweet undertone, reminding Naldy of a wild forest flower.

'How long has it been, Rupert?'

'Too long, Cousin Ralph! It's been too long!' said Rupert. He was smartly dressed in a large black overcoat with a colourful lining and a beautiful grey silk shirt tucked into his neat brown trousers. 'We mustn't let time keep us apart like this again—oh, how rude of me, I haven't introduced myself. I'm Rupert.'

'This is Naldy.'

'It's nice to meet you,' said Naldy.

'The pleasure is all mine, I'm certain of that,' said Rupert, smiling wider to show more of his white teeth. 'Now, tell me, what sort of trouble have you walked into, Cousin Ralph? Wait, shall I get us something to eat or drink?'

Rupert ordered an impressive spread of cured meats and pickled sauces. As they ate, Naldy and Ralph took turns describing their journey so far, sharing details about Diamone, the birdcages, Maverick, and the Devante.

'So, it is books you are searching for,' said Rupert, picking up a slice of cured meat and dipping it in mustard seed sauce.

'Yes,' replied Naldy.

'And how many of these books do you need to find?'

'Eight,' said Naldy, 'we need to find eight.'

'Seven,' corrected Ralph. 'One has been... well, if the parchment Maverick gave us is to be believed.'

'You know,' said Rupert, taking a bite from a salted pickle and then licking his fingers. 'I spent some time in the south with an old commune of witches. They experiment with potions, using plants from Edengar.'

It was clear that Rupert knew nothing about the Devante, and the last dregs of hope Naldy had been cherishing evaporated. Her face must have revealed her disappointment, as Rupert's features softened with pity.

'Don't judge too soon,' he said, locking eyes with her. 'I know potion-making is controversial magic. But what they create is quite remarkable. They use rare flora to concoct marvellous elixirs, including some wonderfully reviving brews. I boarded with them for a few months.'

'How interesting,' said Naldy dryly, knowing that the rare practice of potion-making was little more than a witch's hobby. It was scarcely practised anymore, and rightly so, as its results were often questionable. 'That's not quite what we mean when we say the invention of new spells.'

'Nonetheless,' said Ralph, thrilled by the new information about potions, 'we could go south and enquire. Maybe they know something about the Devante or even use one to help create their potions.'

'If they had a Devante,' said Naldy, 'they wouldn't waste their time stewing tree bark.'

'I'm sorry I can't be more help,' said Rupert, his teeth vanishing behind a frown. 'I've travelled to many places but have never heard about these magical books.'

'The reality is dawning,' said Naldy sadly, 'that we're as likely to come across these books as we would be a living dragon. It's impossible. I knew it would be pointless.'

Rupert ordered another large platter and a fresh round of cider, hoping it would cheer them up. But the abundance of food and drink did little to lift Naldy's spirits. They abandoned the discussion of the Devante, and Rupert began recounting his recent travels.

'You've travelled through the Mortous Woods?' said Naldy, aghast.

'Twice. There and back again. Although I was fortunate because a group of wood fairies decided they liked me and followed me on my return journey.'

'Oh, I hate wood fairies,' said Ralph scornfully. 'I hate all fairies.'

'Oh, but you shouldn't, Cousin! Wood fairies make good company when travelling in dark and deadly places, especially if you are alone. Sure, a fairy can't communicate with you in our language, but they communicate in their own odd little ways.'

'Pests if you ask me!' concluded Ralph.

'Fairies are also gifted at knowing when danger is approaching and predicting the weather. You have to make sure you're watching them closely and interpreting their behaviour.'

'What were you doing in the Mortous Woods?' asked Naldy, but Rupert ignored her question and continued talking about wood fairies.

'When I was on my return journey, I'd stopped at a cave to spend the night. I awoke the next morning and was about to set off when I noticed that the lively wood fairies—who'd been pursuing me for five whole days—didn't follow. They stayed inside the cave.'

'You should have left them there,' said Ralph.

'Oh no, I decided I should remain if they were staying. That evening, the worst storm broke out. I was lucky to be in the cave's shelter. Many large tree branches fell.'

'Dangerous place, the Mortous Woods,' said Naldy.

'I was planning on setting sail to Arkus Day.'

Naldy almost slipped off her chair when Rupert

said this. Only a handful of explorers had ever returned from their travels to Arkus Day—the sole other land discovered. It was rumoured to be far out at sea.

'You went to… to Arkus Day?' said Naldy.

'No, he didn't,' said Ralph, staring reproachfully at his cousin. 'He got as far as the Boat Builder, then did the sensible thing and returned.'

'The Boat Builder lives in a remote seaside cottage,' said Rupert, his eyes glistening as he recalled his travels. 'He is the only person brave enough to live on that side of the Mortous Woods, out on the east coast. The beach is lined with boats people have made over the years, which will never set sail.'

'So why didn't you go? What made you turn around?'

'The Boat Builder refuses to sell anyone a boat,' continued Rupert, 'even though hundreds of excellent boats line the sand. He makes everyone who wants to set sail build their own. He helps, of course. The building takes months, and… you see… by the time my boat was nearly finished, I didn't want to go anymore. Something inside me was urging me to turn around.'

'It was the right choice, too, if you ask me,' said Ralph, raising his glass of cider. 'A toast to turning around.'

'One day,' said Rupert, a glint in his eye. 'I will return, take my boat, and sail to Arkus Day. It's sitting along that stretch of golden sand with all the other abandoned vessels. Waiting.'

Ralph ordered more pints of cider, and Rupert regaled them with more stories. They were so engrossed that Naldy soon forgot about the Devante. They shared an apple pie for dessert in the dwelling's rustic bar while Rupert enacted a gripping account of his run-in with a swamp troll. After dessert, the old, grey-haired dwellingtend croakily informed them that no other rooms were available for the night.

'But you've got other rooms,' said Ralph irritably. 'I haven't seen anyone else staying in them.'

'The roof has... erm,' croaked the dwellingtend. 'You see, it caved in a couple weeks back, and we don't usually receive more than one guest at a time.'

In light of this news, Naldy surrendered the bed so Ralph and his cousin could share it while she endured the lumpy sofa. She hoped this gesture of goodwill would adequately demonstrate her selflessness.

The uncomfortable sofa and the cacophony of snoring kept Naldy awake. Her thoughts soon drifted to memories of her six-year-old self. She recalled standing beside her thirty-year-old mother, preparing sardine and bean sprout sandwiches in the cramped kitchen of the Witch House. Her father was away on another business trip in The Great City.

Naldy's mother wrapped the sandwiches in butcher paper and placed them in her black cloak pocket, then she beckoned young Naldy to follow her outside. She was lifted onto the back of her mother's broomstick.

'Hold on tight, Naldy dear.'

Together, they flew over the Kirkwood Forest's green pines, and Naldy held her mother tightly. The wind blew her mother's long black hair, which smelt strongly of sandalwood.

They landed in a small clearing, and six-year-old Naldy stared at the giant talking tree. She couldn't understand why her parents had given it the family's most prized possession.

'Oak protects it for us, my darling,' her mother said in her soft, silvery voice. 'One day, the book will be yours—when you are older. It is an extraordinary spellbook.'

'But I don't understand why we can't keep it at the Witch House with our other books. The big tree frightens me.'

Something heavy fell into eighteen-year-old Naldy's lap, waking her with an uncomfortable jolt. The curtains had been pulled back to let the sunlight into the room.

'Rupert left,' said Ralph.

'What did you throw at me?' asked Naldy, blinking and slowly adjusting to the light. 'You should have let me sleep in.'

'You know it's almost midday,' said Ralph, sitting on the sofa's edge. 'You've been sleeping for hours.'

She sat upright, picking up what Ralph had flung into her lap. It was a parcel wrapped in brown paper, the shape and weight of a hefty book.

'What is this?'

'A book, presumably,' said Ralph, as Naldy wiped the sleep out of her eyes. She noticed an envelope attached to the parcel. 'Rupert left this morning. Don't worry, he does that, just up and leaves. He doesn't like stagnating in one place for too long. I've been waiting for you to wake so we can open it.'

Rupert had written on the envelope:

Naldy and Ralph,
Ralph, do NOT open this without Naldy and do NOT wake her. Let sleeping witches lie.

'What do you mean he's gone?' asked Naldy. Ralph was staring back expectantly.

'Open it up. I've been waiting all morning.'

Naldy turned the envelope over. It had been sealed shut. She tore the wax seal and read the letter to herself while Ralph read over her shoulder:

My dear Cousin Ralph and dearest Naldy,
Forgive me for sneaking out in the early hours of the morning. I am truly sorry I couldn't be more helpful. I wish you both luck and many adventures on your quest to find these Devante.

Remember, a step in any direction is better than no step at all.

Yours,
Rupert

'Go on then,' said Ralph as Naldy finished reading.

She opened the brown paper, and as suspected, a book was inside. Its cover was fashioned from eggplant-purple leather. On the front, written in silver cursive lettering, read *The Invention of the Spell by Barbra Hexogg.*

'Not a Devante,' said Naldy, flipping open the book's cover. 'No 'H', see.'

'You may as well use that book to get the fire going again.'

'What's wrong with it?'

'Scribblings of a madwoman.'

'You've read it?' asked Naldy, taken aback by Ralph's aversion to Rupert's parting gift.

'Barbra Hexogg,' said Ralph, his brow wrinkling, 'is the witch who wrote that article in the *Heatherton Herald*. She is regarded by all scholars—at least all respectable scholars—as a loony provocateur.'

'Rupert kindly left it for us,' said Naldy, standing to begin folding her bedsheets. 'So, I'm keeping it. You know, I might even read it. It could prove helpful. Besides, *you* were highly interested in her article yesterday.'

'I was interested in Maverick's direct quote. I thought *you* didn't want to go hunting for these Devante.'

Naldy ignored him, bundling her sheets up messily—folding them neatly without the aid of magic was too hard.

At breakfast, Ralph perused the local newspaper while Naldy spent the morning flipping through Rupert's gift.

'You seem in a mood,' said Naldy.

'I've told you that book is a waste of your

time,' said Ralph, turning the page of his *Heatherton Herald*.

'What do you think he meant by a step in any direction is better than no step at all?'

'We are not stepping in *that* direction,' said Ralph firmly.

'Which direction?'

'Miss Hexogg lives locally, doesn't she,' said Ralph, avoiding eye contact. 'But it'd be a waste of our time.'

'Maybe we should meet with her, Ralph,' said Naldy, closing her book. 'Your cousin Rupert seems to think it's a reasonable step. She has written a book about the invention of the spell, and she might be able to help us.'

'Tell me,' said Ralph, folding up his newspaper and looking at her intently. 'Does Miss Hexogg's book about spell invention mention anything concerning the Devante? Or even Hannah Hale, for that matter?'

'Well, not that I can find, but,' began Naldy hesitantly, 'it doesn't mean she doesn't know anything about them.'

'Oh! Come on, Naldy!'

'We're meeting with her, Ralph. I met with your cousin, and you'll come with me to visit Miss Hexogg. I'm not going to spend the morning arguing with you. She lives locally, and it's a step! And a step in any direction is better than no step at all.'

'I'm not sure it'll prove true in this case.'

Chapter Seven

SCONES

Termites had eaten away parts of the wooden front door, and even its brass knocker, resembling a dragon's head, desperately needed a polish. The afternoon sunlight barely glinted off it.

'Are you certain you got the right address?' asked Ralph, staring over his shoulder at the neglected front garden. Unforgiving weeds had strangled everything else in it.

Afraid she might accidentally put a hole in the door if she used too much force, Naldy gently lifted the dragon-shaped knocker and gave a delicate tap.

Initially, they had walked right past the decrepit house, believing it to be abandoned. The paint was peeling, the grimy windows needed a wash, and the tattered curtains were pulled tightly closed.

They waited a few moments, but there was no answer, so Naldy knocked again, a little louder this time.

'See, Naldy, you must have the wrong address. This house is abandoned, as we thought.'

Naldy lifted the door knocker a third time but accidentally pulled it entirely from the door. Ralph erupted into laughter, but Naldy, unimpressed, shot him a scolding glare.

The door swung open.

'I don't see what's funny,' said the wrinkly woman standing before them. Naldy recognised her from the photograph in the newspaper. 'That was a precious gift from the great wizard Beckle Jong himself.'

The doddery woman had a kind face but cold, stern grey eyes. Her white hair was unkempt and wild.

'Come inside and close the front door after you. Gently now,' said Barbra, slowly retreating down the slanted hallway.

'We're not going to follow her, are we?' mumbled Ralph.

But Naldy ignored him and pursued the woman, still clutching the dragon knocker. Ralph grudgingly trailed after her.

The interior of the house seemed in worse condition than the exterior. Mould grew in greyish patches across the walls, and cobwebs filled every corner.

The old woman, bizarrely dressed in an elaborate cloak with delicate emerald green stitching, led them to a small sitting room off the main hallway. The room smelt faintly of old books and paper, and was decorated with dusty antique furnishings.

'Are you here about my article in the *Heatherton Herald*?' asked Barbra, gesturing for them to sit. The sofa was upholstered in a floral print with large pink flowers.

'Umm... no, we're not here about that,' said Naldy, placing the brass knocker on the small table between them as Barbra seated herself in the twin armchair opposite.

'*Arcesso*. They didn't want to publish it, you know,' said Barbra, as a tray of brew floated into the room and rested beside the knocker. The old woman reached for the brewpot, shaped like a gargoyle, and poured three cups of a strikingly vibrant purple liquid. Naldy had never seen such a colourful brew. 'I had to take out a paid page so they would print it. The locals here don't appreciate my journalistic talents. But I'm extremely well-known throughout Kirkwood, and I often have to remind them of that.'

Naldy reluctantly picked up her brew and politely took a sip. The liquid had a sour taste.

'Kineleek tree bark,' said Barbra informatively, taking a sip from her own cup. 'It's from the Mortous Woods. Drinking a brew made from the bark of the Kineleek tree will help build up your immunity to its poison.'

'Umm...' said Ralph, his face scrunched as he recovered from the sour sip of the purple liquid. 'We don't plan on venturing through the Mortous Woods anytime soon. Do you have any regular brew?'

'Life is a strange thing, my dear. You never know where it will lead you. Now, why don't you tell me which of my life's written works has brought you here? I will sign them for a small fee.'

'Miss Hexogg,' said Naldy, putting her cup on a

coaster made of red-coloured wood. 'We are here because we wanted to ask you a few questions. We were recently given a copy of your book, *The Invention of the Spell.*'

'Oh, of course! It's been a while since any enthusiasts have visited me about that old chestnut. But yes, of course, I'll gladly autograph it for you.'

'No, no, that's not exactly the reason why we've come. We had some questions... well, about your book.'

'Questions?' repeated Barbra, her smile waning. 'Oh yes, indeed, questions you say?'

'We wanted to ask,' began Ralph, hesitating briefly, 'well... why you don't mention anything about the Devante in your book?'

Barbra stood at the mention of the Devante and slowly hobbled towards the nearest window, pulling back the curtain to peer out. Naldy exchanged a curious glance with Ralph.

'I've been living on this street for ninety-seven years,' said Barbra, her back to them. 'It has hardly changed in all that time. I grew up in this house, you know.'

'Miss Hexogg?' said Naldy. 'Do you know what a Devante is?'

Barbra turned away from the window, panic-stricken.

'What is it?' asked Ralph, staring fearfully in the direction of the window.

'I've forgotten the scones! Oh, dear!'

Naldy and Ralph watched as Barbra hurried from

the room.

'She is as mad as they come,' said Ralph, with an I-told-you-so expression. 'Are you convinced yet, Naldy? Can we go now? Before she returns with mouldy scones. This brew is horrid.'

'You saw it, didn't you?'

'Saw what, Naldy?'

'The look on her face when you mentioned the Devante,' whispered Naldy. 'It registered with her. She knows something, Ralph. I'm certain of it.'

'Naldy,' he said, exasperated, 'she's bat-crazy. She knows nothing about these Devante—she can barely make a drinkable brew.'

'The world is changing,' blurted Barbra as she re-entered, carrying a plate of greyish scones. 'When I was a young girl, the future seemed brighter. But we are heading into dark times, children, oh, I tell you. I'll just place these scones here. Do help yourself now.'

'Can you tell us what you know?' asked Naldy, ignoring the addition of the scones. 'We'd appreciate any information you could help us with.'

'You're asking me what I know?' said Barbra, returning to her armchair.

'Yes, we're trying to find these surviving Devante.'

'Are you just!' said Barbra, perching on the edge of her seat and gesturing at the scones. 'You must try them, for they are delicious.'

Naldy ignored the scones and pressed on, 'I think you know something, and you're avoiding telling us.

But Miss Hexogg, you don't need to be worried—we want to help protect them.'

'Yes, I know what a Devante is,' said Barbra in a croaky voice. Her stare hardened. 'I had possession of two of them.'

Ralph, who had taken a bite of a scone out of politeness, almost choked on it.

'Two?' repeated Ralph, swallowing the dry scone.

'We were each given two, my sister Betty and I.'

'You have two Devante?' asked Naldy, hope igniting within her.

'Eat now,' said Barbra. 'I've added peppered snudgewall, and it will help keep your magic in fit form.'

'Miss Hexogg,' said Naldy, dismissing the scones again, 'we want to protect these Devante. We think they might be in danger.'

'Since their creation, the Devante has been in danger, child. They always will be.'

'There are people,' remarked Naldy, her tone becoming urgent, 'who are on a mission to see them destroyed. But we want to help protect them.'

'Oh, I'm sorry to tell you,' said Barbra, picking up her cup and sipping. She swallowed the sour brew and smiled. 'You're ninety years too late. One of my Devante was stolen from me.'

'Stolen?' Ralph and Naldy said together.

'Yes, I was betrayed by my own sister Betty. Many years ago, four Devante were gifted to my mother. They are rumoured to have been passed down through generations of Hexoggs. When our mother died, my father gave two Devante to my sister and two to me.'

'These are delicious,' said Ralph, chewing on a second scone. 'Naldy, you should try them. They are more scrumptious than they look.'

'Have another,' said Barbra kindly. 'Have as many as you like.'

'Maybe we can help get it back from your sister for you,' said Naldy optimistically.

'Oh, child, I'm sorry to say my sister lost the Devante. The fool not only lost my Devante, but she lost both of hers, too.'

'Lost them? But lost them where?'

'There's no knowing, is there... lost.'

'Pepper snudgewall, you say?' asked Ralph, swallowing the last bite of his second scone and helping himself to another.

Naldy shot Ralph a disapproving glance before continuing, 'Miss Hexogg, you said your sister stole one of your Devante, but what about the other?'

'The other,' said Barbra, keeping a firm gaze on Naldy, 'is in safe hands.'

'You still have it then?'

'I have passed it on. I don't have any children of my own and no friends to whom I would pass on such a burdensome responsibility. When a self-proclaimed protector came knocking, I was relieved to know my spellbook would be kept safe for many years.'

'A protector?' asked Naldy. 'You mean you've given it away?'

Barbra didn't respond. Naldy reached into her cloak pocket and took out the page of Devante, passing it to Barbra.

'Please, Miss Hexogg. Would you confirm if your Devante is still there?'

'Where did you get this?' Barbra asked curiously, taking the parchment. 'Look, there it is, nice and safe, Metallum. It is fourth on your list.'

'I'm glad to hear it is safe,' said Naldy, relieved. 'May we know who this protector is?'

'You needn't worry,' said Barbra, leaning back in her armchair and joining her hands. 'The protector is an accomplished wizard: he is the mayor of Valingfield, Gatengar, Merrydale and Greenswood.'

'Maverick?' said Naldy, her voice catching as if a lump had formed in her throat. Ralph dropped his half-eaten scone. 'You gave your last Devante to Maverick?'

Naldy's heart pounded.

'But he will destroy it,' said Ralph.

'Oh, nonsense,' said Barbra, unperturbed. 'I handed it to him many months ago, and he will not destroy it. You can see it safely written there on your list! Proof!'

Naldy didn't understand and picked up the parchment. Barbra was right—Metallum was still safely there.

'Are you certain it was the mayor you gave your Devante to?'

'How dare you!' said Barbra, insulted, lifting herself out of her armchair. 'You've come to my house and demanded I tell you about my private matters. Maverick warned me others would come searching for it. You can't take it from me... it is safe with the mayor.'

'Maverick will destroy it,' said Naldy desperately. 'You must ask for it back immediately, Miss Hexogg. You must!'

Naldy's insistence sparked an unexpected anger in Barbra, her grey eyes narrowing into an icy glare.

'Out of my house,' said Barbra coldly, pointing a long finger towards the sitting-room door.

A gust of whirling wind appeared in the sitting room, lifting a stack of nearby books from a rickety shelf. The hefty volumes hovered for a moment, but Barbra gracefully swivelled her crooked finger, sending them flying wildly in their direction. Ralph clambered to the door, shrieking, but Naldy stood her ground, batting away the books.

'Please... Miss... Hexogg,' pleaded Naldy as book after book smacked her hard.

'Out,' demanded Barbra. 'Get out!'

The unrelenting knocks became more forceful with each blow, and Naldy had no choice but to hurry out of Barbra's home, following Ralph.

They were pursued by Barbra's library until they crossed the threshold of the rusty garden gate. The books then circled, frantically flapping their pages, and flew back into the house. The front door slammed shut. A smaller, tattered book had flown too slowly and was flapping desperately against the exterior of the termite-eaten door, trying to get back inside.

'That woman is a loony!' yelled Naldy, her voice filled with frustration. 'She wouldn't even hear us out.'

'Let's not take her too seriously,' said Ralph, shooting his second I-told-you-so expression of the day. 'She was probably making it all up. I bet she doesn't even know what a Devante really is.'

'She's not making it up, Ralph,' said Naldy, turning away from the dilapidated house and making her way along the street. 'She knew about the Devante.'

'We were the ones who brought up the Devante,' remarked Ralph, keeping close behind Naldy. Barbra's was the only house on the street that was in disrepair. 'If she is telling the truth, the bright side is Maverick hasn't damaged it yet. And maybe the old witch is right. Maybe he is protecting it.'

'Do you hear yourself?' Naldy snapped. 'You believe Maverick is going to protect the book after he destroyed my family's spellbook and chased us on your magic carpet? Why would he want to destroy mine but save hers?'

'Maybe he wasn't the one who damaged Rubrum,' suggested Ralph, causing Naldy's nostrils to flare with irritation. 'It could have been someone else who destroyed it. You said so yourself—we never actually saw him with the book.'

'Ralph, he locked you in a room and demanded you tell him where the other Devante were hidden.'

'That doesn't mean he wants them destroyed,'

said Ralph, raising his voice. 'If anything, it simply demonstrates that he doesn't know where they are.'

'How can you believe Maverick wants to protect them? Something strange is happening, can't you see?'

'He might be looking for them,' said Ralph, attempting to lower his voice. 'So he can protect them.'

'Ralph,' said Naldy, rounding on him with a disapproving squint, 'if you believe Maverick is a good man, then perhaps you should be on your way. Leave finding the Devante to me.'

Naldy marched away before allowing Ralph the chance to respond. She continued up the street, breathing heavily. Naldy knew arguing with Ralph would only delay breaking Oak's curse.

She stopped, taking a deep breath. She decided it was best to make an effort. The truth was that Metallum had remained safely on the list, and they couldn't be certain of Maverick's intentions.

'I'm just upset,' said Naldy, turning to face him. But Ralph wasn't upright. He was lying on the pavement, his face contorted in pain, his hands hugging his throat as he tried to frantically inhale air.

'Ralph!'

Naldy ran to him and saw a thick purple foam frothing from his mouth.

'Hang on, Ralph,' cried Naldy, holding her palms firmly to his chest. '*Venenum Remedium.*'

Naldy knew the spell only worked as an antidote

to some poisons, but she also knew that wasn't why her magic had no effect.

'Ralph, I can't do anything. It's still daylight—the curse. Help! Somebody, please, help!'

His condition was worsening at an alarming rate. His eyes rolled back into his head.

'She's poisoned you, Ralph! Somebody, please help!'

Naldy glanced up to see a white-haired woman approaching, and at first, she was relieved to see help advancing. However, her hope vanished as she realised the person coming nearer was Barbra.

'Get away,' called Naldy sternly. 'Don't you come any closer! I'm warning you! You've poisoned him!'

Barbra raised her palms. Naldy felt her entire body drop to the road and drag along the cobblestones against her will, sliding further away from Ralph's side. When her body came to a stop, she couldn't move. She no longer had control of her limbs and found herself paralysed from the neck down.

'Stop it,' shouted Naldy desperately. 'Please, stop it!'

From where Naldy lay, she saw Barbra standing over Ralph's body with her palms outstretched. Naldy called out for help again, but it was of no use. Her own voice sounded like it was coming from a faraway place.

Naldy felt her eyes water, and then wet tears slowly trickled across her cheeks. Her body felt numb, her vision blurred, and she could no longer see anything clearly. But she could hear the nearby trees rustling in the breeze and the muffled sound of Barbra uttering strange, unfamiliar words.

Naldy wondered if she had been poisoned by the purple brew.

Everything faded into nothing.

Chapter Eight

BETTY AND BARBRA HEXOGG

'You've done a wonderful job.'

Naldy heard Ralph's voice coming from somewhere in the darkness. She wanted to call out to him but couldn't speak because her lips wouldn't move. Squinting through the blackness, she tried desperately to locate Ralph.

'These scones are delicious.'

Ralph's voice was clear, as if he were a few metres away, but Naldy couldn't see him through the dense black fog. She wanted to tell him not to eat any more scones because they might be poisoned!

All Naldy could do was listen to the sound of him chewing.

Then, the fog slowly dispersed. A white ceiling came into view. Naldy realised she hadn't been standing in a mist at all—she was lying on a comfortable sofa.

Tilting her head, she noticed Ralph sitting smugly on an opposing sofa.

'The scones,' croaked Naldy, her voice cracking as if she hadn't used it for many years.

'We have company,' said an elderly woman's

voice.

Naldy glimpsed Barbra sitting next to Ralph. She wanted to run, but when her head left the cushion, it pounded heavily with a debilitating ache, and her body wouldn't allow her to move any further.

'Easy now,' said the white-haired woman.

'It's alright,' said Ralph reassuringly. 'You should lie back down.'

Naldy opened her mouth to speak again, but her throat was too dry. She wondered if Barbra had hexed Ralph because he appeared oddly calm considering Miss Hexogg had poisoned him.

'Have some brew,' said the older woman, pointing to a cup and saucer on the hardwood table. 'It'll make you feel better. I apologise if I frightened you.'

'But you...' said Naldy, her voice gravelly, '... poisoned.'

'Quite mistaken. It was not I who poisoned Ralph. It was my sister, Barbra.'

It took Naldy a moment to understand what the woman had said.

'Twins,' the wrinkly woman added, smiling tenderly. 'My name is Betty. The brew will help to revive you. Drink.'

Naldy gingerly lifted herself, realising they were in a completely different sitting room—in fact, they were in another house entirely. The furnishings were dust-free, and the room's decor was homely. Two large emerald green sofas acted as the room's centrepiece. Everything here felt cleaner, and the walls weren't crumbling but were lined with delicate pink blossom wallpaper.

'She saved my life,' said Ralph. 'The brew will make you feel better. You're lucky you didn't eat Barbra's scones.'

Naldy stared at the woman in disbelief. The two sisters were so remarkably identical that she could hardly believe the woman before her was not Barbra.

'I'm sorry for dragging you along the cobblestones,' said Betty. 'But I couldn't allow you to interfere with the anti-poison spell. Complicated things to produce, as I'm sure you know.'

Naldy reached for the cup before her, and Betty offered her a warm, motherly look.

'Ralph has told me everything,' continued Betty, buttering a scone for herself. These scones weren't grey like the ones Barbra had served—these were golden yellow and had a fluffy texture. 'He has told me about your quest to save these books. It's noble of you both to take on such an immense challenge.'

'You're the sister who stole her Devante, aren't you?'

'Barbra told you that, did she? Hmm,' said Betty, taking a bite of her scone. 'I'm her only sister. Yes, I did steal one of her books.'

Naldy was still in quite a bit of pain, but the brew helped ease her throbbing head and soothe her throat. She sat forward eagerly, hoping Betty would divulge more information.

'Ralph has told me your book was also recently stolen from you.'

'You told her about Rubrum?' said Naldy,

shooting Ralph an annoyed glance.

'He did, yes. You've been unconscious for a while. There's been a lot for us to discuss.'

Ralph guiltily picked up the last scone. The empty plate lifted itself from the table and silently flew out of the room.

'You're an Effangale witch?' asked Naldy, surprised that Betty hadn't needed to utter a spell to make the plate soar gracefully into the hall, presumably heading for the kitchen.

'My sister is an Effangale witch too,' said Betty, her eyes narrowing. 'She can cast spells without needing to vocalise them.'

Naldy had heard of Effangales before—those who could cast magic with nothing more than a thought—but the only other Effangale she had encountered until today was Maverick. She had not shared this fact with Ralph because he was already unreasonably scared of wizards.

'Betty might be able to help us on our quest,' said Ralph, retrieving his leather journal and quill from his pocket. He was no doubt scribbling this new information about Effangales.

'You'll help us find and protect the Devante?' asked Naldy.

'There is much to tell. But where to begin?' said Betty, her mouth curling into a frown. 'Our mother left this world when we were born. After her death, the books—the four Devante—fell prematurely into our care.' Betty paused, scanning Naldy's face. 'You look paler than your porcelain cup. We should wait until your energy is restored.'

'No, I'm fine. Please, keep going. The brew is helping.'

'If you insist,' said Betty kindly. 'You see, it was the tradition in our family for the Devante to be passed down to the eldest girl. My mother intended to give me all four books, as I am the eldest twin, granted by only a few minutes. My father disagreed with my mother's wish. He thought it was unfair that I should be given all four books while my sister received none, especially since we were born so close together. When our mother passed away during childbirth, our father decided to give us each two books, despite her dying wish for all four to be given to me, the eldest girl, as per Hexogg tradition.'

Betty hesitated, and Naldy forced her muscles to relax, trying not to reveal how much pain she was still in. This was the closest they had come to uncovering the whereabouts of the Devante.

'Growing up, my sister Barbra had no respect for her books. She found them boring and often neglected the two our father had given her. One day, she left the smallest of her two books, Rosea, out in the front garden. It was a tattered, faded pink book in poor condition. I took it. She always suspected I'd stolen it, and I've always denied I was the thief. But twins have a way of knowing the truth about these things.'

'Did you know the books were Devante?' Ralph asked curiously.

'We always knew the books were special, for they

had survived The Great Witch Hunt and weren't on The Establishment's approved list. But it wasn't until many years later that we discovered they held rare magic.'

'Did you ever try and steal Barbra's other book?' Naldy enquired before sipping her brew.

'Oh, I would have done had I the chance. But after her first book went missing, she guarded the other, Metallum, with her life. It was the more impressive of the two.'

'Do you have them here?' Naldy asked hopefully, perching on the edge of her seat.

'I do not,' replied Betty, causing Naldy to sink back into the sofa's cushions. 'But I know where they are hidden—I was the one who hid them.'

Hope coursed through Naldy, making her instinctively sit upright again. Ralph's half-eaten scone halted midway to his mouth.

'Many years ago,' said Betty, her tone tinged with nostalgia, 'I decided I needed to find a more permanent location for the Devante. It was our seventieth birthday, and as I stared at my sister's face—so much like mine, as you've seen—I realised how terribly old we had both become. Neither of us had children, and I knew there was little time left to find a new home for the books.'

'But they're safe?' Ralph implored anxiously. 'Hidden someplace where nobody can ever find them, yes?'

Naldy could sense Ralph's hope swelling, just as hers was. Perhaps they wouldn't need to search for the books after all. If Betty had hidden them out of Maverick's reach, their quest could end here.

'As you already know,' said Betty, her tone hardening, 'Maverick visited my sister a few months ago, and she irresponsibly gave him her last book, Metallum. I believe she—as I did—feared for the book's survival. She thought he would protect it for her.'

'We have a list of surviving Devante,' said Ralph cautiously, glancing at Naldy. 'I think it might prove Maverick has no intention of destroying your sister's book.'

'Ralph,' said Naldy moodily. 'He wants to destroy them. Just because he hasn't done it yet doesn't mean he won't.'

Betty seemed uncomfortable. She lifted herself from the sofa, picking up the empty brewpot by hand.

'Fresh brew?' she asked, tottering from the room before they could reply.

Ralph cocked his head, bewildered. Neither said anything to the other. It wasn't until they could hear Betty flitting about the kitchen at the other end of the house that Naldy broke the stubborn silence.

'There's something she's not telling us,' whispered Naldy.

'I'd say.'

'I am glad you aren't poisoned, Ralph,' said Naldy softly. 'You're looking much better now, without the purple froth pouring from your mouth.'

'I appreciate you trying to help. When you were

standing over me and uttering spells, I thought you were the one poisoning me. We were lucky Betty was watching us from her curtains.'

'I want you to know,' said Naldy, a little awkwardly but sincerely, 'that I wouldn't poison you. Not only because it wouldn't help me break my curse, but also because... well...'

'Are you saying you care about me?'

'I'm just saying I wouldn't poison you. I thought you were going to die. It was horrible.'

Betty reappeared with a silver tray of mini sweet pastries but without the brewpot. She set the tray on the hardwood table and then reluctantly settled back onto the emerald sofa.

'Help yourself. There's jam-filled or cinnamon.'

'Betty, if you're worried,' said Ralph, happily picking up several mini pastries at once, 'about whether you can trust us...'

'Oh no, it's nothing like that,' Betty replied, folding her wrinkled hands in her lap. 'I think Maverick has no intention of harming Metallum—at least not yet.'

'Yet?' Ralph prompted.

'You see,' explained Betty, 'the Devante, like most things that possess power, have a hierarchy.'

'A hierarchy?' said Naldy. 'You think Metallum is more powerful than Rubrum?'

'Precisely,' said Betty. 'And from what you've told me, I think Maverick might be on a quest to possess the highest-ranking Devante.'

'But why destroy the lower-ranking ones?' Naldy

asked irritably, her head throbbing with frustration. 'That doesn't make any sense. Why doesn't he keep them all?'

'You mentioned you have a list of these surviving Devante? May I see it, please?'

'Naldy,' said Ralph, his eyes darting nervously towards her, knowing she was currently in possession of it.

She reluctantly removed the parchment from her cloak pocket and handed it to Betty. The woman inspected the page closely before handing it back. Betty didn't say anything, but tears welled in her eyes.

'What is it?' asked Ralph delicately.

Betty directed her gaze at the door, and the hot brewpot floated into the room. She took hold of its wooden handle and poured the hot amber liquid into their empty cups, keeping her head bowed low.

'For some time, I have had my suspicions,' she said finally, her voice quivering with what seemed like tremendous emotional pain. 'But this list you've shown me confirms what I have feared most.'

'Confirms what fear?' pressed Naldy.

'For many years, I had hoped—or ignorantly believed—that the Corium had been destroyed. But I can see it there, safely on your list.'

'But what's so special about the Corium?' asked Ralph, noisily chewing on his pastry.

'Have you heard of the witch Hannah Hale?'

'Yes, we've been hearing a lot about her lately,' answered Naldy impatiently.

'When the Devante were created, Hannah feared her invention might be used for dark magic. And so, the Corium was made to control the others— to restrict them from producing wicked spells. Her intentions were good, but her plan had a significant flaw.'

'What flaw?' asked Ralph, setting down his half-eaten pastry.

'And if she banned evil spells,' said Naldy, annoyed at Betty for not getting to her point, 'then what is the issue?'

'The Devante hold powerful magic,' explained Betty patiently, 'likely the most potent to ever exist. Almost any spell can be created with them —except those that were banned. Some Devante-hunters have long believed that Hannah destroyed the Corium to lock the bans in place forever, so no one could ever produce such dark magic using the other Devante.'

'But our list says she didn't destroy the Corium,' said Ralph, his mouth agape and filled with half-chewed pastry.

'And now you see my fear,' said Betty, avoiding meeting their eyes.

'Why bother with all these less powerful books?' said Naldy. 'Why is Maverick searching for these lower-ranking Devante if what he actually desires is this Corium?'

'Because, my dear,' replied Betty, topping up their cups with more brew, 'he doesn't want anyone getting in his way. The other Devante might be unable to create certain wicked magic, but they can still be used to invent many spells. Maverick isn't taking any chances. I think he'll destroy all lower-ranking Devante so they can't accidentally fall into the hands of others.'

Naldy wasn't sure if her head was throbbing from the flood of new information or from her earlier fall. It seemed they had embarked on a much more critical and dangerous quest than they had initially realised.

'Betty, there is something else I don't understand,' said Naldy thoughtfully. 'Something I haven't been able to get my head around.'

'Yes, my dear?'

'How did they find my family's spellbook?'

'My sister's ignorance prevented her from delving too deeply into Devante lore,' replied Betty. She sighed before continuing. 'Her book, Metallum, could have helped her find Rosea many years ago, had she realised the Devante's power and tried. Only recently has Barbra come to understand their true value. You see, a higher-ranking Devante can locate the lower-ranking ones.'

'But that means—'

'Yes,' said Betty, taking a deep breath before continuing. 'Maverick has possession of Metallum, so he can find the locations of the four lower-ranking Devante—three, my apologies—now that he has sadly destroyed Rubrum.'

'Which other books did your mother leave for you?' asked Naldy.

'As I mentioned, Rosea was given to my sister, the book I stole from her,' said Betty, counting on her wrinkled fingers as she listed them. 'It is the lowest-ranking, and Metallum was also passed to her. I was given Caeruleum and Aurum.'

'The Aurum?' repeated Ralph in surprise. 'But that's—'

'It is,' said Betty solemnly. 'It ranks higher than the Devante Maverick currently has.'

It dawned on Naldy that if Betty had hidden the Aurum alongside the Caeruleum and Rosea, Maverick could use Metallum to locate this higher-ranking Devante. It was as if Betty had read Naldy's mind, for she nervously twiddled her fingers.

'I know what you are thinking,' said Betty in a quiet voice. 'I did, foolishly, hide them together. I thought they would be safe. But—'

'If Maverick can see the location of Caeruleum and Rosea,' said Naldy anxiously, 'he will find the Aurum. We must protect them.'

Betty briskly stood, collecting the plate of remaining pastries and the brewpot, which was still half full. Naldy also rose, assuming Betty was eager to beat Maverick to the Devante.

'Sit down,' said Betty firmly. 'There is more I must tell you.'

Naldy didn't sit. She refused to waste any time. Maverick could already be making his way to Betty's hiding place, and they had to get there first before Maverick realised that the Aurum was hidden there, too.

'Caeruleum is next on the list after Rubrum,' said Naldy. 'We must hurry.'

'I do not believe Maverick will seek the Caeruleum next,' said Betty calmly. 'The next book he will go after is the Aurantiaco. Although it ranks lower, it is far easier to access than the books I have hidden. He cannot see the location of Aurum, and he certainly does not know it is hidden alongside the Caeruleum or Rosea.'

'You know where the Aurantiaco is as well?' said Ralph, stunned by their luck. He stood up, pocketing the remaining pastries from the plate Betty was holding. 'We'd best get a move on if we're to get there before Maverick does.'

Naldy couldn't believe their luck either. Just that morning, they had no clue about the whereabouts of any Devante. Now, they were in the company of someone who could lead them to four, and they knew that a fifth was with Maverick.

Betty didn't seem as excited. She shuffled nervously to the sitting room door, stopping when she reached it, the empty pastry plate in one hand and the brewpot in the other. Then, without turning to face them, she said in a quavering voice, 'The thing is, I must tell you that my hiding place was the Edengar Mountains.'

After Betty had said this, she hurried from the room.

'Edengar?' said Ralph in shock, slumping back onto the sofa, squishing the pastries in his back pocket. 'Naldy, there is no way we are trekking through the Edengar Mountains.'

'But, Ralph.'

'That's not happening!'

'She managed to take them there, so Betty must know a safe passage.'

'Safe!' said Ralph, outraged. 'The Edengar Mountains are not safe! People don't return from those mountains, Naldy!'

'Ralph is right,' said Betty quietly. She was standing in the doorway again, her hands empty. 'The Edengar Mountains are not safe. They are a vast and treacherous place, which is why I chose them as the hiding place for the three books.'

'Maverick isn't foolish enough to tackle Edengar,' said Ralph resolutely. 'So, we don't need to worry about him going after Betty and Barbra's spellbooks.'

'He will,' rebutted Naldy. 'He has a Devante, and he'll just invent spells to protect himself along the way.'

Betty seemed impressed by what Naldy had said.

'I'm afraid Naldy is quite right. Navigating the mountains, although still dangerous, is far easier with the help of a Devante.'

Betty hesitated, as if she wanted to share something else but was holding back.

'What is it?' asked Naldy slowly.

'I think there might be something... there is something else you both need to know. I might sound crazy saying it. I have been avoiding telling you this. But I think it is important that you both know.'

Before Betty could say anything more, there was a hard knock on the front door. It echoed eerily up the hallway and into the sitting room. Betty shuffled to the nearest window, bending her head to peek through the sheers, trying to get a view of the front door.

'The silly witch,' said Betty to herself, her face hardening in anger as she pulled the curtains closed, shrouding them in shadow.

'Who is it?' asked Ralph curiously, a speck of fear in his eyes. 'Is it your sister Barbra?'

The knock came again, louder this time.

'No, it is not Barbra,' said Betty, making for the sitting room door. 'It is Maverick. Come with me, quickly now.'

Chests pounding with anxiety, they stayed close behind Betty, hurrying into the long hall towards a small kitchen at the far end. The kitchen had a rectangular table, and the shelves above the sink were stacked with jars of herbs, spices, grains, and a variety of strange raw meats.

Betty collected a leather bag and a broomstick beside the back door, which led out into the rear garden. It was as if she had prepared for this day, knowing she might need to depart in a hurry.

'But how?' asked Ralph, dumbfounded. His brow was sweating. 'How does Maverick know where we are?'

'Barbra must have tipped him off.'

The knock came again—this time, it was so loud it vibrated the floor. They sped out into the beautiful garden, and Naldy wished there had been time to stop and enjoy its peacefulness. It boasted big, blooming roses, and Naldy recognised the strange pink flowers from the print on Barbra's antique sofa.

'Here, take this,' said Betty, handing Naldy a second broomstick that had been leaning on the outside of the house.

'I can't.'

'Can't?'

'I won't be able to fly it. I'm cursed.'

'Oh dear, we'll all have to go on one and hope it doesn't slow us down.'

Betty mounted the broom, and Ralph climbed sceptically on after her. His complexion was paler than Naldy had ever seen.

'I wish Maverick hadn't stolen my carpet,' said Ralph.

Naldy clambered on behind him, holding tightly to his waist. Glancing over her shoulder, through the kitchen window, she saw the front door fall off its hinges at the end of the hallway. The doorway framed the slim silhouette of Maverick, leaning maliciously on his black cane.

Betty kicked off the ground, and the broomstick shot upwards. Naldy feared they weren't flying fast enough. With the weight of all three of them, the broom struggled to gain speed, while Naldy fought to hold on at the far end.

Looking down, she saw Maverick appear in Betty's back garden. She was relieved to see he wasn't carrying a broomstick. But her relief was short-lived as Maverick picked up the broom Betty had offered her moments ago, and Naldy felt guilty she hadn't thought to take the spare with them. *Prosterno* spells flew from Maverick's cane as he leaped onto the broomstick and pursued them— Betty skilfully swerved out of their way.

Naldy gripped Ralph tightly, feeling helpless because she couldn't cast any spells back at Maverick due to her curse.

The three of them on the same broom were too heavy—Maverick was closing in. It was a matter of time before he caught up. Betty lifted one hand off the broom.

'Duck your heads!' she shouted. Ralph and Naldy managed to move just in time as Betty sent a *Prosterno* spell speeding towards Maverick.

The wizard dangerously dipped his broomstick to avoid getting hit, causing Betty's spell to miss him by a long shot. He straightened up and, with a determined jab of his black cane, shot another brilliant black *Prosterno* spell. It whizzed aggressively towards them. Naldy ducked, and the black spell collided with Ralph. He was instantly knocked unconscious, and it was fortunate that Naldy was positioned behind him to hold his body steady as it went limp. Without her, Ralph would have fallen off and plummeted to the ground.

The wind whooshed past them as Naldy struggled to keep both herself and Ralph on the broom. Betty swerved, making turbulent twists to avoid Maverick's unrelenting spells. If Naldy were hit next, both she and Ralph would be at the mercy of gravity—and the only way to undo a *Prosterno* spell was to wait for its effects to wear off.

'Hold tight,' said Betty, calling over the roaring wind.

She directed the broomstick down towards the tall pines of the Kirkwood Forest. Naldy had one hand tightly gripped around the broomstick while her other struggled to keep Ralph steady—he flopped about like a flimsy rag doll.

Betty steered them dangerously amongst the forest's trees, continuing at a neck-breaking pace and dodging hazardous branches. But Maverick was undeterred and remained close on their tail.

They narrowly missed colliding with trees, dodging and swerving this way and that, until Naldy heard a flinch-inducing crunch from behind.

Maverick had slammed into a tall pine tree and fallen to the forest floor. She glimpsed him hastening to his feet—but Betty shot one last purple *Prosterno* spell, which collided with the wizard and rendered him paralysed.

Betty piloted them upwards, out of danger.

Once they were high above the trees again, it was clear that Maverick was no longer chasing them. Naldy expected to see the Edengar Mountains in the distance. Instead, she saw the impressive stone buildings of The Great City.

'I thought we were going to the mountains?'

'We will. But we need to make a detour first.'

Chapter Nine

THE BLECKDALE WITCHERY MUSEUM

'**A**nything for him?' asked the waiter, pointing a long ostrich feather quill at Ralph, who was awkwardly perched unconscious beside Naldy in the bistro's booth.

'A green brew, please,' said Betty with a kind smile. The waiter finished scribbling the order and then left the table.

Betty had levitated Ralph through the crowded cobblestone lanes of The Great City. Naldy had been concerned they would draw unwanted attention. However, the streets had been bustling with all sorts of quirky individuals, so nobody seemed to have noticed—or perhaps cared—that Ralph had drifted along unconscious.

'We passed over a dozen dwellings and bistros on the way here,' said Naldy, brushing her black hair out of her face.

Betty didn't respond—she was preoccupied rummaging through her leather bag, looking for something.

'What's so special about this bistro?' asked Naldy. Again, Betty didn't reply.

Their black cowhide booth was positioned by

the large window of the lively bistro called *The Mortismor,* facing a wide cobblestone street where bicycles and horse-drawn carts passed by. On the other side, Naldy could see broad stone steps leading up to the entrance of the most renowned witch museum, The Bleckdale Witchery Museum. Naldy had never been to The Great City, but she had heard many stories about it from her father.

Ralph grunted and then mumbled something inaudible. His eyes opened and then widened.

'Did I fall asleep?'

'You got hit by a *Prosterno* spell, my dear,' said Betty, closing her leather bag. 'Unfortunately, we could do nothing except wait for it to wear off.'

Ralph appeared dazed as he glanced curiously at the waiters darting across the bistro's black-and-white checkered floor, carrying plates stacked high with lavishly presented meals.

'This isn't the Edengar Mountains,' said Ralph flatly.

'No, it is not,' said Betty, slightly lowering her voice. 'I need to confess something to you both, and you mightn't believe me when I do.'

The waiter, who had taken their order moments earlier, arrived with a green brew and two sweet-looking pink drinks.

'Wave when you're ready to order meals,' he said, placing the drinks in front of them and rushing to attend to a cheery group of witches who were waving the flashy dessert menu.

'Why didn't I get a pink drink?' Ralph asked,

enviously eyeing Betty's and Naldy's.

'Because you were unconscious,' said Naldy.

'Because the green brew will help to revive you better,' Betty explained matter-of-factly. 'We can get you one of these fancy ones after you finish your reviving brew, if there's still time.'

'We don't have time,' said Naldy, unsettled they weren't already on their way to the Edengar Mountains.

'Years ago,' said Betty, disregarding Naldy's remark, 'when I took the three books to Edengar, I knew they had to be left somewhere secure.'

'I don't think you could have chosen a more secure place,' said Ralph, pettishly sipping his green brew. 'Edengar is impossibly secure.'

'I used the power of the Devante to help find a… well… a suitable place. I left the books hidden deep in a dragon's cave.'

'A dragon's cave?' repeated Ralph, wiggling a finger in his ear as if to check whether Maverick's *Prosterno* spell had damaged his hearing. 'Do you mean an old dragon's cave? Like where a dragon *used* to live?'

Betty raised a grey eyebrow and took a sip of her pink drink.

'You mean to say the books are guarded by a… a living dragon?' Naldy asked, starting to wonder if Betty was as unhinged as her twin sister.

'Dragons, as you probably know,' said Betty, 'are solitary creatures who like to have their own space.'

'Dragons,' replied Ralph, 'as we know, are extinct!'

'Endangered, yes,' continued Betty, 'but not extinct. Strangely, all six dragons have set up their caves rather unusually close together, deep within a ravine in the Edengar Mountains.'

'All six!' Naldy and Ralph exclaimed in unison.

Ralph looked as if the revelation might knock him unconscious again.

'Yes, did I not mention that part?' said Betty indifferently. 'Four adults and two younglings. They are the last of their kind, at least in this land. Dragons live for hundreds of years, and I think they might have taken refuge in the ravine since The Great Witch Hunt. Not only were witches burnt during that time, but many other magical creatures were hunted, including dragons. I used the Devante to guide me to any living dragons... and I found the last six.'

'If what you're telling us is true,' said Ralph uneasily. 'Then we really needn't worry about Maverick getting hold of the books.'

'I think you're underestimating Maverick,' said Betty, leaning forward. 'Now, to business. The Edengar Mountains are unfathomably vast, and we would never find the dragon caves without the same aid that Maverick possesses.'

'What aid?' asked Naldy.

'His cane,' said Ralph.

'A Devante,' Betty corrected.

'But we don't have a Devante,' said Ralph, scratching his head as he contemplated how long he had been unconscious. 'Do we have a Devante?'

Betty glanced knowingly out the window.

'The museum,' said Naldy, understanding that Betty was looking at the Bleckdale Witchery Museum.

'It is not only dragons that the museum foolishly believes to be extinct,' said Betty, leaning closer. 'The museum is run by The Great City's Establishment, and The Establishment has long believed that all Devante perished years ago. I'm sure you've both heard of The Bleckdale Witchery Museum?'

'Yes—home to the largest collection of witch and wizard history in existence,' said Ralph fondly. 'But I've never seen anything about these Devante at the museum.'

'Of course not,' said Betty. 'You won't find a single mention of the Devante inside. The Establishment wouldn't dare, for fear they might give witches ideas. They want the legend of the Devante to fade away.'

'I've never been inside,' said Naldy, a bit annoyed at being the only one unfamiliar with the museum's interior. 'But I don't see why we're considering traipsing through a museum when we should be getting a head start on Maverick in Edengar.'

'You won't find a single mention of the Devante, but what you will find is...'

Betty reached into her bag and rummaged around for a moment before pulling out a burnt-orange book.

'Ah. You'll find this,' said Betty, placing the book on the bistro's table.

Naldy was underwhelmed. Granted, it was a beautiful book, with an undeniably pretty engraving of a peacock on its cover, but she couldn't see its significance.

'Is this…?' said Ralph, leaning in to run his hands over the book's cover. 'Is this a Devante?'

'It's not the Aurantiaco,' said Betty, pushing the book closer to Ralph so he could examine it more closely.

'Are you going to tell us what it is, then?' asked Naldy, picking up her pink drink. 'Or how it's supposed to help us?'

'This is a fake,' said Betty, nodding sheepishly at the book. 'It is a fraudulent copy of the Aurantiaco.'

'How is a fake supposed to help us?' asked Naldy, now convinced that Betty was, indeed, as loopy as Barbra.

Ralph's brow crinkled in confusion.

'Oh, child,' said Betty, chuckling. 'We are not taking this one to Edengar. The real one is inside there.'

Betty pointed out the window across the road at the museum.

'But you said—'

'You will not find any mention of the Devante. However, you will find an orange book that holds the earliest record of the levitation spell. It also happens to be the Aurantiaco. We're fortunate that The Establishment hasn't recognised it as a Devante; otherwise, they would have destroyed it long ago.'

'We can't burgle a museum!' said Ralph loudly,

causing nearby tables to flinch and glower at their booth.

'There is no way to navigate Edengar without it,' said Betty, gesturing for Ralph to lower his voice.

'It's not a library,' remarked Ralph heatedly. 'We can't walk in and borrow the book. There are guards, and we'll end up imprisoned.'

'How did you...' Naldy picked up the book to inspect it. 'But how... it even has the indented 'H' inside its cover. And it looks aged.'

'I recreated it when I still had the Aurum,' said Betty, a glint in her eye.

'You seem well-prepared to steal this book,' said Ralph, huffing. 'Why don't you go and get it, while Naldy and I stay here and wait for you? I'll have one of those pink drinks.'

'I am ninety-seven years old,' said Betty. She paused to finish off her own pink drink. 'If I am up for the challenge, surely the spritely young things in front of me are. I cannot manage it alone. The plan I have devised requires more than one of us, and if it required only one, I would have stolen it long ago.'

'You want us arrested!' said Ralph. 'Magic can't be used inside the museum. You want us caught and behind bars.'

'I think we should do it,' said Naldy softly.

Ralph stared at her, outraged.

'We knew this was always going to be difficult,' continued Naldy, meeting his gaze. 'But if you don't want to come with us, don't. Personally, I'm less afraid of the museum and more afraid of the mountains. So, what is it? Are you in or out?'

Ralph sighed and then nodded. 'In.'

Betty waved down the waiter and ordered Ralph his own pink drink. She also ordered a large amount of food, which arrived shortly for them to share. They ate and drank while Betty divulged her plan. It involved stealing a guard's access stone, which allowed its carrier to use magic inside the museum.

For the first time, Naldy was glad to be cursed, as it meant she was given the easier task of swapping the two books rather than the more difficult job of stealing the access stone.

The sun seemed to be travelling faster than usual, and before Naldy could let her lunch settle in her stomach, they were strolling across the sunny street towards the enormous stone museum.

'I do not wish to see any of us put behind bars,' said Betty, holding out the handle of the broomstick she was carrying to stop them so that a horse and cart could pass. 'But it's important to remember: we mustn't, at any cost, divert from the plan, not even to save each other should the worst transpire.'

'I'll distract the guard,' whispered Ralph courageously, repeating their plan aloud as if he'd joined a high-profile spy organisation. 'Betty will secure the access stone, and Naldy will switch the books.'

As they ascended the many steps leading to the impressive building, constructed from large grey stone blocks—the type only old magic could have produced—Naldy couldn't help but ponder if they were entertaining a madwoman's hare-brained scheme.

'How many more steps,' groaned Ralph as they approached the top.

'Why is it called Bleckdale?' Naldy asked as they reached the entrance marked by grand wooden doors.

'You're a witch, and you don't know why it's named Bleckdale?' said Ralph, shaking his head.

'It's what this city used to be called,' answered Betty kindly. 'It once had the largest population of witches and wizards. The name was changed to The Great City during The Great Witch Hunt.'

They entered through the majestic wooden doors, where a stern guard dressed in the standard uniform issued by The Establishment greeted them with a dry smile. Naldy found the guard intimidating in his blue military blazer with gold buttons fastened down the front and his blue felt porkpie hat sitting askew on his head. The room was narrow, with a second pair of smaller maple doors behind a long security desk.

'I'll need your broomstick,' said the guard, holding out his hand.

Betty relinquished the broomstick she was carrying, and Naldy focused hard on keeping her breathing casual. The sight of the guard seemed to have caused her throat to constrict with nerves.

'Cloak pockets, turn them out, please. I'll have to inspect that bag too, madam.'

They emptied their pockets, and the guard

nodded in approval. He then turned his attention to inspecting Betty's leather bag, reaching in and pulling out the burnt-orange book.

'My recipe spellbook,' said Betty sweetly.

The guard gave a curt nod of his blue porkpie hat, returning the book and the bag to Betty.

'Enjoy your visit,' said the guard.

They continued through the second pair of wooden doors into a magnificent entrance chamber. The large room, packed with visitors, had a very high ceiling. Naldy barely had time to take in the lively crowd before her eyes were drawn upwards to a display of dragon bones. They were arranged in the form of a flying dragon, its great wing bones outstretched in mid-flight, taking up nearly the entire ceiling.

'Terrifying,' said Ralph, his mouth agape. 'We're going to journey to the mountains to retrieve books from—I'm sorry, Betty—how many did you say? Six of them? The books are surely safer left where they are now.'

'My dears, as long as Maverick knows where the books are, they will not be safe.'

The older woman had to drag them away from staring at the monstrous display of bones. She led them through the museum's long stone corridors, each lined with glass cabinets displaying various artefacts: a collection of rare crystals, ancient scrolls, elven daggers, bewitched rusty keys, and many other items.

Occasionally, a passage would open into a larger

room filled with more oddities on display. These more spacious chambers had additional corridors branching off from them. Naldy felt lucky to have Betty as their guide, as the museum felt like its own city.

'Don't they have a map?' asked Naldy.

Betty stopped when they came to a vast passage exhibiting old broomsticks.

'These aren't books,' said Ralph, crinkling his nose as he stared at them.

'We mustn't rush to the spellbooks,' said Betty firmly. 'We don't want to draw attention to ourselves, just behave like ordinary visitors and have a little look around.'

Naldy pretended to admire an archaic broomstick. It was made from a long, thick tree branch with a meagre bundle of ragged twigs tied to its end. She read the plaque beside it:

The First Broomstick

Grand Wizard Julian Hereto Blackbard created the first broomstick in 1203. Navigation was difficult, and multiple deaths by broomstick nearly led to the invention's abandonment until Julian managed to refine his design.

'Let us move along,' said Betty before Naldy could finish reading the plaque. They followed her down a large stone corridor, and when they came to a passageway lined with ancient quills, Betty stopped and faced Naldy.

'I believe you'll need this,' said Betty, discreetly handing her the orange book from her leather bag.

Naldy placed it securely in her cloak pocket. She felt a lump forming in her throat, and her palms became unpleasantly clammy. They delved deeper and deeper into the depths of the museum, stopping occasionally to pretend to admire the artefacts. Naldy found she didn't need to feign interest, as most of the museum's displays were genuinely fascinating. They viewed a collection of immaculate robes, magical necklaces designed to bring luck to their wearer, crystal balls with coloured smoke floating inside, and many other curious items.

When they reached the room containing ancient spellbooks, situated five stories below ground, Naldy's nerves peaked. Were they making a foolish mistake by trusting Betty? One thing was certain: Naldy was sure she appeared guilty before she had committed any crime.

The chamber walls were lined with bookshelves behind a thick layer of glass, but the shelves were mostly bare, with fewer than sixty books in the entire room. Naldy had seen many of the titles before.

'I've never been inside this room,' said Ralph. 'It's quite empty. Where are all the spellbooks?'

'Lost to time,' said Betty sadly. 'This is all that remains after The Great Witch Hunt. Most witch families own copies of these spellbooks. You're mainly looking at The Establishment's approved list. Various editions were printed with different titles and slight amendments—usually removing a spell or two. But there are a few others here: rare volumes that survived and were donated to the museum. You'll notice their pages don't turn, and it's rumoured they contain forgotten spells The Establishment doesn't want known.'

'There are thousands more books in other chambers,' said Ralph.

'Yes,' said Betty, 'but none of those are spellbooks. They are mostly lengthy historical accounts.'

In the centre of the room were a few podiums encased in glass. The books on the stands were slowly turning their own pages.

'Now, Naldy, you will need to wait until I've undone the sensor charm,' said Betty quietly, eyeing a guard who had arrived to patrol the long room. 'You'll find the Aurantiaco on the other side of this room. The museum will close in less than an hour, so we'd better get a wriggle on.'

Naldy made her way across the stone floor, passing the guard. She could feel her heart beating loudly and worried the guard might hear it.

The Aurantiaco was resting on a small podium encased in thick glass. Naldy was impressed by the book's likeness to the one in her pocket—they were as identical as Betty was to Barbra.

Mindful not to arouse suspicion with her lingering, Naldy decided to read the small plaque:

The Levitation Spell
Unknown author

Here lies the earliest known record of the levitation spell. Burnt-orange in colour, this spellbook is estimated to have been created before The Great Witch Hunt. Donated to the museum by The Greyfairywell Family Trust.

Naldy couldn't do anything until Betty had stolen the guard's access stone, so she read the plaque several times. After skimming it for the fourth time, she turned her attention to the adjacent podium, which exhibited a black leather book.

Seeing Spells III, First Edition
Glenda Frog & The Establishment's Literary Circle

Esteemed author Glenda Frog, renowned for her influential book Communicating with Witches, *collaborated with The Establishment to create the* Seeing Spells Series. *This volume was intended to educate the non-magical community on identifying and reporting unapproved spells.*

However, the first edition inadvertently included the full texts of spells that The Establishment had prohibited. It is rumoured that witches removed pages to access these forbidden spells. Subsequent editions of the book removed the spells' incantations to prevent misuse.

As the pages turned themselves, Naldy noticed that many had been ripped out, leaving ragged edges.

'Oh! We're so sorry,' said Ralph to the guard. 'How clumsy of me.'

In the reflection of the glass casing, Naldy saw Ralph helping the guard up from the ground while Betty sneakily took the access stone from his belt. Naldy knew they had collided with the guard intentionally, just as planned.

'It's fine,' mumbled the guard dryly.

She positioned herself in front of the Aurantiaco as Ralph and Betty moved towards the exit. Naldy reached into her cloak and took out the fake book. As anticipated, the glass casing vanished, exposing the orange spellbook on the podium. She carefully lifted the Aurantiaco from the stand, but before she could replace it with Betty's fraudulent copy, she felt a hand on her shoulder.

'Naldy, stop! You can't,' said a familiar voice behind her.

Naldy turned and came face to face with someone she recognised.

'Rupert?'

'Put it back,' he urged.

Her heart felt as if it had stopped. There was no time to explain to Rupert what she was doing. Naldy pivoted to face the podium before the glass was restored. The two books were perfect twins, and Rupert's distraction had caused her to forget which was which.

Time was up; the plinth's glass reappeared, leaving the plinth empty. Naldy held both the fraudulent and the real Aurantiaco, still trying to determine which was which.

Chapter Ten

FLIGHT ON THE FIRST

Over Rupert's shoulder, Naldy saw the guard reaching for his belt—only to realise his access stone was missing.

'Run,' said Naldy to Rupert.

The two bolted to the nearest corridor, weaving between podiums. In the passageway, they encountered Ralph and Betty, who were casually strolling.

'Run! Just run!' shouted Naldy.

Ralph was momentarily stunned by the sight of his cousin Rupert and stood frozen in shock. It wasn't until Naldy rushed past him that he snapped out of his daze and started running, with the museum guard pursuing.

'You... really... should have... listened to me,' puffed Rupert, jogging beside her.

They were still five floors below ground level, and Naldy could not see how their escape would be possible. The situation was worsened by the shrieks of surprise from other museum visitors as they raced past.

'The book... it's...'

'Now is not the time, Rupert,' interrupted Naldy as she rounded a corner, narrowly avoiding a large display cabinet showcasing elaborate knight's armour. 'You've ruined our plan.'

They made their way up a flight of stone steps and continued along another corridor where stuffed birds were posed in lifelike positions. Beside each bird was a feather quill fashioned from one of its feathers.

Naldy and Rupert were leading, with Ralph and Betty close behind. But that quickly changed when three more guards rounded the corner ahead, approaching briskly. Guards were now coming from both directions, and the ones who had just joined the chase still had their access stones.

Prosterno spells ricocheted off the nearby display cabinets with loud cracks. Betty and Ralph veered down a narrower side passage, with Naldy and Rupert right on their heels. Betty, now in the lead, was sending impressively quick *Prosterno* spells back over her shoulder at the guards.

'We're still four floors below ground,' said Naldy to Rupert. 'We'll never make it.'

They rounded another corner—to find more guards rushing towards them from the end of the corridor. With no side passages to escape to, they had no choice but to keep moving. It was a miracle that the four of them avoided the numerous whizzing balls of light, though the baffled patrons were not so fortunate.

Betty impressively dodged an oncoming guard,

but Ralph crashed right into him. One of the guards cast a spell to bind Ralph's legs, causing him to drop to the floor. Meanwhile, balls of light continued to ricochet haphazardly off the glass display cabinets.

Betty, Rupert and Naldy managed to weave past the guards, who were focused on restraining Ralph.

'We can't go back,' urged Betty as they turned into another long corridor. 'We must protect the Devante.'

Betty didn't stop running until they reached a passage lined with ancient broomsticks.

The old woman cast a spell to vanish the glass of a nearby cabinet. Naldy recognised the hefty old broom Betty picked up as the Grand Wizard Blackbard's.

'Get on.'

'Will that thing still fly?' asked Rupert sceptically.

But without waiting for an answer, Rupert and Naldy scrambled onto the broomstick. Betty was in the front, followed by Rupert and then Naldy.

'Hold tight,' said Betty, kicking off the ground.

Betty steered them up a flight of stairs, scarcely avoiding more spells from the guards and swerving around shrieking patrons. They made a sharp turn, nearly crashing into a low-hanging chandelier. Its candles extinguished as they sped by, leaving only the light from the glowing crystal balls in the display cabinets to illuminate their path.

Naldy felt disheartened that The Establishment guards had captured Ralph, especially since the broomstick seemed large enough to fit all four of them.

After what felt like an awfully long, stomach-churning flight, they reached the entrance hall, where the monstrous skeleton of a dragon dangled from the high ceiling. As they hurtled towards the exit, they narrowly missed one of its wing bones. Museum guards were rushing to secure the heavy wooden doors.

'We're going to crash,' shouted Rupert, but Betty must have employed a spell to force both sets of doors wide open, and they shot out into the purple glow of the setting sun.

Betty aimed the broomstick skyward, and they flew past the old stone buildings of The Great City, heading towards the shelter of the Kirkwood Forest.

Landing the ancient broomstick proved troublesome. As they neared the pine trees, the broomstick picked up speed, and the ground rushed towards them at an alarming pace.

They were sent toppling forward. Naldy rolled painfully across the forest floor as twigs and rocks jabbed her skin. Her body came to a stop when she collided with a large tree, sending a piercing pain shooting up her left leg.

Betty, who had landed some distance away, stood up, dusted off her dirt-covered cloak, and approached them. She reached into her pocket, took out three long green leaves, and handed one to each of them. Betty ate her leaf, and Rupert followed suit without asking questions.

'What is it?' asked Naldy, staring suspiciously at

the long green leaf.

'Nenderfall leaves,' replied Betty kindly. 'They'll relieve any pain in the body, but it's only temporary.' She turned to Rupert. 'Now, I don't believe we've been introduced.'

'I'm Rupert,' he said, shaking Betty's outstretched hand. Naldy noticed a nasty scratch across his arm from their turbulent landing. 'I'm Ralph's cousin.'

'Well, Rupert,' said Betty, picking up a splintered piece of the broomstick that had shattered upon landing. 'No spell exists to return magic to a broomstick that is this broken. Lucky for us, we have something that can help with that problem. Naldy, pass me the Aurantiaco.'

'What about Ralph?' asked Naldy, still holding her uneaten green leaf.

'He would have been taken to The Great City's prison,' said Betty, picking up another piece of the damaged broomstick from the forest floor.

'We have to go back for him,' pleaded Rupert.

'There is no time,' said Betty sternly. 'We have the Aurantiaco and must make our way to the Edengar Mountains without delay.'

Betty held out her hand to Naldy.

'You don't have what you think you have,' said Rupert.

'We do,' said Naldy, retrieving both the real and fake Aurantiaco books from her cloak. 'The spellbook at the museum was a Devante.'

'Neither of those books,' said Rupert solemnly, 'is a Devante.'

'What do you mean, boy?' asked Betty, fixing her eyes on him. Naldy was reminded of an eagle about to devour its prey.

'When I left you in Heatherton, I came to The Great City to visit an old friend. He was once on the board of directors for The Bleckdale Witchery Museum. I thought he could offer me some information on these Devante, but he had never heard of them.'

'Yes, we know, silly boy,' said Betty, clearly annoyed that Rupert had interfered with their plan. 'The museum does not recognise the existence of the Devante, but you can rest your troubled mind. I'm certain that book is one.'

'This friend of mine,' Rupert continued bravely, ignoring Betty, 'he simply laughed at me. He said there was no such spellbook in existence. But then he went quiet, like he wanted to tell me something but knew he shouldn't.'

'We must make haste,' said Betty, sighing with frustration. 'We must depart if we are to arrive in Edengar before Maverick. Come, help me collect the pieces of the broom. I am old. Do not keep me waiting.'

But neither Rupert nor Naldy moved, and Betty only took a few lumbering steps.

'What did he want to tell you, Rupert?' asked Naldy.

'He made me promise I wouldn't repeat it. He said he could be locked up for disclosing it.'

'Come, get to the point,' called Betty sharply. This

was the most frustrated Naldy had seen her, and the woman's bitterness reminded Naldy of Betty's twin sister.

'He said a spellbook had recently been stolen from the museum,' Rupert explained. 'The museum's board was embarrassed that the book had been taken right under their noses. They are run by The Establishment, after all, so they placed a fake book in its place to avoid public embarrassment.'

Naldy flipped open both orange books. One had the indented 'H' pressed into its inside cover, and she felt relieved.

'You're wrong, Rupert,' said Naldy, holding up the book. 'See, this one has the 'H', so it must be real.'

'My copy has the 'H',' said Betty, suddenly troubled.

'What have we done?' said Naldy, feeling her whole body cramp with tension. 'We've risked our lives only to see Ralph imprisoned—all for a fake book!'

'I went straight to the museum to see if it were true,' said Rupert. 'I was surprised to see you there, and it was pure luck we arrived at the same time.'

'Luck?' repeated Betty, her eyes widening. 'If you hadn't interfered with our plans, we would have switched the books peacefully without causing such a commotion.'

'But I don't understand,' said Naldy, pulling out the parchment from her cloak pocket. 'It was still on the list this morning... look! It's still on the list now.'

They gathered around to stare at the parchment

—there, unmistakably on the page, was the Aurantiaco.

'If it was Maverick who took it,' said Naldy, 'why hasn't he destroyed it? It's too low on the hierarchy for him to keep it.'

'Unless it wasn't him who stole it,' said Betty, frowning. 'We must get moving now, before the sun disappears. There's an old-fashioned town nearby. If you don't want the Nenderfall leaf, Naldy, give it to me.'

She ate her leaf, and the pain from the fall eased. Betty began making her way through the forest, and the others went after her.

The Nenderfall leaves may have masked their physical pain, but they did nothing for Naldy's spirits. She couldn't believe their plan had failed.

'Is there another way?' asked Naldy, dragging her feet through the dirt.

'It will be impossible,' remarked Betty, 'to navigate the Edengar Mountains without the aid of a Devante. We must find out who stole it from the museum, and we must steal it from them.'

'And what about Ralph?' asked Naldy tetchily, kicking pinecones as they went. 'We must go back. We cannot leave him in prison for trying to steal a book, especially since it is a fake. It's not fair!'

'The prison of The Great City is not just bars and bricks, my dear. It is the highest-security prison in the land, protected by old magic.'

Naldy stopped walking, feeling disappointed. Rupert stopped as well, while Betty continued slowly ahead.

'She is right, you know,' said Rupert sombrely. 'Nothing can be done if he has been taken to The Great City's prison. I'm sorry, Naldy.'

'Don't you care? He's *your* cousin!'

Rupert returned a defeated look and then went after Betty.

Naldy felt she had let Ralph down. She imagined him sitting in a high-security prison cell, believing he had helped secure the Aurantiaco, unaware that the book they had stolen was just another fraud. As they ambled along in silence, with the light fading, Naldy pondered who this unknown thief might be and whether they would help or hinder their quest.

When they arrived at the nearest town, the glowing full moon hung high in the sky. Like the other towns in the Kirkwood Forest, Little Lithgow was dotted with small cottages and narrow cobblestone streets, and the entire village was surrounded by tall pines.

They made their way to the dwelling, a building covered in black moss with a sign above the door reading: *Gorge and Blood Place.*

Inside, they took seats at a rickety table beside a crackling fire. The room was gloomy, its windows almost entirely concealed by the dark moss. They sat in silence, solemn and defeated, sipping on pints of dark yellow ale.

Naldy had barely taken a mouthful of her ale when excruciating pain shot up her left leg.

'What is it, Naldy?' asked Rupert, concerned.

The agony was so intense that she collapsed onto the table, knocking over her pint. The glass shattered, and its contents spilt onto the floor.

She let out a long, harrowing cry.

Naldy felt her body lift out of her chair. Her mind was foggy, and her skin cold as if a winter's mist had descended. She could see the blurred image of a room with three beds and sensed she was in a small space, but the fog was so thick she couldn't make out much else.

'Can you use a spell to ease the pain?' asked someone in a panicked voice.

'I cannot mend broken bones, boy,' replied a woman's voice. 'The magic does not exist for an injury this severe.'

'Can't we give her some more Nenderfall leaves?'

'Not unless you want to journey to the Edengar Mountains and back again.'

Naldy's blurred vision gradually disappeared into blackness.

She must have fallen asleep because the next thing she felt was a damp cloth being gently dabbed on her forehead. The bright glare of the room briefly stung her eyes, and her left leg ached.

'How are you feeling?' asked Rupert, sitting on the edge of her bed, holding a wet cloth. Naldy glimpsed Betty, fast asleep, in the adjacent twin bed.

'What time is it?'

'It's early,' replied Rupert, offering a weak smile. His face was paler than usual, with dark shadows under his eyes. He seemed as if he'd been hit with an aging curse. 'I'm glad to see you're awake.'

'My leg feels a lot better,' lied Naldy, lifting her body into a sitting position, but Rupert gently pushed her back down again.

'You need to rest.'

'We don't have time to rest. Maverick is probably halfway through the Edengar Mountains, and we still need to find out who stole the real Aurantiaco.'

'Betty made me promise that I'd make sure you rest.'

'Is she alright?' asked Naldy, glancing over at Betty.

'I think the excitement at the museum was a bit too much for her.'

'She doesn't look well.'

'She's alright,' replied Rupert tenderly. 'She said the Nenderfall leaves have worn off and left her feeling weak. But she hasn't broken anything, so it's *you* we need to keep an eye on.'

'Broken anything?'

'I don't know if you should look,' said Rupert squeamishly.

Ignoring him, Naldy pulled back her bed covers. Her left leg was wrapped in a white muslin cloth with a long stick acting as a splint.

'Betty said the magic doesn't exist to heal wounds or broken bones,' said Rupert, avoiding her eyes. 'I'm lucky I have some basic first aid knowledge from all my travels. I've wrapped it, but you must stay off it until it heals.'

'How am I going to navigate the mountains with

a broken leg?'

'You won't be navigating anything until you recover,' said Rupert. 'I went out early this morning and bought you a gift.'

'A gift?'

Rupert bent down, and from underneath the bed, pulled out a sleek wooden cane with a cat's head sculpted into its handle.

'Is my leg really that bad?' asked Naldy.

'I've gotten Betty one too,' said Rupert, smiling as he reached beneath the bed to retrieve a second wooden cane, almost identical to the first.

'No,' blurted Betty from her bed. 'I may be ninety-seven but I'm not using a blooming walking stick.'

Naldy chuckled as she pulled herself into a sitting position, determined to prove she was ready to set out for Edengar. Her left leg felt hot as she lowered it to the floor. She stood up slowly and took a few wobbly steps. A sharp, intense ache travelled up her leg, forcing her to sit back on the bed to relieve the pain. Naldy picked up one of the cat canes and tried again. Using it didn't ease all the discomfort, but it did help a little.

'We need to start thinking about who stole the real Aurantiaco,' said Naldy as she unsteadily walked around her bed. Rupert grinned at her.

'You need to rest,' said Betty, sitting upright. Naldy ignored her.

'This friend of yours who lives in The Great City, Rupert. Could he help us?'

'He found it baffling that the museum wouldn't

publicly announce the book's theft,' said Rupert. 'But I believe he has already told me everything he knows.'

'It doesn't make sense,' said Naldy thoughtfully. She sat to ease the pressure on her leg. 'Why has the museum kept the theft a secret?'

'It's impressive how similar both of these books are,' said Rupert, picking up the two fake Aurantiacos from the bedside table. 'Betty, it seems your fake is more impressive than the museum's.'

'I did create it using a Devante,' said Betty from her bed.

'You'd think the museum would have done a better job,' added Naldy. 'Forgetting obvious details like the indented 'H'—how silly!'

Rupert's expression intensified, and he hastily got up from the edge of Naldy's bed, heading for the door.

'Where are you going?'

'I'll be back. I might know how we can save my cousin.'

'Rupert, come back. Tell us how.'

Rupert had hurried from the room before replying. Naldy felt exhausted, as if she hadn't slept for many days. She lay back against the pillow and closed her eyes, trying not to focus on the discomfort in her body. Over the next few hours, Naldy kept pondering what Rupert's plan might be to free Ralph. Eventually, she drifted into a deep sleep.

Chapter Eleven

HERETO'S BROOMSTICK

'**N**aldy! Naldy, wake up!'

She opened her eyes in alarm.

'What is it?'

'The indented 'H',' said Rupert.

Both Betty and Rupert were sitting on either side of her bed. The morning sun streamed through the curtains as Naldy sleepily sat up. Betty looked worse than Rupert—pale, with dark rings around her eyes.

'What time is it? I'm so exhausted. You insisted I needed rest, and now you've gone and woken me.'

'We have a plan to save Cousin Ralph,' said Rupert, a spark of hope flickering across his weary face.

'From The Great City's prison?' asked Naldy.

'Ask yourself this,' said Rupert, smiling, 'why would the museum create a replica that's perfectly exact in every way, except for one obvious detail?'

'A mistake,' suggested Naldy, the throbbing in her leg causing her to wince.

'We think,' murmured Betty faintly, 'the museum might have left the indent off on purpose.'

'But why would they do that?' asked Naldy.

'A museum's job,' said Betty, 'is to protect history. Their sole purpose is to preserve and protect historical artefacts. If the museum left off the indented 'H', they might have done so intentionally.'

'Yes, but why?'

'Museums,' said Rupert, waving his hands around to emphasise his point, 'are in the business of protecting originals. I have a feeling whoever stole the Aurantiaco has no intention of returning it to the museum. This leaves us with an open opportunity.'

'Neither of you is making any sense,' said Naldy, annoyed they had woken her.

'We should let her rest a few more hours,' said Betty, her eyelids drooping as if she might nod off herself.

'Listen, Naldy,' said Rupert, ignoring Betty's suggestion. 'We have a meeting with the museum's board tonight in The Great City.'

'A meeting?' repeated Naldy, wondering if she had heard correctly.

'Don't you see, Naldy? They left off the indent on purpose. The museum needs a way to ensure nobody tries to return a counterfeit copy. It's also why they haven't publicly announced the book's theft. They left the 'H' off so they could tell an original from a fake.'

'Why do we have a meeting with the museum's board?'

'We're going to return our Aurantiaco,' said Betty, offering a small smile as she squinted, 'in exchange for Ralph.'

'But we can't,' Naldy protested. 'They'll never believe it. We'll all end up locked up.'

'They have agreed to meet us tonight,' said Rupert with a hint of joy. 'I requested we meet in a public space; it should give us a better chance of escaping if things go wrong. We'll meet at the bistro, *The Mortismor*, where you and Betty had lunch two days ago.'

'Two days ago?'

'You've been asleep for that long, my dear,' said Betty tenderly. 'Your body has been through a lot of stress. You needed the rest.'

'You let me sleep for two whole days!' exclaimed Naldy, outraged at the lost time. 'We should be on our way to Edengar—that's where Maverick will be. Do you really think they'll believe Betty's imitation is the real thing?'

'I think it's worth a shot,' said Rupert.

'And if we all get caught?' asked Naldy, concerned by Rupert's grand plan to free Ralph.

'Then our quest comes to an end,' said Betty matter-of-factly. 'But we don't have any leads on the whereabouts of the real Aurantiaco, and we can't navigate Edengar without a Devante—only a fool would try. So, the right thing to do is to focus on freeing poor Ralph, if we can.'

There were still many hours before they were due to leave for The Great City, and Rupert and Betty firmly instructed Naldy to continue resting. But she was too anxious to relax, knowing they were losing precious time. Although Naldy had initially thought freeing Ralph was a good idea, she now believed it best to shift their attention to searching for the real Aurantiaco—possessing it might even help them free him.

The afternoon arrived, and Betty had a generous serving of food delivered to their room: fresh fruits, warm bread buns, and a pot of hot brew. After they had finished eating, Naldy spent the rest of the day in bed, trying to ignore the discomfort in her leg.

'Can't you mend it with magic?' pleaded Rupert wishfully.

'Oh, of course I can,' Betty replied sarcastically. 'I've just been waiting for you to ask.'

'The magic doesn't exist,' said Naldy from underneath the covers. 'If one of these Aurantiaco were real, we could invent the necessary magic. Oh, how I wish we could—my leg is throbbing horribly.'

Before departing, Betty tossed the museum's fake Aurantiaco into the small fireplace. She entrusted Naldy with her own fake, the one she had previously fashioned using the Devante. Naldy carefully stowed it in her cloak pocket, and together, they stepped out into the crisp, cold afternoon air. Little Lithgow, being a conservative town, didn't sell broomsticks or any magical items. Rupert had arranged for a horse and cart to take them to The Great City, but it had yet to arrive.

'I hope you'll consider coming to Edengar with us, Rupert,' said Betty, leaning on her cane as they waited patiently outside the dwelling. Seeing Naldy with hers, Betty felt more at ease relying on the walking aid. 'I believe you could be of great help to our quest.'

'I've been to those mountains,' said Rupert, rubbing his hands together to keep warm. 'I spent three days there and have no intention of ever returning, except maybe to visit the witch commune on the edge of Edengar.'

Betty's lip thinned in disappointment. Naldy leant on her wooden cat cane to ease the pressure of her injured leg.

'Let's start by getting Ralph out of prison,' Betty whispered to Naldy. 'Then, later, we can try to convince him to join us on the journey through the mountains. His experience might prove useful.'

'There won't be any of us journeying to the mountains,' added Naldy under her breath, 'if we don't find a Devante first.'

A small cart, drawn by a petite grey pony, arrived and an elderly man descended to greet them. Rupert handed the wrinkled man fifteen currents.

'We best be off if we're to make it before sunset,' said the old man.

The three of them squeezed into the cart's uncomfortable wooden seat behind the driver's bench. The man leered at Betty and Naldy as he took his place up front. It was fortunate Rupert had arranged their transportation, as Naldy got the sense that the driver might have refused to take them had he known prior that they were witches.

'Arms and legs all in?' grumbled the man

unenthusiastically, giving the reins a gentle flick. The pony set off at a surprisingly quick trot, considering its size.

The journey beneath the grand trees of the Kirkwood Forest was mostly peaceful, except for the persistent pain in Naldy's leg, which intensified whenever the cart hit an unforgiving bump in the road. The wrinkled man wasn't keen on conversing with witches, but Naldy was glad of this, as their minds were heavily burdened with the task ahead. The chilly breeze carried the comforting scent of pine, and soon the last rays of the sun were swallowed by the encroaching night. They were taken aback when the driver pulled the pony to an abrupt stop.

'This is as far as I'll go,' the man croaked. 'There are all sorts of strange folk in that Great City, and I'll not venture any closer.'

They climbed out of the cart, their bottoms sore from the rigid wooden seat.

'There is a broom shop on this side of the city,' said Betty, leaning on her cat cane as the old man drove the cart away. 'We have some time to spare and should purchase a couple. We might need to make a quick getaway, and it seems we're going through broomsticks at a remarkable rate.'

The moonlight provided ample light as they made their way through the forest to the edge of The Great City. Rupert and Betty were considerate enough to let Naldy set the pace.

The shop was located on the outskirts, oddly

sandwiched between two much taller, more modern buildings. A small, paint-chipped sign in the shop's window read *Hereto's Broomsticks.* Naldy might have overlooked the store, dismissing it as deserted, if not for the flaking sign.

'Here-toes,' read Rupert.

'It's pronounced heh-reh-toe, dear,' said Betty, glancing warily up the street before turning the wrought iron handle shaped like a broomstick.

A brass bell on the shop's door tinkled as they entered. Naldy was surprised to find that the interior starkly contrasted with the store's weathered exterior. The inside was well cared for, with a gleaming wooden floor and recently polished wooden walls.

'Sorry,' called a young boy from somewhere inside the shop. 'We're closed—moments ago. You'll have to return tomorrow.'

The store was narrow but stretched a long way back.

'We're here to buy a broomstick,' called Betty, peering around for the boy. 'In fact, we'll be needing two.'

Mounted on the wooden walls were countless old broomsticks. Naldy had never seen so many in one room. Each broom was expertly crafted from various woods and twigs, with a handwritten card attached detailing its history and price.

'We won't leave without them,' said Betty impatiently.

'Is that you, Miss Hexogg?' asked the boy, peeking

out from behind one of the shelves at the far end of the shop. 'I am terribly sorry—I didn't realise it was you.'

The boy bounded over to them with a large, toothy grin. He appeared to be no older than ten and carried a broomstick and a bottle of polish.

'Welcome,' he said excitedly, bowing low. 'Welcome back to *Hereto's Broomsticks,* Miss Hexogg. It is an honour.'

The boy had curly reddish-brown hair and freckled cheeks. He turned to Naldy and bowed low.

'My name is Hereto, which was my father's name, and my grandfather's name, and so on and so forth. I am at your serv—'

Hereto's enthusiasm faltered as he glanced up at Rupert's face. He took a step backwards.

'Broomsticks were designed by witches, for witches,' Hereto continued, lowering his voice to add, 'and wizards.'

'Right, well...' began Rupert, but Hereto cut him off.

'I am most sorry, oh kind gentleman, but we only sell to—'

'They are for us, Hereto,' Betty interrupted.

'Oh! For you, Miss Hexogg?' said Hereto, his eyes widening. 'Oh, beg my pardon. I see this other lovely angular-faced woman with a cane, also a witch. Two broomsticks, did you say? Yes, two witches, two broomsticks!'

'Something with speed, if you have it,' said Betty.

'Of course, only the best for you, Miss Barbra

Hexogg,' said Hereto, bowing even lower. The boy then shuffled to the shop's far end, disappearing into a stockroom.

'He thinks I am Barbra,' explained Betty once Hereto was well out of earshot. 'He's a huge fan of my sister's scribblings. The perks of being a twin, I suppose.'

'Heh-reh-toe...' said Rupert thoughtfully. 'I've heard that name before.'

'Yes, I am not surprised,' said Betty warmly. 'This family invented the magic for flying broomsticks. Every broom is a *Hereto's* broom. The magic to create new broomsticks was lost during The Great Witch Hunt, destroyed by The Establishment. Still, the Hereto family produced enough brooms before that to keep them in business for many centuries.'

'Why did they destroy the magic,' asked Rupert, 'but not the brooms?'

'Oh, they did,' replied Betty. 'The Establishment ordered that all magical broomsticks be burnt, and a great many of them were. But, you see, it's difficult to distinguish a magical broomstick from an ordinary one unless you're a witch or wizard. Even regular townsfolk use broomsticks for sweeping, which is why so many survived. Plus, *Hereto's* was prolific in crafting them.'

'Right,' said Hereto, scampering back up the aisle with two ancient-looking brooms. 'Do you have a preferred wood or a specific twig in mind?'

'Something fast, Hereto,' said Betty impatiently.

'Oh, yes, these are both durable and speedy. But I

have many options. There's a lovely walnut—'

'These two will do just fine, thank you. And before you ask, we don't need the brooms gift-wrapped.'

'Of course, of course,' said Hereto, bowing low again and handing over the broomsticks. Betty reached into her cloak pocket to retrieve some currents.

'They're all quite old, aren't they?' said Rupert, eyeing the nearest broom mounted on the wall.

Hereto turned snobbishly away from Rupert before taking the currents from Betty. 'I thoroughly enjoyed your latest article in the *Heatherton Herald,* Miss Hexogg. As you know, I subscribe.'

'Oh, yes, thank you, Hereto.'

'You were quite right in saying magic is at risk,' said Hereto, pausing to cast a disparaging glance at Rupert. 'These townsfolk—they take advantage of our magic when it suits them, but treat us like second-class citizens. Your article was a riveting read.'

Betty gave Hereto a forced smile and handed the broomsticks to Rupert.

'Carry these, would you, Rupert, dear?'

Hereto's jaw dropped in horror as Rupert gladly accepted the brooms, and Betty sauntered towards the store's exit.

Hereto's priceless reaction lifted their spirits as they walked through the streets towards *The Mortismor.* But their mood soured when they reached their destination.

'It's a trap,' said Naldy, noticing the bistro's blinds were pulled closed. Under the yellow glow of the streetlights, it looked sinister.

'No, I don't think it's a trap,' replied Betty, scanning the street. 'If it were, they'd have already arrested us.'

They cautiously approached the bistro's maple doors. Naldy's leg was still throbbing, but the adrenaline helped distract her from the pain. She wished she didn't need the cane, which made her feel vulnerable. Rupert carried the broomsticks they'd bought from *Hereto's,* but Naldy knew they were useless and couldn't see how they would help them if trouble arose inside the bistro.

Upon entering, they were relieved to find that nothing attacked them. Naldy was surprised to find no patrons—only a few figures standing in the shadowy corner. The space was nothing like it had been just a few days prior. Apart from a rectangular marble table occupying the centre of the room, surrounded by eight magnificent wooden chairs, all the other furniture had been packed away.

'Welcome,' said a spindly woman from the other side of the dim room, staring down her long, pointed nose. Her black hair stretched to her waist. 'We do appreciate you coming.'

The woman's bony hands gestured for them to sit before she resumed whispering to four others huddled in the shadows at the far end of the bistro. Naldy, Betty and Rupert exchanged a brief look and, without speaking, decided it was safe to take a seat.

Once Naldy was seated, she noticed two stern-faced guards standing in the shadows. Between them stood Ralph. Naldy almost didn't recognise him; he appeared tired and deflated, unusually distant. His eyes met hers—but there was no sign of recognition.

The whispering group in the shadows broke apart and joined them at the table, taking the five seats opposite. The pointy-nosed woman settled in the central chair.

'I am Sallandra Wunkle, the head of The Establishment and the chairman of the board for The Bleckdale Witchery Museum.'

Naldy's stomach did a few somersaults as she glanced at the faces and recognised two men. At first, she thought her mind was playing tricks on her, until Sallandra proceeded to introduce the party.

'We also have the other three board members of The Bleckdale Witchery Museum present this evening: acclaimed historian Franny Fantispot; award-winning scholar and mayor of Jasberg, Hilda Vulen; mayor of Valingfield, Gatengar, Merrydale, and Greenswood, Maverick Gadswell; and last but not least, esteemed artefact authenticator Getergrin Bomtayle—who will be ensuring the legitimacy of the artefacts you have agreed to return. Do you have any questions or concerns before we proceed?'

Naldy had a million questions whooshing through her mind, the biggest of which was why Maverick and Getergrin were present and pretending not to know each other.

'No questions,' croaked Betty softly.

'Wonderful,' said Sallandra in an authoritative tone. 'If there are no questions, we shall proceed. Our chief concern is the recovery of the stolen artefacts. As head of The Establishment, I have the authority to release a prisoner from The Great City's prison, should I so desire. I am sure we all agree that a swift exchange would be ideal, so let us not waste time. The book, if you please.'

Naldy reached into her cloak pocket but suddenly hesitated.

'I do have a question,' said Naldy, her voice breaking nervously.

'A question? Yes, of course. What is it?'

'How do we know you'll keep your word? How do we know you won't lock us all up once we've returned the Deva—sorry—the book containing the oldest record of the levitation spell?'

'I am magically bound by The Establishment's code and must keep my word,' said Sallandra, facing the guards and giving them a quick nod. Her nose looked longer in profile. 'But to ease your concerns...'

A change came over Ralph's demeanour, and he instantly appeared more relaxed and like himself.

'An Effangale witch?' asked Betty aloud.

'An Effangale wizard,' corrected Sallandra. As if to demonstrate, an extra chair magically soared across the room and took its place next to Naldy. 'Why don't you join us at the table, Ralph?'

Ralph stared around the room, bewildered, as if

he didn't know how he had arrived at this moment.

'Naldy?' said Ralph. 'Is that really you?'

'I'm sure your friends will be kind enough to explain everything in time. But for now, why don't you take your seat?'

Ralph made his way to the table and sat next to Naldy, who offered him a half-smile to try to ease his worried look.

'Does that quell your concerns?' asked Sallandra. Without waiting for an answer, she continued, 'Good. Shall we proceed?'

Naldy reached into her cloak and pulled out the small, burnt-orange book. Ralph bit his lip and shook his head.

'Naldy, you can't,' protested Ralph, realising they were trading the book for his freedom. 'We need that book.'

'It's okay, Ralph,' said Naldy, shooting him a firm stare, hoping he wouldn't interrupt and jeopardise their plans.

Naldy calmly placed the book on the marble table. Sallandra nodded to Getergrin, who reached across and pulled it closer to himself.

Naldy's heart felt as if it had stopped beating. Getergrin took out a small magnifying glass from his floral waistcoat pocket and inspected the book with one eye closed. He wasn't letting a millimetre go unscrutinised. First, he studied the book's spine, then its covers. He opened the book and delicately thumbed through its middle pages, pausing now and then to rub them tenderly between his chubby fingers. After an excruciating ten minutes, Getergrin set the magnifying glass down.

'Hmmm,' said Getergrin, holding the book up to his ear, tapping it lightly and listening. It didn't make any unusual sounds—it was, after all, just a book. Getergrin opened his mouth to proclaim his verdict. 'It is the original. The true and honest artefact.'

Naldy wasn't sure she'd heard him correctly. It wasn't until the faces on the opposite side of the table broke into relieved smiles that she realised Getergrin had confirmed their fake to be authentic.

'Wonderful,' said Sallandra, placing the book inside a cloth bag with the museum's name stitched in gold lettering and passing it to Maverick. 'We are glad this precious artefact is back in our care. I must ask, how did you manage it? Getting in and out of the museum without anyone noticing has baffled our expert team for months. They've been trying to figure out how you broke in, stole the book, and somehow bypassed every security measure.'

There was a brief pause as none of them knew how to respond. The real thief who stole the actual Aurantiaco was the only one who knew the answer to that question.

Naldy knew that once Maverick destroyed the book, he would see the Aurantiaco still on the list and realise it was nothing more than an impressive fake.

'You almost got away with stealing the oldest record of the levitation spell,' said Sallandra, 'and you would have, had you not gotten greedy and returned to steal the broomstick.'

A lump formed in Naldy's throat.

'Let us continue,' said Sallandra, folding her long arms on the table. 'Which one of those broomsticks is the Grand Wizard Hereto Blackbard's?'

Chapter Twelve

THE PACT OF PACTS

'The deal was the book,' said Betty, leaning forward in her chair.

'The deal,' replied Sallandra, smiling, 'was that you would return the items stolen from the museum. Several guards witnessed you flying out on Grand Wizard Hereto Blackbard's broomstick. We will not let your friend go, nor will you leave here, unless both stolen artefacts are returned.'

Naldy's broken leg throbbed horribly, and she felt nauseous. It felt as if her broken bones were reminding her of where Grand Wizard Hereto Blackbard's broomstick really lay—snapped into pieces somewhere in Kirkwood Forest.

Naldy considered how quickly she might be able to hobble towards the exit, and she placed a trembling hand on her wooden cat cane in preparation. Before she could stand, Rupert picked up one of the old broomsticks they'd purchased from Hereto and placed it on the marble table.

'Fine,' he said confidently, 'you can have the broomstick back too, but you should have been clearer with us from the outset and told us that you wanted both stolen artefacts returned.'

Naldy felt beads of sweat forming on her forehead. She knew there was no chance Getergrin would believe any old broomstick from *Hereto's* was the Grand Wizard Hereto Blackbard's.

Betty shifted uncomfortably and placed a hand on her cat cane, as if she, too, was considering fleeing.

Getergrin picked up the broomstick, inspecting the wood with his magnifying glass.

Naldy stared at Maverick, his greasy hair brushed back, and his black cane leaning against the table. This was the man who had stolen and destroyed her family's spellbook. A wave of anger rose within Naldy, but she forced herself to shift her focus from the mayor to the broomstick Getergrin was intently examining. She knew it was a matter of time before he announced it as a fake; he had no reason to lie and declare it the original, especially now that he believed he had possession of the Aurantiaco.

Naldy knew they had to make a run for it. She stood up.

'It is the original,' announced Getergrin hurriedly.

Naldy had a hard time concealing her surprise. To cover the awkward fact she had hastily stood, she stretched her body, pretending that sitting for so long had been taxing for her injured leg. She could sense Betty shifting uncomfortably beside her.

'It is Grand Wizard Hereto Blackbard's first

broomstick,' repeated Getergrin. 'Safe in the museum's possession again.'

'Thank you. Good to hear,' said Sallandra. 'The museum is glad to have these magical historical artefacts returned.'

Betty stood up and stretched as well.

'Before you go,' said Sallandra, a sweet smile teasing the corners of her thin lips, 'a word of warning to you all. We will not be so lenient if there is a next time. I would give serious consideration before deciding to pay the museum another... hmm... unwelcome visit.'

No spells came flying at Naldy's back as she limped towards the exit, and the only sounds following her were the footsteps of Betty, Rupert and Ralph. She reached the bistro door and stepped out into the darkened street. The cool night air brushed her face, and Naldy instantly felt refreshed.

'We need to move,' said Betty, ushering them across the road to the museum steps. 'We mustn't think we are out of the thick of it—not yet.'

The moon must have dipped low, as the stone buildings blocked it from view, but the streetlamps provided plenty of light. They stopped on the museum's bottom step.

'Why did you do it?' asked Ralph, clearly frustrated. 'You should have left me and made your way to Edengar.'

'A thank you would suffice, Cousin Ralph.'

'You need the Devante to get through those mountains. More than you need me.'

'It's a fake,' said Naldy, and she quickly explained to Ralph that the spellbook they'd stolen wasn't the real Aurantiaco and that someone had beaten them to it.

'I can't believe we've gone through another one,' said Betty, holding out the single broomstick that hadn't been relinquished and letting it float at waist height in mid-air. She didn't climb onto it. 'Naldy, hop on. Come on, Ralph and Rupert, too. You must take the broomstick immediately and get away from here.'

'We're not leaving you here,' objected Rupert, as Naldy lifted a leg over the broomstick.

'Get on, Ralph,' said Betty impatiently. Ralph obligingly—and somewhat awkwardly—climbed on behind Naldy. 'Rupert, you too.'

'We can all fit,' said Rupert, climbing on behind Ralph and squishing against him to prove his point.

'The more of us on the broom, the slower it'll go. You'll need speed.'

'Where should we meet you, Betty?' asked Naldy.

'I'm sorry to say I am all out of plans. We don't have time to talk, for they could change their minds at any moment. You must get going.'

Rupert climbed off the broomstick.

'Rupert,' scolded Betty.

'They'll be faster without me. Maverick and Getergrin are after the both of you. I'll stay with Betty.'

'But where are we to go?' asked Naldy, refusing to leave without them. 'We don't have a Devante, and we can't go to Edengar without one.'

'We can send you a message, Betty,' suggested Ralph, 'from the Tebellos when we find a town.'

'You mustn't,' said Betty firmly. 'The Tebellos have been compromised before. Besides, I hate to admit it, but without a Devante, I am at a loss as to how I can be of any help. You must find another way.'

'But we can't do it without you,' said Naldy stubbornly. 'We need your help to lead us through the mountains.'

'I do not know the way,' said Betty, her expression pained.

'But you took the books to the mountains,' said Ralph.

'That was over twenty years ago,' said Betty, a great sadness spreading across her face. 'I do not remember where the ravine is. You will need to find the Aurantiaco or another of the Devante. I fear it is the only possible way. I hope our paths cross again, but I cannot offer your quest anything more.'

'Our quest!' repeated Naldy furiously. 'You're the one who took the books to the mountains! You're the one who didn't keep a close enough eye on your sister's Devante! You let her give it to Maverick, and now you're abandoning us! Well, we don't need your help anyway.'

Naldy kicked off the ground, and the broomstick shot upwards above the city's twinkling lights.

'Now why did you go and do that?' said Ralph, baffled.

'Oh, shut up,' said Naldy bitterly. It only took her

a few minutes to regret speaking so rudely to Betty, and her eyes welled with tears. She wished she had said goodbye properly and allowed Ralph to say his goodbyes, too.

Naldy wanted to turn back but knew it was too late—doing so would be too dangerous. The museum's board members might realise the artefacts they had returned were fakes and could come after them. The wind rushed past their ears, and Naldy could see the darkness of Kirkwood Forest ahead, but she had no clear idea of where they should go.

Ralph didn't say anything for a while. They flew over the tops of the forest's tall trees, with The Great City's burning lanterns shrinking to tiny lights far behind them. Naldy found herself longing for a cosy bed.

'Do you think they'll be alright?' asked Ralph over the whoosh of air.

'I think Betty has left us in the lurch, Ralph.'

'I'll tell you one thing,' he replied, changing the subject. 'I'm looking forward to a good dinner. Prison meals were some of the blandest food I've tasted.'

A loud bang erupted behind them, and Naldy felt Ralph slide closer to her in a panic.

'We're on fire!' called Ralph in distress.

'Fire?' repeated Naldy, turning her head to see the tail end of the broomstick ablaze.

Naldy scanned the sky, searching for the source of the unexpected fire. Thick black smoke trailed behind them, and the flames hungrily consumed the twigs of the broomstick.

'Naldy! You've got to do something! Put it out!'

She steered the broomstick towards the forest, the flames whooshing violently as they sped downward.

'I'm beginning to think Oak cursed me so that every broomstick I touch falls to pieces,' Naldy muttered.

'It's night, Naldy! Use your magic!'

'Witches can't conjure water out of thin air, Ralph. If we get to the ground, I can use dust to put it out!'

As they neared the forest floor, it became clear that saving the broomstick was no longer an option; they would be lucky to save themselves. Naldy fought to maintain control as the trees loomed closer, rushing towards them at an alarming speed. The broomstick swerved wildly, branches swatting them as they descended. With a heavy thud, they struck the ground and tumbled off the burning broom. Naldy felt the splint protecting her leg snap, followed by Ralph crashing into her back as they came to a sudden stop. A sharp pain jolted up Naldy's left leg, as if it had been broken a second time.

The only light came from the bright orange flickering of the almost entirely ravaged broomstick —it was too late to save it, even with magic.

'I don't think I can stand up,' said Naldy, holding her injured leg. She could see the bone protruding through her skin. 'I've lost my cat cane.'

'You couldn't have just put it out with water?' asked Ralph, lifting himself gingerly. He seemed to have landed without any severe injuries, thanks to Naldy cushioning his fall.

'I told you, Ralph, I can't create water from thin air. Magic has its limits.'

'Unless you have one of these,' said a familiar voice from the darkness of the pine trees.

A vertical curtain of water floated in mid-air, slowly moving through the forest towards them. Naldy had never seen anything like it. Both she and Ralph were mesmerised by the shimmering surface of the strange wall of water, too stunned to react. The burning broomstick's flames were beautifully reflected on its surface.

'What are you?' asked Ralph, frightened.

The floating stream halted a few metres from them. Naldy, still on the ground, hesitantly raised her palms, though fear held her back from attacking the river. Little fish swam within it, and there was something else—something hidden behind or within the water.

Suddenly, the stream splashed to the forest floor, revealing Maverick and Getergrin, who had been concealed behind it.

'*Comburite*,' Naldy called instinctively, but her fireball evaporated as soon as it left her palms.

'Now, now,' said Maverick, clicking his tongue. 'Play nice, won't you.'

The forest floor had become a muddy mess from all the water, and the burning broomstick sizzled as the liquid pooled around it. Naldy remained seated, lacking the strength to stand without her cane's support.

'*Prosterno*,' shouted Naldy, but Maverick was quicker, and her spell evaporated again.

'You don't want to play nice?' asked Maverick, slowly taking a few steps into the mud where fish squirmed helplessly. He stopped and leant on his cane. 'You've both been quite difficult to track down.'

Ralph looked nervously at Naldy, but there was nothing she could do; she was too weak from the fall to duel with the wizard.

'It was a rather impressive fake you returned,' said Maverick, smirking. 'The museum now believes they have saved another ancient book, which is being safely returned to its chamber.'

Naldy tried to stand, but the pain was too great.

'But you see, Getergrin and I were not so easily fooled. We knew the book you returned was not the real Aurantiaco. We knew this for certain because the book I have here'—Maverick pulled a burnt-orange book from his cloak—'this is the real Devante.'

'The real Aurantiaco?' asked Ralph in a concerned tone. 'But what do you mean?'

'You didn't think we fell for your tricks at the bistro, did you? Sallandra and the others might have, but Getergrin and I know better.'

'But if you took the real Devante yourself,' said Ralph, clenching his fists and squaring his shoulders, 'why haven't you destroyed it? What do you want with them?'

Maverick didn't answer. Getergrin folded his sausage-like fingers across his floral waistcoat.

'I don't believe you,' said Naldy, attempting to stand again, but the pain was too debilitating. 'You're lying. You're angry because someone got to the real Devante before you.'

'Look here, Getergrin,' said Maverick mockingly, 'the children need proof.'

Maverick flipped open the orange book and began reading from it.

'*Sanitatem   Restituere*,'   uttered   Maverick confidently.

It was a spell Naldy had never heard before, and for a split second, she thought Maverick was cursing her. Then her leg throbbed with agonising pain. Naldy screamed, and Ralph charged at Maverick —but Getergrin intervened, grabbing Ralph and wrestling him to the soggy ground until he was sitting on top, holding Ralph's face in the mud.

Her leg felt as though someone were hacking at it with a saw.

And then it stopped.

Ralph ceased struggling against Getergrin's grip and stared at Naldy, his face filled with anxiety.

'What have you done?' she asked, reaching to touch her leg. It took her a moment to realise she was no longer in pain. She could feel that the protruding bone was no longer there.

'Do you believe me now?' asked Maverick, using the end of his cane to drag a small branch into the flames of the burning broomstick, causing the dwindling fire to rise higher. 'I have healed it for you. Only a real Devante could produce such magic.'

Naldy lifted her black cloak to examine her leg more closely. Maverick had been telling the truth; the Aurantiaco had not only healed her bones but also her skin—there wasn't even a scar.

'It was a trap, wasn't it?' accused Naldy. 'You stole the Aurantiaco from the museum, but why? Why did you place a fake there? Did you just want to see who would come for it?'

'Clever girl,' said Maverick patronisingly. 'After burning Rubrum, we knew anyone with knowledge of the Devante would try to protect the Aurantiaco at the museum. It is the most well-known of all the Devante.'

'You were the only ones,' said Getergrin, his fingers still pressing Ralph's face into the mud. 'Nobody else came to check on the Au-run...the Orintargo.'

'Aurantiaco,' corrected Maverick.

'We don't know where any of the other Devante are,' declared Naldy hurriedly. 'So you may as well just leave us alone and let us go.'

Maverick ran a hand through his greasy, slicked-back hair before reaching into his black leather cloak to retrieve a brilliant, silver metal book.

'Metallum,' said Ralph in awe, gazing up at the book as it reflected the fire's dancing flames.

'My dear boy, aren't we familiar,' said Maverick coldly. 'You know your Devante well for someone who claims to know nothing about them.'

Naldy was itching to shoot another spell at Maverick's smirking face. But she knew it would do no good, for he was too skilled a wizard.

'Your fake Aurantiaco was an impressive copy. However, your Grand Wizard Hereto Blackbard's broomstick—well...' Maverick stifled a laugh. 'What a dismal display.'

'Let us go,' said Naldy, climbing to her feet—her leg really was completely healed.

'The fire needs more fuel,' said Maverick threateningly, holding the Aurantiaco and Metallum over the flames. 'Don't you think, Getergrin?'

Getergrin chuckled.

'Please,' said Naldy, 'we really don't know anything more than you do.'

Maverick dropped the orange book, and the flames surged as the spellbook caught fire. Ralph let out a yell of horror.

Naldy raised her palms, desperate to save the book, but Maverick silenced her spell before the words could leave her lips. It was too late—the Aurantiaco was already turning to ashes.

'But it couldn't have been the real book,' said Naldy in disbelief, as tears began to pool at the edges of her eyes.

Getergrin chuckled again before shifting his position, dropping his full weight onto Ralph's legs, and settling himself more comfortably. Ralph groaned beneath the heft of the round man.

'Check the list you ran off with,' said Maverick

coldly, lowering Metallum away from the blaze.

Naldy reached into her pocket and pulled out the parchment. Her heart sank as she discovered Maverick had been telling the truth—the Aurantiaco was no longer written there.

'I've given you the chance to play nice,' said Maverick bitterly. 'But it seems you would prefer I use force. There's no use pretending you know nothing about the Devante.'

'We don't know where the Corium is,' blurted Ralph.

'And even if we did,' added Naldy sourly, 'we wouldn't tell you!'

'Let me make myself clear. Getergrin and I have already done you a great favour by lying about the authenticity of your fraudulent artefacts.'

'It's time for you to do us a favour,' said Getergrin, pressing hard on Ralph's face.

'You only helped us,' said Ralph, his voice strained, 'because you couldn't question us about the Devante if we were locked behind bars.'

Maverick flipped through Metallum's pages.

'Okay,' said Naldy, 'we will help you.'

'No, Naldy!' Ralph protested. 'You can't!'

'I will tell you where a higher-ranking Devante is,' said Naldy, knowing there was no chance of them winning in combat, especially with Maverick in possession of a Devante.

'Naldy, you mustn't,' objected Ralph.

'But we must make a *Pactum Pactorum*,' said Naldy, glaring at Maverick. 'If we are to help you, we need to know you'll keep your word.'

'A *Pactum Pactorum?*' repeated Maverick, startled. 'How untrustworthy of you.'

'What's a *Pactum Pactorum?*' asked Getergrin, a little frightened.

'It is a binding pact,' answered Maverick, grinning amusedly. 'Such little trust.'

'Why should we trust you?' said Naldy sharply. 'You have proven your word is not worthy.'

'What are your conditions?' asked Maverick, gesturing for Getergrin to let Ralph go.

Getergrin reluctantly released Ralph, who clambered to his feet, his face stained with mud. Maverick and Naldy locked eyes, neither of them blinking.

'I, Naldy Elahline, hereby agree to reveal the location of a higher-ranking Devante, and you, Maverick Gadswell, must agree to let Ralph and me go unharmed. *Pactum Pactorum.*'

'Agreed,' said Maverick. '*Pactum Pactorum.*'

There was a flash of light, and purple smoke erupted between them. The smoke didn't rise but drifted eerily to the floor before vanishing.

'Naldy, you can't!' said Ralph. 'Please don't tell him.'

'She has no choice now,' said Maverick, leaning casually on his cane. 'The *Pactum Pactorum* will force her to keep her word.'

'I don't care. You can't tell them, Naldy!'

'It will extract the information from her and punish her if she doesn't give it willingly.'

'I will keep my end of the deal,' said Naldy, squinting her hazel eyes. 'And you will keep yours, as you must. The Aurum is sitting in a dragon's cave alongside Rosea and Caeruleum, deep within the Edengar Mountains.'

'Naldy! Why? Oh, why did you tell him that?'

'It's okay, Ralph.'

'And the Corium?' asked Maverick. 'Where is it located?'

'The Corium?' repeated Naldy, a smirk breaking at the corners of her mouth. 'That was not part of our *Pactum Pactorum,* Maverick. I promised to tell you the location of a higher-ranking Devante, and I believe I've fulfilled my part of our contract.'

Maverick nearly slipped from the support of his cane. Getergrin bit his lip, unsure of what had just happened.

'I've had enough,' said Maverick, thrusting his cane forward. Two jets of dark blue light shot from the tip, hurtling towards them. Ralph squealed—but the lights circled back and zoomed in Maverick and Getergrin's direction, knocking them off their feet. They landed comically in the wettest part of the mud.

'Your agreement was that you would let Ralph and me go,' said Naldy confidently, then added, 'unharmed.'

Naldy strolled off into the darkness. She heard Ralph let out a disbelieving laugh before he turned and set off after her into the forest.

Chapter Thirteen

ENTER ONE WHO SEEKS ANSWERS

'Why are you walking so fast?' asked Ralph once they were well out of earshot of Maverick and Getergrin. 'You made a *Pactum Pactorum*. They can't harm us.'

'Maverick has Metallum,' said Naldy, pushing aside tree branches as she walked, 'which means he can simply create a spell to override the *Pactum Pactorum*. I'm sure he will realise it soon enough.'

She had decided to stay clear of the main roads.

'Can we go a little slower, please?'

'No, we can't, Ralph,' said Naldy, pushing on through the darkened forest. The moonlight was obscured by ominous clouds.

'Couldn't Maverick just use Metallum to create a spell to find our location?'

'I don't know, Ralph,' said Naldy uneasily. It was something she hadn't thought of. 'Hopefully, it's one of those banned spells Betty told us about. Keep up.'

'Can you at least create some flame so I can see where I'm going?' asked Ralph agitatedly. 'I keep walking into cobwebs.'

Naldy ignored Ralph's request and continued on.

'I don't think you should have told them where

the Aurum is,' said Ralph stroppily.

'They would have found the Aurum regardless of whether or not I told them its location. They already have a Devante that can lead them to Rosea and Caeruleum, and it'll be next on their list.'

'Yes, but now they won't waste any time going after it,' said Ralph bitterly, brushing away another cobweb. 'It's over, Naldy. Don't you see? We haven't got a shot now!'

'Ralph!' said Naldy tensely. 'I've saved you on multiple occasions, so can you please keep all your negativity to yourself and just focus on keeping up.'

'I'm trying to be realistic,' said Ralph, lowering his head miserably. 'We don't have a Devante, and we don't know where any of them are. Betty said there's no chance of navigating the Edengar Mountains without one.'

'Go home, then! If you've had enough, just go home! You're not a witch or a wizard, so you should be off on your merry way, and I'll save the Devante by myself. We should have left you in The Great City's prison.'

Naldy regretted her harsh words the moment they left her mouth.

'I didn't ask you to save me,' said Ralph under his breath, walking behind her. 'I do appreciate it—but you can't blame me. I didn't ask you to.'

The trees were thicker in this part of the forest, and Naldy found it more difficult to avoid being swatted by branches.

'*Lucere*,' said Naldy, and a small ball of floating

light appeared above her palm, illuminating the trees around them.

'Thanks for the light,' said Ralph.

Naldy knew that getting angry would delay lifting Oak's dreaded curse. 'Let's just find the nearest town, Ralph, and check ourselves into its dwelling.'

'Don't you think Maverick will check the nearest towns?'

'Maverick is more likely to head straight to Edengar to collect another three Devante.'

Naldy couldn't help but dwell on Ralph's criticism. Had she traded their freedom for the destruction of another three Devante?

Neither spoke again until they emerged from the forest and stood on the outskirts of an impoverished town.

'We can't stay here,' said Ralph, eyeing the decrepit buildings illuminated by flickering streetlamps.

'I know it's a grubby-looking place,' said Naldy, wrapping her cloak tightly around her body, 'but it's turning chilly, and I'd rather not walk any further.'

'No, it's not that,' said Ralph, pointing to a hand-painted wooden sign. 'Look!'

The sign read: Gatengar. Naldy instantly recognised it as one of the towns where Maverick was mayor.

'I think we'll be alright,' said Naldy hesitantly. 'But to be safe, let's not use our real names.'

The town's buildings had an ominous character.

Many roofs had jagged black edges, as if they had been ravaged by fire—it seemed the inhabitants hadn't the heart, or perhaps the currents, to properly repair the damage. They headed straight for the dwelling, where Ralph awkwardly offered fake names to the doddering woman behind the bar.

'Bobby and Anna Buckwater, was it?' asked the toothless dwellingtend, dunking a limp chicken feather quill into an ink bottle before writing their names in the ledger. 'Just the one night, then?'

Naldy nodded.

'Just passing through,' added Ralph. 'We'll be on our way tomorrow morning.'

The toothless woman grunted before collecting a brass key from the wall behind her.

'This way,' croaked the woman, leading them down a short hallway to their room. 'Breakfast will be served at sunrise. Night, dears.'

'She gives me the shivers,' said Ralph as the woman tottered away. 'The people here are very different from those in Maverick's other town, Greenswood.'

The room was small and poky, and its furnishings had collected an unhealthy layer of dust. One of the twin beds sagged in the middle, and Naldy insisted on taking it, hoping the small gesture would break her curse—though similar compromises had never seemed to help.

She lay awake, listening to Ralph's snoring, wondering if Oak had given her the wrong instructions on how to break the curse. Despite everything she had done to prove her selflessness, the curse remained stubbornly in place. She was beginning to think she would be cursed forever.

The following day, Naldy awoke with the sunrise and headed to the dwelling's bar for an early breakfast.

The toothless dwellingtend was sleepily shuffling around the empty bar, still in her pink nightgown.

'I'm doing scrambled eggs and beans,' the woman said, pouring Naldy a hot brew. 'Sit yourself down, and I'll bring it over.'

Naldy chose the round table in the shadowy corner, furthest from the window, as it seemed the least grimy.

The woman soon delivered a mug of hot brew along with a plate piled high with scrambled eggs, toast, tomatoes, beans, and mushrooms.

'There you go, and I've got seconds and thirds waiting if you'd like more,' said the toothless woman.

Naldy wasn't feeling hungry; she was too preoccupied with her thoughts. She stared at her plate, wondering if Ralph, like herself, felt the heavy ache of failure. It wasn't like him to sleep in. When the dwellingtend approached the table for the third time—hoping to collect an empty plate—Naldy finally picked up her fork and started eating.

'Is there something wrong with your food?'

Naldy was surprised to see the dwellingtend settle herself in the seat opposite.

'Or perhaps there's something else on your mind?'

Naldy managed a weak smile. She didn't feel like chatting.

'There's no point denying it,' said the toothless woman. 'I know something's the matter because you've let your breakfast go cold.'

'Oh, it's nothing,' lied Naldy. 'Only an upset stomach.'

'Okay, you don't have to tell me if you don't feel comfortable. I'll bring you some stewed Greel to help settle your stomach.' She stood and started to leave the table but stopped suddenly. 'The Winterborough Town Fair is this evening, and it's only three miles west of here. It might help lift your spirits—they're always a lot of fun.'

The woman made her way back to the wooden bar to prepare the stewed Greel, while Naldy finished her breakfast. The news of the nearby town fair deepened Naldy's gloom, stirring memories of the last one they'd attended—which had ended with Ralph and her locked up in birdcages.

When the dwellingtend returned, she brought a cup filled with a strange liquid that resembled floating seaweed in cold, murky water. Naldy was relieved the dwellingtend didn't linger to watch her drink it, and she pushed the cup away from her the moment the doddery woman left the table. Almost three hours passed before Ralph emerged.

'You've missed breakfast,' said the toothless woman scoldingly. Naldy got the impression the dwellingtend suspected Ralph was the cause of her sorrow.

'You should have woken me,' said Ralph to Naldy, settling into the empty seat opposite her. 'We don't have time to waste.'

'It's not as if we have anywhere to be,' said Naldy, eyeing the messy tangle of hair on top of Ralph's head. He licked his palm and began trying to flatten it.

'Naldy, we need to get to Edengar.'

'The chances of us ever finding the dragon caves without having possession of…'

Naldy didn't finish her sentence. She had spent all morning failing to formulate a new plan.

'We could go back to Heatherton,' Ralph suggested optimistically. 'We can tell Betty we can't do it without her help.'

'I got the impression she's helped us all she can,' said Naldy. 'I don't think there's any more she can do for us.'

Naldy habitually picked up the cup in front of her and took a sip—getting a mouthful of what tasted like old socks. The cold Greel. She spat it back out immediately.

'She's the one who has been to the caves,' said Ralph, still fidgeting with his hair. 'Betty must be able to remember at least some of the way.'

'I think I made a huge mistake in telling them the Aurum was in the caves with the other books. I think you may have been right.'

'We'll never get to the caves before they do,' said

Ralph, leaning his elbows on the table and placing his chin in his hands. 'Not when they have a Devante!'

'No,' replied Naldy. 'Perhaps we should try to find Lignum and the Corium?'

Ralph leant back in his chair, glancing uneasily at Naldy. From his bleak expression, she could tell he thought going after Lignum or the Corium was a bad idea—the sad truth was they hadn't the slightest inkling of the whereabouts of either.

'I'll order us both some hot brew,' said Ralph, scrunching his nose at Naldy's cup of cold Greel before heading over to the dwellingtend.

When Ralph returned to his seat, he was agitated, fiddling with the corner of the table.

'I was wondering... well...'

'What is it, Ralph? Spit it out!'

'Did your parents,' mumbled Ralph hesitantly, 'maybe leave you any clues or hints?'

'My parents?' echoed Naldy, taken aback.

'They had possession of Rubrum, didn't they? You said yourself they were the ones who hid it in the forest, so I thought they might have known something more.'

Naldy felt heat rising in her cheeks. Was Ralph right—had her parents known their spellbook was one of the famed Devante all along, and simply never told her? She was beginning to suspect that their disappearance had something to do with it.

The dwellingtend approached the table with a fresh pot of brew, placing a clean cup in front of

Naldy and a dirty, chipped one in front of Ralph.

'What's up with her?' asked Ralph as the dwellingtend walked away sourly.

'I think she might believe you're the cause of my despair,' said Naldy. 'She wouldn't be entirely wrong.'

Ralph lowered his eyes, biting his lip. Naldy got the impression he wanted to continue discussing her missing parents. She stared at him, raising her eyebrows expectantly.

'Are they... well...' continued Ralph, busying himself by pouring the brew. '...you know?'

'My parents aren't dead, Ralph,' snapped Naldy irritably. She took a sip of the hot brew and accidentally burned her tongue. In truth, she couldn't be certain they hadn't died. A Devante might have helped her find them if they were alive, but now she wondered if revealing the location of another Devante to Maverick had ruined her chances of ever seeing them again. Her forehead felt clammy. 'They didn't know about the Devante, and I don't want to talk about them.'

'Do you think Oak could help us?' asked Ralph.

'That old fool,' said Naldy, still angry at the tree for cursing her. 'He might be wise regarding some matters, but I doubt he'd know where to find the highest-ranking Devante.'

Ralph didn't push the point, and she was thankful for that.

'I don't understand why you're helping,' said Naldy, blowing on her brew to cool it faster. 'It makes sense for me—I'm a witch—but why are you helping?'

'Things could get worse for everyone if one person possesses all that power,' said Ralph. 'Come on, then—we can't navigate Edengar without a Devante. So let's figure out where someone would hide the most powerful spellbook. What about the Mortous Woods?'

'The woods are not small,' said Naldy. 'Or safe.'

'I wish they were still serving eggs,' said Ralph, his stomach grumbling. 'I suppose lunch won't be far off.'

'Oh, Ralph, That's it!'

'I was hoping we wouldn't have to visit the Mortous Woods,' said Ralph drearily. 'But I suppose it does make sense to search for Lignum or the Corium there. It seems like the sort of place someone would hide something.'

'No, not that,' said Naldy. 'Eggs, Ralph!'

'The dwellingtend said that breakfast service has finished.'

'No, no, Ralph. Not breakfast. *Eggs.* Dragon eggs.'

Ralph's face crinkled in intense concentration as he tried to decipher the cause of Naldy's sudden excitement.

'Oh, Ralph, isn't it obvious,' she said, leaning forward happily. 'The woman who was selling dragon eggs at the town fair.'

Ralph scrunched his face tighter.

'She must know where the dragon caves are,' explained Naldy excitedly. 'Remember, Betty told us she used the Devante to find the last surviving dragons in this land. It must be where that shabby woman got her eggs!'

'If her eggs are even real,' said Ralph.

'If we're honest with ourselves,' said Naldy, 'we haven't got any chance finding Lignum or the Corium—not without any real leads. But we might have an actual shot at saving Rosea, Caeruleum and the Aurum if we have a guide through Edengar.'

'Yes, but first, we need to find the woman who sells those dragon eggs,' said Ralph doubtfully. 'And then convince her to take us to the caves, which might prove difficult considering the last time we were in her company, we broke one of her expensive eggs and stole her scroll.'

'I think I might know where we can find her.'

Naldy told Ralph about the Winterborough Town Fair, which the dwellingtend had mentioned to her earlier that morning. When lunch service began, they ordered trays of pickled meats and vegetables. Naldy's portion was unquestionably larger when the food was brought to the table. The dwellingtend glowered suspiciously at Ralph as they ate. When she came to collect their plates, Naldy tried to explain that her misery was not caused by her travelling companion but rather by their failure to save a magical book called a Devante. Yet, mentioning the spell-inventing books seemed to make the woman distrustful of her as well, and for the rest of the afternoon she eyed them both with suspicion.

The weather outside turned gloomy, and they spent the day drinking goblets of brew in the bar.

'If it keeps this chill up,' said the dwellingtend, placing another log into the flames of the glowing fireplace, 'Winterborough will have the quietest town fair they've seen yet.'

She tottered away to serve an old man coming in for a pint of cider.

'If it is quiet,' said Ralph, worried, 'it'll make it hard for us to go unnoticed. I don't particularly want to end up behind bars again.'

That evening, after settling their bill, they set off on the three-mile walk to Winterborough. The weather was chilly, and both Naldy and Ralph had upturned their cloak collars to keep warm. The sky threatened rain as more grey clouds swept in overhead. They trudged along the dusty road that wound through the tall pines of the Kirkwood Forest.

As they walked, Naldy tried to devise a plan to convince the stallkeeper to take them to the dragon caves. She thought kidnapping might be a good choice, but Ralph pointed out they'd have difficulty abducting a stallkeeper during the middle of a town fair.

'Don't you remember how loudly the woman could shriek?' said Ralph. 'Thieves! Thieves!'

By the time they arrived on the edge of Winterborough, dusk had turned into night. The town's largest field was illuminated by a golden glow from lanterns strung from the many pavilion tents.

They made their way past thatched-roof cottages, towards the vibrant fair.

'It is quiet,' said Ralph, peering around at the meagre crowd wrapped tightly in their woollen shawls, bracing against the biting night air.

'Come, we might be able to purchase a broomstick,' said Naldy, entering a majestic pavilion tent. A large painted wooden sign at the entrance read: *Enid's Items for Witches, Wizards and Wannabes.*

'Can't we try a magical carpet instead?' asked Ralph wishfully. 'I do miss mine.'

To Ralph's disappointment—and Naldy's relief—there were no magic carpets for sale. However, they did manage to buy an overpriced old broomstick.

They explored the stalls, keeping their eyes peeled for any sign of the stallkeeper who sold dragon eggs, but after passing *Plants, Shrubs, and Seedlings* for the third time, they began to doubt whether the dragon lady was attending the Winterborough Town Fair.

'Maybe she went out of business,' suggested Ralph as they turned a corner and ambled along another row of tents.

'Wait, Ralph, look!' said Naldy, pointing to a familiar sign: *Enter One Who Seeks Answers.*

'Oh, you have to be joking,' said Ralph glumly. 'I don't want that fortune teller to see us. Quickly, let's go this way before she comes out and recognises us.'

'Wait, maybe she knows where we can find the stallkeeper? She was at the same fair last time.'

'Or she might have us locked away for ruining her

tent during our last visit.'

Naldy was already making her way inside, and Ralph begrudgingly went in after her. The overpowering scent of thyme and rosemary made Naldy feel instantly nauseated. She placed the broom they'd purchased in the wooden holder by the entrance, then let herself be overwhelmed by the ceiling-to-floor drapes of red and black fabric.

'You really think the crazy fortune teller will help us?' asked Ralph stroppily as they wound through the labyrinth of fabric. 'I must be mad coming through here with you a second time.'

Naldy was certain the maze of fabric had become longer and more complicated since their previous visit.

'Diamone was right about the prediction regarding Oak,' said Naldy, trying to remain positive as they came face-to-face with a dead end. 'She might be able to help us. Should we go underneath the fabric?'

'No, I don't think Diamone would like it if we did that. Let's just go back this way. We should ask one of the other stallkeepers instead.'

Naldy was confident they had taken the same path back, retracing their steps, but somehow they found themselves in the centre of the maze. Diamone was sitting at the low wooden table, her glass ball atop it, surrounded by dozens of candles with blue flames crackling. Her eyes were closed, and her frizzy brown hair framed her face. Ralph quietly beckoned for Naldy to follow him back the way they'd come—but it was too late.

'Welcome, old friends,' said Diamone without opening her eyes. 'Take a seat, please, for the session is in progress.'

Ralph glanced longingly at the exit. Naldy signalled for Ralph to sit, and he reluctantly perched on the uncomfortable cushion next to her. Diamone, seated opposite, kept her eyes tightly closed.

'Diamone... umm,' said Naldy after a brief moment of silence. 'We need to ask you something.'

'Yes, you have come seeking answers,' she said, waving her palms showily over the glass ball. 'The session is not for you, though, my dear. It is for him.'

Diamone's eyes snapped open, and she stared intently at Ralph.

'For me?'

'Yes, you, with the strawberry-blonde hair. Place your hands on the table, please. The mystical energy is strong.'

Ralph hesitated, deciding to leave his hands safely in his lap.

'Come now, for the magnetic atmosphere is waiting for you,' said Diamone dreamily.

'No, no,' said Naldy, becoming restless. 'We need to ask you about the woman who—'

'The session requires complete silence,' she said firmly. 'The future is waiting to be heard. Hands on the table, please, and thank you.'

Ralph obligingly placed his fingers on the wooden table. As he did, the glass ball glowed a smoky blue.

'You have a question?' asked Diamone. 'Something you want answered.'

'Yes, we do,' said Naldy.

'Not you, my dear,' said Diamone, turning and smiling airily at Ralph. 'Him.'

'We have a question, yes,' said Ralph nervously. He kept his fingers on the table, and Diamone shut her eyes again before Ralph continued. 'We are looking for the lady who sells the dragon eggs. Do you know her?'

'The mystic energy is intense tonight.'

'Do you know where we can find her?' asked Ralph, ignoring the fortune teller's theatrical hand-waving.

Diamone began to mumble under her breath. Ralph glanced at Naldy, his expression suggesting he thought this was a clear waste of their time.

He removed his hands from the wooden table; as he did, the candles in the room extinguished themselves, leaving only the phosphorescent glow from the glass ball.

'Yes,' announced Diamone clearly, 'the ambience is the perfect balance of present and future. I can see further than I have seen for some time. You have a question, so please ask it while the room is humming with notes from the future.'

'We are looking for'—but Ralph was interrupted by Diamone.

'A way to navigate the Edengar Mountains,' she said in a quiet, mousy voice. Her eyelids twitched as if the eyes beneath were darting about energetically.

'Yes, it is one of your options. You could go that way.'

'Yes,' said Ralph, dumbfounded. 'We need to travel through Edengar.'

'You seek three Queens of the mountain,' continued Diamone softly. 'But these all-powerful Queens are guarded by six ancient beasts. Do you want to know if death will come to your Queens? And if it might come to yourselves?'

Diamone opened her eyes and stared into the glass ball. Naldy couldn't see anything but the glowing blue light.

'Yes, I see death,' said Ralph squeamishly. His expression indicated he could see more than an illuminated glow.

'Yes,' said Diamone sadly. 'Death awaits should you venture there.'

'There is an oak tree on fire,' said Ralph, horrified.

'Yes, it burns, and the flames fly high. The tree is being consumed by searing fire.'

The candles in the room reignited themselves, and the glow from the glass ball extinguished. Diamone blinked a few times, lifting her gaze to them—almost expectantly.

'As you know, that will cost you twenty currents, please,' said Diamone sweetly.

'Twenty currents!' said Naldy, outraged. 'To predict death and a fortune you've already informed us of!'

'Excuse me,' she said, taking great offence. 'A fortune I've already told you? Oh, how dare you! I never repeat my predictions and do not perceive people's pasts.'

'You told us the same prediction last time,' said Naldy irritably. 'Granted, it has already come true, so you did well there. But don't think I'm giving you another twenty currents for the same fortune.'

'Did you mishear me, my dear?' she said, staring vaguely. 'I do not predict the past. That is not something I have ever done, no. Pointless predicting the past, for it has come and gone. I predict the future.'

'But you haven't, have you?' said Ralph, eager to leave. 'You told us exactly what you told us last time and just added death. I'm glad you didn't do it through me this time. We won't be paying you another current.'

'A proxy?' said Diamone, highly intrigued. She scratched her frizzy hair. 'How impressive of me. I've never managed a fortune by proxy before. Are you certain it was I who did it?'

'Yes, and it has already happened,' said Naldy. 'Oak was on fire, and I saved him from burning. But look, that's enough. If you want twenty currents, how about I give you that to tell us where the stallkeeper who sells dragon eggs is?'

'Naldy,' said Ralph, eager to depart, 'let's just ask one of the other stallkeepers.'

'Harmony Esterfield,' said Diamone slowly. 'The dragonologist is whom you seek.'

'The woman who sells dragon eggs, yes,' remarked Ralph. 'We want to know where she is.'

'I'm sorry, my dears, but she is dead.'

'Dead!' said Naldy, shocked.

'Quite dead, yes,' confirmed Diamone. 'She became paranoid someone was watching her. And now she is gone.'

'I'm so sorry,' said Ralph sincerely.

'Listen,' said Naldy, 'we need to find out how she came into possession of her dragon eggs.'

Diamone stood and made her way to the corner of the room, vanishing behind the folds of the red-and-black fabric.

'Harmony Esterfield,' said Diamone from behind the cloth. 'She was once part of a dangerous commune.'

'You know where she got the eggs from?' asked Naldy.

'Oh, yes,' came her airy voice. 'The commune Harmony belonged to had entrusted her with them. An isolated commune of witches living in the south. But if you take that path, death awaits you there.'

'She got the eggs from a commune of witches?' asked Ralph.

Diamone emerged from between the folds of fabric, carrying the pieces of a smashed dragon eggshell.

'The evil witches from the commune gave Harmony the burden of travelling with the eggs, and they wanted her to deliver them.'

'Deliver them where?' asked Naldy curiously.

'I do not know, but Harmony thought she was being followed,' said Diamone darkly, sprinkling the broken eggshells on the small wooden table.

'Presumably by the very people who'd sent her on the quest with the dragon eggs. Poor old Harmony Esterfield didn't want to return to the commune of witches, and she insisted that she couldn't. She travelled with us from town fair to town fair... until...' Diamone clasped a hand over her mouth, gasping dramatically. 'I should not be telling you this. Eggshells are all that's left. All of the eggs were smashed. And Harmony... gone.'

'We need to visit these witches down south,' Naldy said to Ralph.

'The commune left her with no money,' said Diamone. 'Us poor sellers must make a living. The eggs were all she had left to trade.'

'We should be on our way,' said Naldy, placing twenty currents onto the table amongst the eggshells.

Diamone closed her eyes again and went into a meditative state. She didn't speak another word until Ralph and Naldy finally found the parting in the fabric that led from the central room into the maze.

'Remember what I have said. I do not predict the past. Only the future.'

Chapter Fourteen

THE WITCH HOUSE

I t felt like an eternity since the night Naldy had left the Witch House to visit Oak, hoping to collect a blood-freezing spell.

'I'll never get used to this,' said Ralph, sitting behind Naldy on the broomstick, holding tightly onto her waist as cold air rushed by.

'We're nearly there,' said Naldy. She was glad to be flying home at last.

'Ok-k-kay,' stammered Ralph through chattering teeth. 'I still think we should head to Heatherton to seek Betty's advice first.'

'We've been over this, Ralph,' said Naldy. 'There's no time. Maverick and Getergrin are probably already making their way through the Mountains! Betty told us not to use the Tebellos, as they could be watching it. Flying to Heatherton will delay us. We have to do this on our own.'

'I just don't think walking blindly into an evil commune of witches is wise. Witches who killed Harmony Esterfield!'

'Never mind that, Ralph,' said Naldy as they approached the edge of the forest. 'Remember, your cousin Rupert spoke about a commune of witches down south, and he stayed with them for a while.'

'And if the evil witches aren't happy to help us? If they decide they'd rather kill us instead of helping?'

'I'm sure we will be fine,' said Naldy, steering the broomstick towards the ground.

'But what about Diamone's prediction?' said Ralph, concerned. 'Only death awaits. It was in her crystal, Naldy.'

'Whose death did you see?'

'It wasn't specific,' replied Ralph, shuddering. Naldy knew his sudden tremble wasn't caused by the cold air but by the memory of the crystal-gazing session. 'I didn't see whose, but I could feel it. It was... a feeling. A very strange feeling.'

'No more talk about Diamone's silly predictions. Legs at the ready, Ralph. Let's not crash another broomstick.'

They landed with a soft thud in front of a two-storey stone house. Behind them, the edge of the Kirkwood Forest loomed, its tall trees casting eerie shadows. The land stretching beyond the house was flat and empty, and the silhouette of the stone building's jutting turrets nearly blended with the night sky.

'There,' said Naldy, pleased with her landing. 'We managed to do it smoothly for once.'

'It is much easier with all this clear land around us,' said Ralph, squinting up at the darkened house. 'Where are we?'

'Don't you recognise it? It's the Witch House.'

'Oh, of course,' said Ralph, realising he was familiar with it.

'We'll spend tonight here. We need to rest, and it's too late to continue south. The morning will break before we'd make it, and with it, my curse will come into effect.'

'It's spooky at night,' said Ralph, staring ominously up at the old stone building with its sharply slanted roof.

'This must be exciting for you,' remarked Naldy cheekily, clutching her broomstick as she marched up to the poky wooden porch. 'No more lurking in the forest. You finally get to see the inside of a witch's house.'

'I wasn't lurking,' said Ralph guiltily. He followed Naldy up the creaky wooden steps. 'I was observing you. In your natural habitat.'

Naldy shot Ralph a scathing look before pushing the door open, revealing a darkened hallway. Ralph let out a squeal as a skinny black cat jumped out and began winding its way inquisitively through his legs.

'Smookers,' said Naldy. 'Leave Ralph alone.'

The cat took off into the night, disappearing under the trees of the Kirkwood Forest.

'I leave a window open so he can come and go as he pleases. He enjoys hunting for himself.'

Once inside, Naldy faced an odd contraption: a small golden bowl propped up at waist height by two ornate golden legs.

'*Comburite.*'

A small flame ignited in the golden bowl, and moments later, the sconces lining the walls of the cluttered hall sputtered to life, followed by the cobwebbed chandeliers in the inner rooms.

'My great-grandmother invented it,' said Naldy, watching Ralph stare at the mess crowding the hall. 'She enjoyed creating inventions like this. Come this way, and mind you don't knock the shelf there.'

Naldy led them into a cramped sitting room filled with generations of accumulated furniture: chairs, tables, dressers, and cabinets—all overwhelmed with odd knick-knacks or piles of dusty books. In the corner, a fireplace crackled, also ignited by Naldy's grandmother's magical contraption.

'I've never seen anything like this,' said Ralph, casting curious glances in every direction, attempting to take everything in.

'Sorry about all of the junk. One of these days, I'll get around to sorting through it all.'

Naldy signalled for Ralph to settle into one of the cosy armchairs by the fire. He had to remove a pile of books before he could sit. Naldy walked to the window, pulled the dusty drape open, then sat in the armchair beside Ralph.

'To think,' she said, smiling to herself. 'I covered these windows because I didn't want you peeking in, and now I've let you walk right into my sitting room.'

Ralph brushed some black cat hair from the armrest.

'*Arcesso,*' said Naldy, and a small black cauldron

soared into the room. Its metal handle hooked onto the welded fireplace crane, positioning itself over the flames. A tray with an empty pot and two cups soon glided in after it.

Ralph stared anxiously at the floating tray, worried it wouldn't find anywhere to land amongst the clutter. After circling the room, the tray finally settled on an upended trunk of spellbooks lying on the floor beside them.

'It must be nice,' said Ralph as the liquid in the small cauldron reached a bubbling boil, filling the air with the earthy scent of brew. Naldy returned a puzzled expression, not understanding what he meant. 'You know, being able to use magic to do things like making brew. It must take away some of the pressure of everyday living.'

'For someone who writes about witches,' said Naldy, forcing a smile, 'you seem to know very little.'

'That's why I was observing you,' said Ralph. 'To learn.'

'Spying on me, you mean,' said Naldy, feeling agitated. She muttered a spell, and the hot cauldron lifted itself, gliding over to them as Ralph's eyes widened in wonder. The cauldron tilted, pouring brew into the sturdy pot resting on the tray. As the cauldron returned to its place over the fire, she lifted the pot by hand and filled their cups with brew.

'The truth is I was frightened of you,' continued Ralph. 'It's why I kept at a safe distance on my magic carpet.'

'Most townsfolk are afraid of witches,' said Naldy.

'Ever since The Great Witch Hunt.'

'I suppose it's silly of us.'

'Let me teach you a little about our kind,' said Naldy, shifting in her chair to face him. 'Spells might seem easier at first glance, but a spell takes as much energy out of a person as doing the task by hand.'

'Really?'

'Yes,' said Naldy, her frustration mounting. Ralph's misconception that spellcasting required minimal effort was a common one peddled by townsfolk. 'People often think magic is an easier option, but it's just another option—one that still requires effort.'

'I always thought it was simply babbling some strange words,' said Ralph, 'and flailing your palms around.'

He laughed at his own joke. Naldy was not impressed.

'I'll set you up in the guest room,' said Naldy, forcing herself out of the comfort of her armchair. 'We should get some sleep. We'll use my father's broom to get to the witch commune tomorrow night. It'll be much faster and more comfortable than that overpriced one we bought in Winterborough. Bring the rest of your brew, and I'll show you to your room. The house is a bit of a maze.'

Naldy led Ralph up a crooked wooden staircase and along a hallway lined with more antique furnishings. The guest room was a sizeable, draughty chamber. She fetched extra woollen blankets and an old pair of her father's pyjamas from the hallway cupboard.

'I can't stop thinking about Diamone's prediction,' said Ralph as Naldy laid the extra blankets on the bed for him.

'I wouldn't take it too seriously,' said Naldy, shaking her head. 'I think she was confused.'

'Yes, but the feeling of death... it felt serious.'

'Diamone's prediction has already come true—I saw the oak tree on fire myself. We shouldn't worry.'

'But what if someone tries to set the tree on fire a second time? Shouldn't we warn Oak?'

'Why would they do that?' asked Naldy, eager to retreat to the comfort of her own warm bed. 'Oak doesn't have possession of a Devante, not anymore. We just need to focus on getting to the witch commune. Finish your brew and blow out the candles. Goodnight.'

But as Naldy walked to her bedroom and settled beneath her woollen blanket, she couldn't help but wonder if Ralph was right. Was the oak tree going to be set on fire again?

It must have been early morning when a howl woke Naldy with an uncomfortable jolt. The room was shrouded in dull blue light, and she knew sunrise couldn't be far off.

'Naldy! Come quickly!'

She recognised Ralph's strained and frightened voice echoing down the hallway. She'd almost completely forgotten that he had spent the night in the Witch House. Naldy wondered if Ralph had been woken by one of the rats that had set up their home inside an old trunk filled with broken quills, which she'd promised herself many times she'd discard.

Jumping out of bed, still wearing her long white nightdress, Naldy made her way along the cluttered hallway, her palms outstretched, ready to cast a spell.

'Ralph? What is it?'

She rounded the corner and found him standing in her father's old blue pyjamas that she'd lent him. He was staring fixedly at one of the doors leading off the hallway.

'What happened?' asked Naldy. 'Your howl gave me quite a fright.'

'Be quiet,' said Ralph, raising a hand to urge her to listen. He didn't take his eyes off the wooden door.

Naldy strained her ears, but all she could hear was the occasional creaking of the old house.

'Don't you hear that?' asked Ralph, pointing at the study door. 'There's something in there.'

'It's the house, Ralph.'

'No, Naldy,' he said insistently. 'There's something strange in there.'

Naldy cautiously approached the closed door.

'*Aperio.*'

The door shot open, but Naldy couldn't see or hear anything unusual. The study was empty, apart from its usual clutter.

'Maybe you had a bad dream, Ralph?'

'It wasn't a dream,' he replied, pushing past her and navigating the limited floor space strewn with neglected items. He disappeared behind an antique desk.

'Maybe it was the wind?' suggested Naldy as she entered behind him, nearly knocking over a glass gas lamp sculpted to resemble a sea serpent.

'It's coming from inside there,' said Ralph, pointing to one of the drawers of the ornate cherry wood desk. Naldy stopped to listen.

'I don't hear anything. *Aperio!*'

The desk drawer didn't open. A golden tinge shone through the thin curtains covering the window.

'The sun is up,' she said, pulling at the drawer, which refused to budge. 'I can't open it, Ralph.'

Naldy lowered her ear to the drawer, but she still couldn't hear anything from inside.

'Wait! It has stopped,' said Ralph.

'What did it sound like?' asked Naldy.

'It was like a soft ringing, but more crystal-like. It woke me up. I can't believe you didn't hear it!'

'Whatever it was,' said Naldy, beginning to navigate her way out of the cluttered room, 'it's gone now. I wouldn't worry about it, Ralph. This house is bursting with unusual junk. We're up now, and I may as well get breakfast started.'

Ralph was still eyeing the drawer suspiciously.

'Are you coming?'

He reluctantly made his way downstairs after her to the kitchen, where she began preparing breakfast.

The kitchen was the least crowded room in the Witch House, though it still had every size of pot, pan, and cauldron one could think of packed into its cabinetry. Ralph remarked that the mismatched crockery burdening the shelves reminded him of one of the Winterborough Town Fair stalls.

It wasn't until after they had finished their toast at the round wooden table that Ralph stopped talking about the strange ringing he had heard earlier.

'I'm worried about these evil witches,' said Ralph glumly. 'I think we may be asking too much of them, and I question whether they'll take us to the dragons —even if they know where they are.'

Naldy stood and carried their empty plates to the sink, beginning to wash them by hand due to her curse. 'There's no such thing as an evil witch, Ralph,' she said, scrubbing furiously, annoyed at having to do the chore by hand. 'There's good and bad in everyone.'

One of the ceramic plates snapped in half under the force of her cleaning.

'Well, I think there might only be bad in Maverick,' Ralph replied, stifling a laugh. Naldy tossed the broken plate into the rubbish bin.

They couldn't set off until Naldy's magic returned, so Ralph spent most of the day writing in his journal while Naldy filled a rucksack with food, bottled water, and other things she thought might be helpful for their journey. She even found some old dried medicinal herbs in the back of the pantry, which she was certain were no longer potent, but packed them anyway.

'Don't forget the matches,' said Ralph, glancing

up briefly from his writing.

'Did I forget to tell you I'm a witch, Ralph?'

'A cursed witch,' mumbled Ralph as he wrote another sentence in his journal.

'We won't need a fire during the day, as we will be busy climbing mountains. I'm perfectly equipped to light fires once night falls.'

'And what if the dragons get you, and I'm the last one left to carry out the mission, eh? I don't want to freeze to death.'

'What are you scribbling about in that thing anyway? You better not be writing about my house —or me—for that matter.'

Ralph didn't answer her. Naldy set about searching for matches, though she doubted any would be found amidst all the bric-a-brac.

The afternoon was uneventful until Smookers brought in a dead bird, forcing Naldy to chase him out. She flopped onto the sofa beside Ralph, exhausted from a long day of packing and running after Smookers.

'I'll get dinner started soon,' said Naldy.

'I can help if you like.'

'I can manage it. We should head off once it gets dark to ensure we arrive before sunrise.'

Ralph sat upright, dropping his journal and listening intently. It was late afternoon, and Naldy knew she lacked the magic to defend herself should something go awry.

'Don't you hear that, Naldy?'

'I don't hear anything,' she replied, concerned.

Ralph stood and made his way up the staircase, drawn by a noise Naldy couldn't hear. She trailed after him, concerned Maverick might be luring them upstairs. But as they reached the study door, she realised how unlikely that was—if Maverick had found them, she knew he wouldn't bother hiding. Besides, the wizard was far more likely to already be on his way to the dragon caves.

'It's getting louder,' said Ralph, making his way into the study and heading straight for the desk. Naldy lingered in the doorway. 'I think it's calling me. Do you have a key for—' but Ralph didn't finish his sentence. He began tugging at the drawer, using his full weight. On the third pull, it gave way, and Ralph toppled backwards into a precarious stack of long-forgotten items. Naldy entered the room and peered into the open drawer. It contained some old parchment, a few quills, and a glass inkwell.

'It's some old stationary, Ralph. Must be the scholar in you that was attracted to it.'

Ralph lifted himself from the stack of items he'd fallen into, which included a dusty spellbook, a broken telescope and a collection of half-burned pillar candles.

When he approached the desk, he lifted the parchment and tossed it aside. Beneath the stationary was a small silver chain earring with a little green emerald stone dangling from its end.

'It stopped,' said Ralph, picking up the earring. 'This is the thing that was ringing.'

'I told you it would be some old silly trinket. I've

never seen that before. Who knows who it belonged to? It looks like something my crazy Aunt Geraldine would have worn. You can have it if you want.' She reached into the drawer to see if she could find the matching pair. 'I couldn't tell you where the other is.'

'Can I really keep it?'

'Be it on your own head. But don't blame me if it poisons you in your sleep. I wouldn't put it past Aunt Geraldine to have fashioned something dangerous. Come on, Ralph, I've still got to get dinner started before it gets dark, and we've got a long journey south tonight.'

Naldy navigated her way out of the disorganised study. 'Are you coming?' she called to Ralph, who was still staring at the earring. 'You'd think you'd never seen magic before.'

Naldy spent the afternoon making a butternut pumpkin and potato pie. She wasn't a skilled cook, but it was her great-great-grandmother's recipe, and she'd made it many times before, so she was confident she'd get it right. However, halfway through peeling her third potato, her fingers cramped, and she realised she had never made the pie without the aid of magic.

When dinner was finally in the oven, she found Ralph running his hands over the small, delicate earring, holding it up to the light to better examine the emerald stone. For some reason, she found this annoyed her even more than his incessant journal writing had.

'It's just a worthless trinket, Ralph. Come and

help me set the table, please.'

Ralph obliged, pocketing the antique earring.

The sweet smell of the pie wafted through the air as the last rays of the sun glistened through the kitchen windows. Naldy served up large slices for each of them.

'It should be dark soon, and we'll be able to head off.'

Her father's broomstick was leaning against the kitchen wall alongside Naldy's leather rucksack.

'Naldy, this pie is delicious,' said Ralph, shovelling a large bite into his mouth.

'My grandmother's recipe,' Naldy replied with a smile. 'It'll be a nice night for flying, and not as cold as last night. I don't think we'll come up against any wind or rain.'

'Just an entire commune of evil—sorry—of ordinary witches.'

'My dad's old broomstick will be much more spacious.'

Naldy put down her fork and walked to the pantry to retrieve a bottle of unopened apple cider she'd found while searching the cupboards for supplies earlier that day. She filled two small crystal glasses.

'To protecting the Devante,' she said, raising her glass.

Ralph raised his glass as well, though his expression was sullen.

'What is it, Ralph?'

'I can't help but think we're walking to our

deaths,' he replied, placing his fork on the table and giving a pained look. 'All three Devante in the dragon caves are still on the list. What if Maverick and Getergrin have already made it to the caves and were...'

'Were what?'

'Killed by the dragons.'

'I don't think we've gotten rid of Maverick and Getergrin that easily,' said Naldy, taking a sip of the apple cider. 'Don't worry, Ralph. You've got your lucky earring to help you now.'

'You laugh, but I think we've had our fair share of luck already,' said Ralph, taking another mouthful of pie. 'I'm curious about the earring. Why could I hear it, but you couldn't?'

'Aunt Geraldine probably mucked up the jinx and made it so it can only be heard by townsfolk instead of witches when lost.'

'Can we have seconds?' Ralph asked, taking another big bite.

'I've packed the leftovers for a midnight snack on the way to the commune. We've got everything we'll need. You'll be happy to know I found some old matches—though we won't need them.'

After dinner, Naldy packed the remaining apple cider into her leather rucksack, and they made their way out into the cool night air.

The sky was a grey-black, and a few stars had come out to see them off. The trees of the Kirkwood Forest loomed, unmoving in the still night.

'Ready?' asked Naldy, climbing onto the

broomstick and casting a saddened glance back at the Witch House.

'I don't know if "ready" is the right word,' said Ralph, hesitantly climbing on behind her.

Smookers emerged from the trees and leapt onto the bristles of the broomstick. Ralph started as Smookers settled himself comfortably.

'You'll need to stay here,' scolded Naldy. Smookers jumped off the broom, letting out a disgruntled meow. 'Edengar is too dangerous. Sorry, Smookers. If you're going to hunt wildlife, make sure it's for food and not fun.'

She kicked off the ground, and they shot up into the night sky. Naldy peered down at the Witch House again, but it was too dark to see anything.

She had never flown south before, as she'd never had any reason to, and her parents had always told her the land was mostly barren.

As it turned out, her parents' description was generous; the flight was excruciatingly uneventful, and the ground below was eerily flat, appearing bottomless in the darkness. Only every hour or so, when they passed a lone stone house with its twinkling lights, did Naldy feel a flicker of excitement, glad to witness something other than the dark and empty plain.

After a few hours of flying, they stopped for a midnight snack, which consisted of generous helpings of Naldy's pumpkin and potato pie. Despite Ralph's frequent complaints of nausea from all the flying, he eagerly devoured second and third helpings.

They sat in an empty field, where Naldy lit a small fire using magic, providing just enough light to see while they ate. The darkness around them felt vast and endless, and Naldy wondered why anyone would choose to live so far away from the Kirkwood Forest, where most of the towns were.

After finishing his pie, Ralph lay back in the soft grass.

'I could fall asleep here,' he said.

Naldy feared he might do just that, so she rushed to pack their things and put out the fire.

'Right, off we go. There is no time like the present.'

'Can we have a little nap?' pleaded Ralph. 'Please, the back of the broomstick is awfully uncomfortable.'

'Once dawn breaks, I won't be able to fly us anymore. Come on, Ralph, it's time to go.'

He sulkily mounted the back of the broomstick.

They'd been flying for another three hours when Naldy saw the light breaking on the horizon. She panicked, mistaking the stretch of twinkling lights for the rising sun. Naldy was relieved to realise the glow was coming from the witch commune.

'We're nearly there, Ralph! Perhaps another half hour.'

Ralph's face rested against her back, and he was fast asleep, snoring softly. Naldy was surprised he hadn't toppled off the broomstick, but since he seemed balanced enough, she let him sleep until they got closer to the commune.

As they approached, Naldy could make out many small cottages, all within the confines of a large stone wall that encircled the town.

She dipped the broomstick to jostle Ralph awake. He sat upright, pretending he had been alert for the entire flight.

'We're not climbing those,' said Ralph, nodding at the enormous black shapes in the distance—the silhouette of the Edengar Mountains.

Naldy lowered the broomstick, and they sped towards the ground. She had decided it was safest to dismount outside the walls of the witch's commune. They landed smoothly in front of two giant stone statues depicting witches bent over cauldrons. The sun had not yet risen.

'We're getting better at landing,' Ralph remarked, as if he'd played a part in Naldy's final descent.

The statues appeared to mark the official entrance to the commune. Between the two gigantic stone figures was a large gap, wide enough to fit a horse and cart through, and beyond it was a road leading further into the village. From either side of each statue, the high stone wall stretched out and around the many cottages inside.

'What's the point of having a huge wall?' Ralph asked, staring at the formidable statues. 'I mean, shouldn't there be a gate or something?'

'I don't know,' said Naldy, glancing around for a gatekeeper or any sign of life.

'Even if there were a gate,' said Ralph, 'we could

have flown over it, I suppose.'

'Walls like these could be hexed,' said Naldy, taking a few steps closer to the opening. 'I'm not entirely convinced this gap isn't hexed, and it could be dangerous to pass through without an invitation. Where is everybody? The village seems eerily quiet.'

'Asleep, probably. There's smoke coming from the chimneys.'

'Hello! Anybody here!?' called Naldy.

'Don't wake them up, Naldy! Let the witches sleep. Let's just wait here until the sun rises.'

Naldy approached the beginning of the dirt road and stepped onto it, crossing the threshold to stand within the town's walls.

'Well, that was foolish,' said Ralph testily. 'You could have burst into flames or something. Then what was I supposed to do? Walk back across the plains?'

'Come on,' said Naldy bluntly. 'We need to find someone in charge, and we don't have time to wait for them to wake.'

Ralph followed her, closing his eyes as he passed between the two enormous stone witches. They had barely taken three steps along the road when they heard an old, croaky cough from behind them.

'Welcome to the witch commune. What business do you have here?'

An old man with many wrinkles, elegantly dressed in a dark green cloak with golden buttons, stood in the gap in the wall, blocking their exit.

Naldy hesitated. She had packed everything they

might need for the journey in her rucksack—but she had completely forgotten to plan what they would say to the commune's witches once they arrived. Ralph spoke first.

'Hello,' he said nervously. 'We are here... well, you see... because we want to talk to you about, erm...'

'Harmony Esterfield,' interrupted Naldy.

'Harmony?' asked the old witch, intrigued. 'How wonderful. Harmony Esterfield, you say? Yes, please wait here.'

The old witch walked straight through the back of one of the giant stone statues, apparently vanishing into solid stone. It took Naldy a moment to realise that the witch couldn't actually walk through rock. The back of the statue was made of tiny stone beads, positioned so closely together that the statue appeared solid when the beads were still.

'He doesn't look evil, does he?' asked Ralph, glancing around the empty town. 'He seemed rather friendly and appeared to know Harmony, at any rate.'

Moments later, the old witch emerged, carrying two wooden cups with smoke rising from them. He handed a cup to each of them.

'Welcome,' said the old man warmly, narrowing his strangely youthful eyes. 'We rarely get visitors to our humble town. People avoid being close to Edengar. You must have had a long journey; do drink up, for you must be thirsty.'

The old witch smiled, staring at them expectantly. Naldy took a small sip of the smoking liquid, finding it surprisingly sweet. Ralph, however, stared ominously into his own wooden cup.

'Thank you,' said Naldy, glancing at Ralph, who hadn't yet taken a sip. 'We need to speak to whoever is in charge.'

The old witch nodded but remained silent.

'It's a time-sensitive matter,' added Naldy, but the old man's attention remained fixed on Ralph. Naldy glanced at Ralph intently, urging him to be polite and take a sip.

'It's quite good, actually,' said Ralph, after swallowing a small, suspicious sip from his wooden cup. 'What's—'

But halfway through speaking, Ralph's voice was abruptly cut off, and his cup tumbled from his hand. Naldy opened her mouth to speak, but no words came out. She wanted to run, but her legs felt glued to the ground. It was as if she had been paralysed—nothing would move now except for her eyes. The reality sank in—they *had* been paralysed. Naldy felt a surge of frustration for having drunk the liquid. Had they learnt nothing from when Barbra had poisoned Ralph with the scones?

Eight other sweet-looking elderly witches, dressed in matching dark green cloaks, emerged from the giant stone statue. Naldy was astonished that all of them could fit inside it.

Before Naldy could see their faces, someone plucked the wooden cup from her frozen fingers and lifted her off the ground. She was carried through the stone curtain into the back of the statue. To her surprise, instead of a cramped hollow section, she encountered an impressive wooden staircase winding around a massive stone pillar, descending deep into the earth.

The witches carried them down the staircase for what felt like quite a distance, until they must have been deep below the ground. They emerged into an enormous underground cavern. Naldy could see a large stream of water running through the centre, flanked by wooden cottages.

On the cavern walls were six giant torches, each the size of at least two people, their flames burning brightly. She realised that the small cottages above ground must be empty, as the actual town was evidently built underground!

Naldy and Ralph were carried inside one of the wooden cottages and laid on the floor. The room had no furniture, only the rickety wooden floorboards. Naldy noticed that each old witch had a small leather satchel tied around their waist, with glass phials filled with coloured liquids neatly poking out of the top.

'Call her,' said the old witch who had initially greeted them at the entrance.

Naldy desperately wanted to talk, to explain to the witches why they had come. But she couldn't move anything except her eyes, which darted frantically from side to side.

'Clear the room,' said another elderly witch. 'She is coming.'

Everyone departed, leaving Naldy and Ralph

lying motionless, wondering who was coming.

Chapter Fifteen

IN THE BEGINNING

Naldy's stomach churned with guilt. Had they come this far only to foolishly drink a strange potion from a commune of evil old witches?

'Do you think it's because you mentioned Harmony Esterfield?' asked Ralph. He was lying on his back next to her, staring sadly at the ceiling.

'You can talk!' said Naldy, realising her speech had also returned. She could now move the rest of her face, and her head gradually regained movement.

'We know they don't like Harmony Esterfield,' said Ralph bitterly. 'They killed her, remember? I don't know why you brought her up.'

'I panicked. I should have said we know your cousin.'

'Yes, you probably should have said that instead.'

'Okay, I admit, mentioning Harmony Esterfield was a mistake,' said Naldy, trying to move her arms and legs but with no success. 'I didn't want to mention the dragons or the books, and she was the next thing that popped into my mind.'

'Let's hope our movement is restored before the

old witches return,' said Ralph.

A door creaked open. It took Naldy a moment to realise the sound wasn't coming from the cottage entrance but from a trapdoor beside them. The floorboards had shifted, and an elderly woman emerged from the hole in the floor. Her eyes were kind, but her heavily wrinkled face gave the impression she had seen much in her life.

'You do look awfully familiar,' said the woman as she climbed the last stair and stood over them. 'Your movement will return shortly.'

She wore the same dark green cloak as the other witches who had carried them through the cave, an identical leather satchel tied around her waist with odd-shaped potion bottles poking out from the top.

'We don't know Harmony Esterfield,' said Ralph desperately. 'But we know Rupert.'

'Rupert?' repeated the owlish woman, breaking into a smile. 'Yes, we know that name. It is a name that is welcome here.'

'Rupert is my cousin,' said Ralph. 'Harmony is... well... we accidentally broke one of her eggs at a town fair. But we don't know her personally.'

'We entrusted Harmony with taking several eggs across the land,' said the woman softly, her voice carrying a calming huskiness. 'She was supposed to carry them to The Bleckdale Witchery Museum.'

'She didn't deliver them?' asked Naldy.

'Oh, no, she did try,' said the woman, heading towards the main door of the cottage, which led out into the cavern. She opened it slightly and spoke to the witch standing guard—the same man who had greeted them above ground by the statues. 'Hestern, prepare us for the tunnels.'

'Certainly, Odorf,' replied Hestern, and he briskly marched away.

'Our sources tell us she took them all the way to the museum,' said Odorf, closing the cottage door. 'But the museum didn't want the eggs. They'll exhibit dragon bones in their foyer, but not fresh dragon eggs.'

Naldy tried to move her legs and arms, which tingled slightly.

'No movement yet?' asked Odorf, lifting Ralph's floppy arm and letting it fall back to the floorboards with a thud. 'Well, that's all right. Your limbs will come around soon.'

'We don't have your eggs,' said Ralph hurriedly.

'No,' continued Odorf, 'according to the museum, dragons are extinct. Harmony Esterfield should have returned the eggs to us once the museum told her they did not want them, but she never returned.'

'We didn't want to buy her eggs,' said Ralph. 'She tried to sell them to us, but we didn't buy them. We don't have them.'

'No need to fluster yourself,' said the woman. 'I am not placing blame. We were foolish to think the museum would help us protect the species and to believe they would assist in reintroducing dragons to the rest of the land.'

Naldy could feel her legs and arms slowly regaining movement—she could even twitch her fingers. She was pleased she'd soon have control of her body, though she wasn't sure how they would escape. The sun had likely already risen outside, despite the darkness inside the enormous cavern, which meant Naldy wouldn't be able to perform magic.

'The museum,' continued Odorf, 'is run by stubborn people who would not believe us, even with proof. They did not want to admit they were wrong about the extinction of dragons.'

Naldy felt control over her body return.

'You can move again? Good, good,' said Odorf, approaching the hole in the floorboards. 'Follow me, if you please.'

Ralph sat up, rubbing his legs. The elderly woman had already gone through the trapdoor, and Naldy realised that if they wanted to escape, now was the time. But before any discussion could be had, Ralph descended the steps.

Naldy sighed before climbing into the hole in the floor. The stone steps led steeply downward to a wooden door, where the old woman and Ralph waited patiently.

'In we go,' said the woman, pushing the door open.

Inside was a spacious room, with the floor, walls, and ceiling fashioned from the natural rock. As expected, there were no windows. The room's furnishings were elegant and beautifully crafted, creating a cosy atmosphere. A small kitchen table sat in one corner alongside a wood-fired oven, its stone chimney extending into the ceiling. There was a small wooden bed, along with a sofa and a matching armchair.

'Welcome to my humble home,' said the woman, gesturing for them to sit. She brought over a small platter of bread and cheese before settling into the armchair opposite them.

'We should get better acquainted,' the woman said with a pleasant smile. 'My name is Odorf, and I am in charge here at the commune. I am also a member of The Seagull Society.'

The woman proudly indicated a small silver pin of a seabird fastened to the breast of her cloak.

'The Seagull what?' asked Ralph bluntly.

'They are seabirds.'

'We need your help,' said Naldy, uninterested in hearing about the old witch's devotion to birds.

'Yes, I heard you talking about books and dragon caves. But before we discuss those, let's start with names, shall we? I've told you my name. It is Odorf. Now you must tell me yours.'

'I'm Naldy, and this is Ralph.'

'Splendid,' said Odorf. 'The next question I'm most curious to receive answers to is this: what are your intentions with these books?'

'Intentions?'

'Yes,' said Odorf, picking up a piece of aged cheese. 'I believe I'm correct in thinking you are going to collect the Devante—oh, yes, I know what is hidden in those caves—but what will you do with them?'

'There's a man who is after the books,' said Naldy. 'He wants to destroy them.'

'But we want to save them, that's all,' added Ralph, suspiciously eyeing the food.

'Yes, saving things is noble enough,' said Odorf, eating another piece of cheese. Ralph placed his hands beneath his thighs, resisting the temptation to eat the gooey wedge in case it was poisoned. Odorf glowered at him. 'But it can be problematic, especially when dragons are involved. Do you believe you would be a more suitable guardian for these Devante than the six dragons?'

'Well—'

'You both think you are better equipped than an entire family of ancient beasts?'

'This man named Maverick,' said Naldy quickly, 'he will stop at nothing to eradicate the books. You can help us, or we'll search the blooming mountains ourselves if we have to!'

'Maverick? Yes, I know that name,' remarked Odorf, her voice unsettled. 'A name that is not welcome here. He is the wizard who came across Harmony Esterfield and our eggs.'

Naldy shared a concerned look with Ralph.

'We are told that on Harmony's return journey from the museum,' said Odorf, leaning forward a little, 'this wizard, Maverick, crossed paths with her. He was the one who turned the unborn dragons into magical scrolls, using the magic of the Devante to do so. You see, a dragon egg can hatch centuries after it has been laid, for inside the shell, the unhatched dragon remains alive for hundreds of years. They simply require the love of their mother to hatch. But Maverick sacrificed the baby dragons.'

'She's dead,' whispered Ralph nervously.

'Well, now'—Odorf rubbed her wrinkled forehead—'what we feared has happened, then.'

'But you didn't kill her?' asked Naldy without thinking.

'Kill Harmony Esterfield? Heavens, no! We simply wanted to find her to retrieve our eggs. It was unlike her not to return to the commune.'

'But why was she trying to sell the eggs?' asked Ralph. 'Why was she afraid to return here with them?'

'I am not sure. Dragon properties are potent and very valuable. She would have received a better price for the eggs before they were modified by that wizard.'

'Why would Maverick alter the eggs for her?' wondered Naldy aloud.

'Unless...' Odorf trailed off, deep in thought.

'Unless what?'

'Unless his intention was to harm the eggs. You said yourself he was on a mission to destroy the Devante. Maybe it isn't only the Devante he wants gone...'

Odorf went silent, her wrinkled face deep in thought, worry plaguing her eyes.

'What is it?' asked Naldy gently.

'Perhaps Maverick wants to eradicate all magic,' said Odorf slowly.

Naldy felt goosebumps travel up the back of her neck. She had a strange feeling that what Odorf had said was true. Diamone's first prediction rang in Naldy's mind: *Only you can save magic.*

'You could guard them here,' suggested Ralph. 'Protect them from Maverick for us?'

'No, no. We are much too old for that. Protecting ourselves is effort enough. I will guide you through the mountains, but I must warn you—'

'It is a dangerous journey,' interrupted Naldy impatiently. 'We know.'

'When should we leave?' asked Ralph with a hint of fear.

'We must leave now,' said Odorf, standing. 'We must reach the caves before this wizard does. Hop skip.'

'At least we can take some proper guards along with us,' said Ralph, caving to temptation and picking up a handful of cheese.

'It must be just the three of us,' said Odorf. 'Travelling across the Edengar Mountains with a crowd is dangerous; it can draw unwanted attention.'

Ralph frowned as they climbed the stairs behind Odorf and stepped through the trapdoor into the empty cottage above.

'I was hoping you'd be my guard, Ralph,' Odorf said jokingly.

She led them out into the cavern, and now that they were no longer paralysed, they could see things more clearly. More cottages were crammed into the space than Naldy had initially thought. She noticed that the ground wasn't a hard stone surface but was covered in black, mossy grass. The stream trickled slowly along the length of the cavern.

Many more witches were flitting about the place, all wearing the same dark green cloaks with golden buttons and potion satchels tied around their waists. They were all elderly; there didn't seem to be a youthful face around.

'This way,' said Odorf, leading them towards the closest cavern wall.

Many wrinkled witches were happily fishing in the nearby stream, while others sat outside their cottages, peacefully sipping brew. The giant burning torches attached to the rock walls produced a pleasant yellow glow over the entire place. It was unlike anything Naldy had seen before, and she almost completely forgot they were deep underground.

'Something is swimming down there,' said Ralph, peering disgustedly into the stream.

'Have you never seen a gally fish before?' asked Odorf, shaking her head. 'Their scales, when powdered, are an essential potion ingredient.'

Naldy gazed into the water and saw ugly green shapes wriggling along the bottom. They were the size of her cat Smookers and had bulging black eyes. These were unlike any fish Naldy had ever seen.

The old male witch who had initially greeted them approached, carrying two rucksacks. Naldy recognised her own and took it as the witch handed it to her with a smile.

'Thank you, Hestern,' said Odorf, taking the other rucksack from him. 'May you be safe and protected while I am away.'

'The village will miss you while you are gone, Odorf.'

'Don't I get a rucksack?' whispered Ralph to Naldy.

'You'll both take turns carrying it,' said Odorf. 'You are not used to the journey through the mountains.'

About eighty other grey-haired witches emerged from their cottages to see them off. There wasn't a youthful face in the crowd.

'Hestern?'

'Yes, Mam.'

'Keep the Viligogs fed, won't you?' instructed Odorf. 'Three times a night.'

'Of course, and may your journey see you safely returned to us.'

'Gosh,' whispered Ralph to Naldy. 'I didn't expect us to be leaving this fast.'

'Time ticks quickly,' said Odorf, stopping to face the crowd that had gathered. Odorf bowed her head, and the group lowered theirs in return. They stayed like this, silent, for an uncomfortable amount of time. Naldy noticed that even Ralph had bowed his head.

Then, Odorf turned to make her way up the staircase, with Naldy and Ralph following her.

'I don't feel good about this,' Ralph said to Naldy.

'Do we have any other choice, Ralph? It's our only path to those books, and at least we have a guide now.'

For someone in such a hurry to leave, Odorf was climbing the spiral staircase rather slowly. Naldy thought speed was essential if they were going to make it to the dragon caves before Maverick and Getergrin.

'Patience,' said Odorf to Naldy, who had been close behind. 'There's plenty of time to get to the caves.'

They emerged from the statue's stone curtain, and Naldy was momentarily blinded by the sun's brightness. As her eyes adjusted, she realised that the layout of the ancient town above ground mirrored the one below.

'This way now,' said Odorf, shuffling along the dirt road winding between the cottages. No one else was in sight, and the enormous mountains loomed eerily nearby, their snow-strewn peaks reflecting the sunlight.

'Do any witches live in those?' Ralph asked, pointing to the cottages.

'Oh, no,' replied Odorf. 'Some of them are used as storerooms. We used to live in them, above ground, but that was a long time ago, before The Great Witch Hunt. Ah, this is the one we want here.'

Odorf stopped outside one of the cottages, reached into her green cloak, and pulled out a short rusty key to open the building's door.

'But aren't we going to the mountains?' asked

Naldy, staring inside the empty room. It was similar to the one where the witches had placed them while they'd been paralysed.

Odorf entered the empty cottage and slowly lowered her creaking knees to the floor. With her wrinkled fingers, she pried at a joint between the floorboards. It gave way, sliding aside to reveal a gap big enough to climb through. Naldy could see a stone staircase leading into the darkness below.

'A tunnel,' Ralph said excitedly. 'I'm so relieved we don't have to fly.'

'Fly? Oh no, one cannot fly across Edengar. It's far too dangerous,' Odorf replied, slowly hobbling down the stone stairs and disappearing into the darkness. 'These tunnels are ancient, so do be careful.'

As Naldy descended, she couldn't shake the suspicion that this might be a trap. When the stairs levelled out, she stepped cautiously onto the flat ground, her nerves on edge.

'Odorf?' Ralph called. 'Can't you create some light? Naldy is cursed, so she won't be able to. Please, I can't see a thing.'

'Keep walking,' echoed Odorf's voice from the darkness up ahead.

Naldy was shocked at how skilfully Odorf had managed to navigate the dark, for her voice seemed to come from quite a distance up the tunnel. Naldy stretched out her hands and took tiny steps, afraid she might knock into something.

Suddenly, a flood of golden light filled the tunnel as many torches burst into flame, their glow illuminating the rough, rocky walls where they were perched in ornate brackets.

Naldy noticed the floor was made of hand-painted tiles with a faded regal pattern.

'I don't like being underground,' said Naldy timidly.

'It is some distance to the other side,' said Odorf, moving along the torch-lit tunnel. 'If you want to turn around, now would be the time. This tunnel is as old as I am, so mind your step if you choose to come along.'

Naldy and Ralph paused, exchanging a grim look as they steeled themselves for the journey ahead. The flickering flames cast dancing shadows on the rough stone walls.

'Here we go,' Naldy said, trailing after Odorf.

'Why does it feel like this is the beginning?' asked Ralph, running to catch up.

'Because,' she replied, 'I think it is the beginning.'

Weeks went by—or at least it felt like weeks to Naldy. The absence of sunlight made it hard to gauge exactly how long they'd been journeying through the tunnel. Odorf eventually informed them it had only been four days. They were all fatigued and had scarcely spoken as they trudged along. The uneven, rocky walls seemed endlessly monotonous. Naldy had initially found some pleasure in observing the regal tiles on the tunnel's floor, but even they had become tiresome. The further they went, the more chipped and cracked the tiles became, leading to frequent stubbed toes and numerous trip-ups.

It didn't help that the deeper they went into the tunnel, the fewer flaming torches there were. The darkness would become pitch black before gradually brightening again.

'Why don't we take one of them with us?' grumbled Ralph, still limping from a recently stubbed toe. 'I'm sick of not being able to see anything.'

'This place was built using ancient magic,' remarked Odorf dryly. 'If you take one of the torches from its bracket, all of them will go out, and they only relight if you're at either end of the tunnel.'

Naldy felt that she was ill-prepared for the task ahead. Each time she stopped to check the list she was surprised to find the Devante still clearly written on the parchment. The longer they spent underground, the more an ominous dread grew inside her. She did not openly share her concerns with the others, as she didn't want to dampen their already low spirits.

Odorf stopped in the middle of the tunnel.

'Are we sleeping here?' asked Ralph, throwing himself hopefully onto the floor. 'Please tell me it's night. I don't think I can walk much more.'

'Yes,' said Odorf, spreading knitted blankets from her leather bag onto the cold tiles. 'We'll sleep here tonight.'

They settled on the blankets, and Odorf retrieved three goblets and a flask of fresh water from her rucksack.

'Whoever built this place,' said Ralph, removing

his shoes to rub his feet, 'has no understanding of comfort. It's so dreary down here.'

'Our people built this tunnel as a safe passage to the mountains,' replied Odorf, passing them each some pumpernickel bread. 'We sometimes journey to Edengar to collect rare flora and exotic insect species for our potion-making.'

'Are we far under the mountains then?' murmured Ralph, his voice betraying his fear at the prospect.

'We have been far beneath them for most of this journey,' said Odorf. 'These mountains are greater than many realise and stretch quite a distance.'

They finished their bread and water and readied themselves for bed. The light meal eased an ache in Naldy's joints, which she hadn't been aware of until it was gone.

'Odorf?' Naldy asked as she lay on her blanket.

'Yes.'

'Something has been worrying me.'

'What is it, dear?' replied Odorf softly.

Naldy wanted to confide in Odorf about the nagging feeling growing inside her—the sense that something terrible was imminent and that failure loomed. But she decided against it.

'I think I might know why the museum refused your dragon eggs,' she muttered instead.

'You do?'

'Getergrin,' said Naldy softly. 'He's working with Maverick. Getergrin is the artefact authenticator for the museum. He must have declared Harmony's eggs to be fake.'

'And why do you think he would have done that?' asked Odorf. 'When they are real.'

'Maybe,' suggested Ralph, fussing with his knitted blanket, 'so Maverick could destroy the eggs without the museum caring. There's also a question that's worrying me: if it wasn't the commune that killed Harmony Esterfield, then who was it?'

'Maverick?' suggested Naldy.

'Possibly,' said Ralph, sounding unconvinced. 'But why would Maverick alter her eggs, set her free, only to go after her later? I mean, she was selling eggs at his town fair!'

'Perhaps,' began Odorf, 'it was to avoid drawing suspicion. Come now, let us sleep for a few hours. There'll be ample time for speculation when we continue through the tunnel tomorrow.'

Odorf rolled over, and nothing more was said. Naldy saw Ralph fiddling with the emerald earring between his fingers. When sleep finally overtook her, she was plagued by nightmares of never-ending tunnels.

'We should be moving now,' said Odorf, gently shaking Naldy awake. They packed up their things and strapped their rucksacks onto their backs. 'We still have quite a distance to cover.'

The tiles became more treacherous as they trudged on; sometimes, they were missing entirely, leaving jagged exposed rock for them to step over. Time seemed to slow to a crawl, almost to the point of stopping. Naldy was uncertain how many days and nights they had lumbered through the underground passage.

When they first glimpsed a small circle of white light ahead, Naldy was convinced she was hallucinating. It wasn't until Odorf proclaimed, 'Ah, the end,' that Naldy felt joy coursing through her.

They all quickened their pace, eager to exit the tunnel and feel the sunlight on their faces. There was no door on this end, and Naldy was grateful for it, as the expanding light was a comforting sight.

Once they reached the exit, Naldy could see nothing but a blinding wash of white light. She squinted, standing at the tunnel's opening, the cool breeze brushing her face, waiting for her eyes to adjust.

Once her vision sharpened, Naldy saw they were standing on a ledge halfway up a large rock wall. There was no obvious way down, and the rock wall opposite stretched even higher.

Naldy mistakenly peered into the ravine, where both rock walls narrowed inward, almost meeting at the bottom but leaving a small, perilous gap.

'Is this the ravine where the dragon caves are?' Ralph squeaked nervously, backing into the shelter of the tunnel.

Naldy couldn't see any caves on either side of the ravine's rock, and Odorf let out a hoarse laugh, clearly unaware that Ralph's question was serious.

The old woman stepped onto a set of precarious stairs leading downward. The steps had been carved into the rockface by an unskilled hand, and their roughness had made them nearly invisible to Naldy at first.

'Are we meant to follow her?' asked Ralph, unimpressed.

'You won't find dragons here!' Odorf called back as she descended. 'The ravine we're heading towards is much larger than this one—and much further away, too.'

By the time Naldy and Ralph reached the bottom, Odorf had already leapt across the gap and was climbing a second set of steps scaling the opposite rock wall.

'How deep do you think it is?' wondered Naldy, gazing into the darkness of the chasm.

'I don't know,' said Ralph, bending to pick up a small stone from the rocky floor. 'Let's find out.'

'No!' shouted Odorf's echoing voice. She was eyeing Ralph sternly from a quarter of the way up the opposite rockface.

'But I just want to see how far the bottom is,' called Ralph, still clutching the rock.

'Put that rock down, you fool,' Odorf snapped. 'These mountains aren't empty. Believe me, you don't want to upset anything living in this part of the land.'

Ralph didn't argue—he placed the stone carefully back on the ground before jumping over the dark crevice.

When Naldy leapt across, she felt a gust of wind surge upwards from below. She approached the second set of stairs and, as she ascended, became convinced that these were spaced further apart.

Relieved, she hoisted herself up from the last step and was greeted with a breathtaking view. Endless mountains stretched across the horizon in every direction. The tips of the taller peaks were dusted with snow, while vast expanses of stunning trees covered the lower slopes.

'It's extraordinary,' said Ralph, stunned by the beauty of the view. 'I could live here.'

'You do not want to live here,' remarked Odorf. 'You'll soon tire of its beauty once you witness Edengar's uglier side.'

Chapter Sixteen

SADDLES WITHOUT HORSES

T he weather was warm, and the towering trees provided plenty of shade to walk beneath.

'Watch the rock there,' said Odorf as they descended another slope.

'You know, come to think of it,' said Ralph, delicately placing one foot in front of the other, 'I've come to see the benefits of flying.'

'I've already told you,' said Odorf, making her way down the mountainside with surprising agility, 'there are things in this part of the world you do not want to be seen by. Flying on broomsticks is out of the question.'

'Seen by what?'

'Creatures roam these skies. We are much safer keeping our feet firmly on the ground.'

The rocky slope eventually evened out.

'We continue along here until we reach the river,' said Odorf, 'and then up to the snow gums and across the ridge there.'

Naldy and Ralph were impressed that Odorf didn't require a map for navigation. The group's morale lifted for the first time in a long while as a cool breeze drifted pleasantly across their faces.

The trees around them soon thickened, and the sky gradually turned a dull blue-grey as night approached.

'I can hear water,' said Ralph, stopping.

'The river,' replied Odorf, setting her rucksack on the ground. 'We'll set up camp here tonight. It's too late to approach the water now, so we'll fill our bottles in the morning.'

Odorf reached into her rucksack and pulled out an umber-coloured fabric, loosely folded. She placed it on the forest floor and waved her hand over it. The material unfurled into a medium-sized tent, just big enough for a person to stand in.

'It's not luxurious,' said Odorf, 'but it's warm inside.'

Naldy made her way through the opening and was surprised to find three simple hammocks.

'How many days will it take us to reach the caves?' asked Ralph, entering the tent and happily climbing into one of the hammocks.

'That depends,' replied Odorf.

'On what?'

'On what Edengar dishes up. Without any major obstacles, we could arrive at the dragon caves in as little as two weeks.'

'Two weeks! That long!' said Naldy, shocked.

'If we're lucky, yes,' said Odorf. 'But we shouldn't expect Edengar to play nice. It will more likely take us three to four weeks. I'll light us a fire outside and get dinner started.'

Odorf left the tent to prepare dinner. Naldy climbed into the hammock beside Ralph's and found it extremely comfortable.

'To think,' said Ralph, pulling the emerald earring from his pocket to examine it, 'I thought the Kirkwood Forest was intimidatingly large.'

'It's not too late to turn back,' said Naldy.

'Turn back? I'm not taking on that tunnel alone.'

'I don't want anything to happen to you, Ralph,' said Naldy softly.

'I intend to make it to those caves,' replied Ralph sternly, climbing out of his hammock. 'If *you* want to turn back, *you* can!'

'I don't want to turn back. I'm just saying…'

'Good. Then please stop pretending the weight of this journey is solely your responsibility. I want to be here, Naldy. Now, let's go out and help Odorf with dinner, shall we?'

Odorf was skinning a wild rabbit when they exited the tent.

'How did you catch that so quickly?' marvelled Ralph in awe.

'With a little help from magic,' said Odorf, snapping the lid shut on a hexagonal glass phial and returning it to her satchel tied to her waist. 'Hegervege potion—rabbits adore the smell of it.'

Odorf was adamant she didn't require assistance preparing the rabbit and asked Ralph and Naldy to search for some wild mushrooms.

'But be sure to stay away from the river!'

They didn't have to wander far from the tent

to find plenty of button mushrooms growing abundantly under the nearby trees.

'I'm beginning to see the appeal of Rupert's travelling lifestyle,' said Ralph as they returned with armfuls of the edible fungi.

Odorf finished cooking dinner and served each of them a hearty helping of the fire-roasted rabbit and mushrooms.

'It's so peaceful out here,' commented Naldy, glancing up at the sky as the first stars of the night emerged.

After dinner, when they retired to their hammocks, the soft crackle of the dying fire just outside blended with the low hum of night insects, lulling them to sleep. Occasionally, a distant howl or the cry of some unfamiliar animal would echo through the night, but Naldy felt safe within the warmth and comfort of the tent.

The next few days passed uneventfully as they clambered up and down mountainsides. The weather remained sunny, and they always found plenty of wild forest food. This was not the Edengar Naldy had heard of. Apart from aching limbs, the journey so far had been unexpectedly serene, leaving Naldy with a growing sense of unease at their unlikely luck.

The sun continued to shine over the picturesque landscape, and they even stumbled upon a strange, green stump-like bush that yielded juicy, sweet pink berries.

'Oh look, the Dendah bush is in bloom,' said

Odorf, plucking a berry and popping it into her mouth. 'Hard to find these, as they usually grow in the most difficult-to-reach places—like the sides of cliffs.'

They joyously filled their cloak pockets with the delicious vibrant fruits.

It wasn't until they reached a mountain covered with twisted snow gums that the trouble Naldy had anticipated emerged.

'We're going through there?' asked Naldy, shuffling towards the tangled maze of stunted trees that stretched to the mountain's tip.

'We are,' said Odorf, 'unless you want to add another month to our journey to the caves. Stay close now.'

Odorf stepped through an opening between two low, claw-like snow gums, and Naldy and Ralph reluctantly followed. The stumpy, greyish trees were slightly taller than Ralph's head, their contorted branches bristling with hazardous, spiky points. The dead-looking, leafless trees grew so close together that there was only enough space to weave through one behind the other.

'Keep your head down, Ralph,' said Odorf in a reprimanding tone.

'Why must we keep our heads low?' Ralph whispered to Naldy.

'I don't know,' Naldy replied. 'Just do as you're told.'

They were impressed that Odorf knew which path to take, as the labyrinth presented many choices. After an hour of winding this way and that, Naldy stood on her tiptoes, peering over the leafless trees to see how far they'd come. The jagged branches were sharp enough to pierce the skin, and Naldy knew it would be impossible to climb over them.

A black crow swooped and landed on one of the gnarled branches of a nearby snow gum.

'Hello, little fella,' said Naldy to the black bird. The crow began cawing loudly.

'I told you to keep your head down, girl,' said Odorf sharply. 'Make haste.'

'Make haste?' Ralph echoed questioningly.

Odorf sprinted through the maze without pausing to explain, and Naldy and Ralph hurried after her. The crow pushed off its branch and took to the skies, mirroring every turn they made.

'This way,' said Odorf anxiously, urging them to quicken their pace.

'It's only a bird,' Naldy panted. The path was so narrow that the branches scratched against their bodies as they raced through.

'We must lose the crow,' said Odorf, 'before it calls its master.'

Naldy, who was at the rear, struggled to keep up. She rounded a corner and was met by three diverging paths, with no sign of Odorf or Ralph. She didn't know which direction they'd gone.

'Odorf?' called Naldy, the crow circling overhead. 'Odorf! Ralph? Where are you?'

The bird landed nearby on one of the crooked

branches, mockingly staring at her with its black, marbled eyes. Its shrill caw echoed.

'They've left me behind!'

Naldy shuddered as dread set in, and the air seemed to leave her lungs. She was certain she would die amongst these wretched snow gums.

'There you are!' Odorf growled, emerging from the central path with a panic-stricken Ralph in tow. 'I said to stay close! Quickly now.'

Odorf hastened onward, and they raced after her. As they rounded a corner, the old woman pulled them beneath the cover of one of the larger trees. They heard the crow fly past, unaware of their hiding spot.

'We'll wait here for a little while,' said Odorf, catching her breath.

'I was calling out to you,' said Naldy, 'but you'd gone. What did that crow want with us?'

'Do you think these snow gums grew naturally in the shape of a labyrinth?' snapped Odorf, tentatively peering at the sky to check if the bird was really gone. 'I won't tell you again: these mountains are home to dark creatures and darker witches. Evil festers in these parts. Don't trust anything, not even the birds.'

'And to think,' said Ralph, gulping air, 'I was beginning to enjoy these mountains.'

'Let's continue on,' said Odorf, lifting herself up. 'Stay close, like I told you to.'

With a gesture and a scolding glance, Ralph indicated that Naldy should walk ahead of him. The fear Naldy had experienced was enough to sharpen her wits for the rest of the journey through the snow gums.

To Naldy and Ralph's disappointment, the end of the maze led them to a bleak, rocky cliff, fully exposed to a biting wind.

Naldy scowled at the steep drop—a sheer ninety-degree angle without any steps. She was sure they hadn't packed rope long enough to reach the rock-strewn bottom.

'Now what do we do?' asked Ralph, staring expectantly at Odorf.

Odorf turned to the great divide and chanted a string of foreign words.

Naldy peered across and saw another mountaintop a short distance away. Odorf finished her chanting.

'Are we meant to fly across?' Naldy asked. 'It's a short distance. Surely we won't be noticed by anything.'

'We walk,' Odorf replied, as if it were obvious.

'Walk? But where are we to walk?'

'We brought rope,' said Ralph, squeamishly eyeing the cliff face. 'We could try to fling it across and hope it catches on a small boulder.'

'Some of the enchantments in these mountains are centuries old,' said Odorf, her feet precariously close to the edge. 'There are remnants of ancient magic all throughout these parts.'

Odorf took a step off the cliff, but—much to Ralph and Naldy's relief—gravity didn't pull her to the bottom. Instead, as her foot touched the air, solid ground materialised beneath her. The surface was only visible around her feet, making it appear as though she were floating on two plates of solid rock.

'It's been made to look like the tip of the mountain,' said Odorf, noticing Ralph and Naldy's dumbfounded expressions. She smiled. 'But the top is actually that higher peak up there. It's a unique enchantment, powerful magic. We're not standing on the true mountaintop.'

Odorf continued walking up the mountain, the solid ground appearing with each of her steps. As she lifted her feet, the ground vanished behind her.

'Come now, don't be shy. The real ground will come into view as your foot touches it.'

'You want to go first?' offered Ralph, shooting Naldy an uneasy glance.

'Alright,' said Naldy, hovering a foot over the edge. 'Here goes.'

Naldy placed her foot down—her inner thoughts ringing alarm bells, warning her that she would fall—but solid rock appeared as her foot struck the ground. The uneasy feeling didn't lessen with each terrifying step, and her mind refused to accept that she wouldn't plummet into the chasm below.

Ralph cautiously placed his feet exactly where Naldy's had landed.

When they reached the actual mountaintop, the harsh wind ceased. Naldy noticed the enchantment couldn't be seen from this side—the perilous drop they had crossed now appeared solid.

'I've never seen magic like that,' said Naldy, finally able to appreciate the illusion now that she was no longer standing on it.

'But now what?' asked Ralph, surveying the view.

They stood on the peak of the highest mountain for miles around, but there still didn't seem to be any safe way forward. Instead, they were met with a more enormous, much steeper chasm.

'No!' shouted Odorf as Ralph hovered a foot dangerously over the mountain's edge. 'This one is not an enchantment. This cliff is real.'

Terror flashed across Ralph's face as he backed away from the cliff.

'I thought I was getting the hang of it,' said Ralph, sitting on a nearby rock. 'How do we get across, then? Please tell me we don't have to clamber over another set of terribly crafted stairs.'

'There are no stairs here,' said Odorf, reaching into her leather rucksack and searching for something.

'It's oddly quiet up here,' said Naldy, feeling the warmth of the setting sun on her face. 'There's snow on those mountaintops, and they're lower down.'

'Ah, here it is,' said Odorf, smiling as she pulled out their folded tent. 'We'll stay here tonight. This mountain has been magically protected and is a safe haven.'

'Safe?' said Ralph disbelievingly. 'It seems awfully exposed if you ask me.'

'It is safe,' Odorf repeated, calmly waving a hand over the tent as it unfolded before them.

'I doubt we will find any wild rabbits up here,' said Ralph sadly.

'I think I have some apple cider,' said Naldy, reaching into her leather bag. She fished out the bottle from the bottom of her rucksack. 'This should help lift our spirits.'

'I wish we had some of your pie left, Naldy,' he said longingly.

As the sun disappeared, Odorf lit a fire. Its smoke curled slowly upwards, reaching six or seven metres before swirling away in a violent wind. Naldy had the strange feeling they were sitting inside an invisible, bubble-like enchantment.

'So,' said Naldy, pouring the last of the apple cider into their cups, 'how are we getting off this mountaintop?'

'We fly,' said Odorf.

'But didn't you say—'

'Not on broomsticks.'

Ralph and Naldy exchanged puzzled looks. Odorf reached into the rucksack resting beside her, pulling out three sizeable brown saddles. They were clearly enchanted to fit magically inside, much like Ralph's magic carpet, which Maverick had flown off with. The worn leather was creased from many years of use.

'Flying horses?' said Ralph curiously. 'If the saddles fit in your rucksack, surely you could have brought broomsticks?'

'I wouldn't risk flying across these parts, at least not with the piglinns about.'

'Piglinns?' repeated Naldy, noticing the firelight reflecting off the long metal chains attached to the saddles.

'Have you got flying horses in your rucksack too?' Ralph asked jokingly.

'Don't be silly,' said Odorf, frowning. 'Horses cannot fly, boy. And even if they could, we wouldn't fly them here—it would upset the piglinns. You don't want to risk upsetting them. Carnivores, you see.'

'What is a piglinn?' queried Naldy softly, uncertain whether she wanted to hear the answer.

'They are somewhat like pigeons and bob their heads back and forth when in flight, but they're a little bigger. A lot bigger, I should say.'

'How big is bigger?' asked Ralph, wrinkling his forehead.

'The adults come up to about your nose.'

'Giant pigeons!'

'Piglinns,' Odorf corrected him. 'I suppose they share many similarities with pigeons—not their size, of course. They have a crest on their heads—a brilliant green, the most wonderful feather you'll ever see, and the most expensive. You'll make some pretty currents if you can get your hands on one.'

'We're quite exposed up here,' said Ralph, shifting agitatedly. 'Are we safe? I don't want to be eaten by a giant pigeon in my sleep.'

'We are perfectly fine, as I've already told you. The piglinns won't come out of their nests until the sun breaks.'

'So, what are the saddles for?' asked Naldy suspiciously.

'For the piglinns, dear.'

Naldy realised from the woman's serious expression that she wasn't joking—they would be flying atop these giant birds.

'I'd only just gotten used to broomsticks,' said Ralph, lowering his head as if he might burst into tears.

'We should get some sleep,' said Odorf wearily, standing to stretch her limbs. 'We must be up early and wide awake before the piglinns come by.'

Neither Ralph nor Naldy had the spirit to ask Odorf how exactly they would capture piglinns to ride. Odorf took herself to bed, leaving Naldy and Ralph sitting around the crackling fire.

'You should stop obsessing over that thing,' said Naldy, noticing Ralph was turning the emerald earring over in his hand.

'I feel like it's protecting us,' said Ralph. Naldy shook her head, and Ralph quickly changed the subject. 'Are the Devante still on the list?'

Naldy retrieved the parchment from her pocket. She saw the Corium, Lignum, Metallum, Caeruleum, Rosea, and the Aurum safely listed there. She nodded.

'You seem a bit low,' he said gently. 'I know this quest feels unlikely to succeed, but the Devante are still on the list, and we have Odorf's help, so we mustn't lose hope yet.'

'It's not that,' said Naldy as salty teardrops fell,

catching in her mouth. 'Seeing Rubrum missing... it's difficult. I don't understand why my parents didn't tell me Rubrum was one of the Devante.'

'You said it yourself that your parents probably didn't know,' Ralph replied kindly.

Naldy didn't respond. She couldn't understand how they wouldn't have known, especially since her parents had given Oak the book and asked him to protect it.

'How old were you when they disappeared?'

'I was twelve,' said Naldy, wiping her wet cheeks on her cloak. 'One night, they left, and they never returned. They didn't even leave a note.'

'I'm so sorry, Naldy.'

'I don't know where they went or why they disappeared. I always thought someday they would return. I believe the Devante could help me find them, or at least help me find out what happened to them. We need to save the Devante before Maverick gets to them. Perhaps then, I can finally get some answers.'

Ralph didn't say anything.

'We should go to bed,' said Naldy, yawning, though she didn't move from her comfortable log.

'We do have to be up early,' Ralph agreed, standing, then added sourly, 'to learn how to ride piglinns. Gosh. Goodnight, Naldy.'

Ralph approached the tent but paused at the entrance. He turned to face Naldy, who was still sitting by the fire.

'We will save them,' he said confidently. 'We

won't let Maverick destroy any more.'

Naldy smiled, and Ralph lingered for a moment before entering the tent.

Naldy stayed awake for a couple more hours, staring into the dancing fire and pondering the impossible task ahead. She knew that saving the Devante might be her last chance to discover what happened to her parents. Perhaps her last hope of finding them. Eventually, she picked herself up off the ground and made her way sleepily inside the tent, where Odorf and Ralph were already snoring.

The question of how they would capture piglinns was answered early the next day, which came a little too soon for both Naldy and Ralph's liking.

'Any minute now, we should see them come by,' said Odorf, standing in the first rays of brilliant sunshine. The tent was packed away, and all three stood looking out over the vast abyss, each holding a leather saddle. 'We must land on piglinns from the same family,' Odorf continued. 'They always travel in groups. We wouldn't want to upset them by splitting them up.'

'Not upset them?' Ralph mumbled to Naldy. 'We're supposed to capture them and saddle them up. How do we do that without upsetting them?'

Naldy yawned, wiping at her sleepy eyes. She wished she had gone to bed when the others retired. Naldy tried to mentally jolt herself awake, but it was useless. She had slept poorly, with nightmares of giant birds chasing her.

'Here they come,' called Odorf gleefully. 'Saddles

at the ready.'

Naldy peered into the distance and saw three birds flying in their direction. They didn't seem as big or scary as they had in her nightmare.

'They're rather cute, actually, aren't they?'

As they came closer, Naldy noticed their heads bobbing awkwardly as they soared, giving them a rather silly appearance. They looked remarkably like giant pigeons, each with a captivating green crest of feathers.

'Like this,' said Odorf, holding up her saddle in a brief demonstration. 'They'll come close to the cliff to search for food, and you throw your saddle, then jump after it.'

'Jump?' Naldy repeated, not sure she had heard correctly.

'I think I definitely prefer broomsticks,' said Ralph, his face turning paler as the birds approached. 'They won't mistake us for food, will they?'

'When we land on the piglinns, they'll get a bit of a fright—they're not the smartest creatures— but they'll soon forget we're there. We'll fly a few mountains across, but we can only go so far.'

'Can we just fly the rest of the way to the dragon caves?' asked Naldy, hoping to give her aching legs a rest.

'No, a few mountains along there are nistles nesting, and they eat piglinns, so we'll need to dismount before then. Here they come. Ready yourselves!'

Naldy no longer felt sleepy. Her adrenaline had kicked in, and her heart was pounding heavily. Ralph stood beside her, holding his saddle limply, as if he might faint. But there was no time to console him, for the piglinns were now directly below them. Naldy was astonished at how close they flew to the mountain's rocky wall.

'Now!' called Odorf loudly.

The next few moments happened quickly. Odorf threw her leather saddle haphazardly off the mountaintop. To both Naldy and Ralph's surprise, it landed neatly on one of the piglinn's feathered backs. Odorf then jumped from the cliff and landed effortlessly atop the saddle, as if she were some sort of piglinn-riding expert.

Without having time to think, Naldy threw her own saddle off the cliff and was surprised when it landed squarely on the second piglinn's back, as if by magic. Her stomach leapt into her throat, her mouth dried up, and terror struck—she no longer felt capable of moving her limbs.

Slam! Her legs had worked, and she'd jumped from the cliff, colliding with the saddle. But just as she felt secure atop the flying creature, it began weaving and bucking in a panic-stricken tantrum. Naldy lunged forward and grabbed the metal reins, certain she would be thrown off by the piglinn's wild bucking.

Then, to her relief, the turbulence stopped. Naldy's piglinn had calmed itself and was now flying smoothly, almost gracefully, despite its awkward head-bobbing. There was no need for Naldy to hold the reins, as the bird's flight was steady, but she kept a firm grip on them as a precaution.

The sight of the elderly woman atop the giant pigeon-like bird was rather comical, and Naldy chuckled to herself as her piglinn coasted behind Odorf's.

She turned around to check how Ralph and his creature were getting along—but Ralph wasn't on top of any piglinn! He was still standing on the mountaintop, holding his saddle over his head, while his piglinn viciously pecked at him.

'Odorf!'

She had already noticed Ralph's failure to mount his bird and made a sharp U-turn. Naldy's piglinn glided after Odorf's without her needing to direct it.

'The daft boy!' cried Odorf as their creatures approached the mountaintop. Naldy noticed that her piglinn was beginning to excrete saliva the closer they got to Ralph.

'Here, Ralph!' Odorf shouted, throwing down a rope and pulling hard on her piglinn's metal reins to stop it from landing and joining the attack. 'Wrap it around yourself!'

Naldy's piglinn was determined not to miss a meal. It flew right past Odorf, landed on its short, stumpy legs, and bobbed its head aggressively in Ralph's direction.

Still cowering underneath his saddle, Ralph struggled to fend off the relentless attack of the rogue piglinn.

Naldy pulled tightly on her reins, but the piglinn was much stronger than she had anticipated.

Ralph struggled to slip Odorf's rope around himself while dodging the two rogue piglinns' hungry pecking.

'Control your bird, Naldy!' Ralph shouted angrily, narrowly avoiding a snapping beak.

'I'm trying,' called Naldy, pulling as hard as she could on her reins, but it was useless, for the creature was too strong.

Odorf looked unimpressed.

Ralph finally succeeded in securing the rope around his body, but then he froze with terror as he was dragged by the rope towards the cliff's edge.

'No! No! No!' he cried.

Odorf had steered her piglinn away from the mountain, and Ralph's body was reluctantly dragged off the cliff. He dangled from her rope, swinging back and forth. Naldy's and Ralph's rogue creatures followed eagerly, as if he were a tasty, dangling snack.

'Hold on!' Odorf cried, beginning to pull him up.

Odorf managed, with a great heave, to pull Ralph onto the back of her saddle. The pursuing piglinns relaxed into a glide, and Naldy's piglinn let out a disappointed squawk—an unusual sound, not at all like a pigeon, reminding Naldy of a high-pitched sneeze. The piglinns now flew peacefully in line.

'Ralph!' called Naldy. 'What happened?'

'The silly boy!' said Odorf, responding for him. 'He was too afraid to jump.'

The rest of the flight was uneventful, and Naldy was grateful for it. It was unexpectedly serene sitting atop the feathered bird, with the spectacular mountains rolling by. It wasn't just the scenery that piqued Naldy's interest; she found herself fixated on the piglinn's beautifully exotic green crest. The feathers were unlike any Naldy had seen before, and she was tempted to pluck one from her piglinn's head, but she didn't dare risk upsetting it.

Almost two hours later, Odorf informed them they'd be dismounting shortly. Thankfully, this proved far more straightforward than mounting. Odorf guided them to a river nestled between two mountains, where the creatures happily stopped to drink the fresh water. They jumped off their grey-feathered piglinns and hurried to the shelter of a nearby pine tree. Odorf kindly collected the saddles for them.

The feathered creatures didn't seem to notice the riders had dismounted, and once they'd satisfied their thirst, they flew off.

'I can't believe I didn't get to fly my own piglinn,' said Ralph, watching the three gigantic, pigeon-like birds disappear into the distance.

'You should have jumped,' replied Odorf firmly, 'like I told you to.'

—Chapter Seventeen—

PROMISED RAIN

Edengar had already presented them with challenging tasks, but nothing proved as arduous as simply walking. Every muscle ached constantly.

'Can't we find some of those Nenderfall leaves?' asked Naldy. 'Don't they grow in these blooming mountains?'

'They do, yes,' said Odorf. 'We've passed plenty of Nenderfall trees.'

'Then why aren't we eating the leaves?' said Naldy.

'Because they're out of season,' Odorf explained. 'The leaves are poisonous this time of year. They're only safe to eat if picked while in season.'

Naldy sighed, rubbing her aching legs.

They rose early each morning, stopping for brief breaks throughout the day. By the time they finally settled in their hammocks each night, their limbs had stiffened uncomfortably.

The further they ventured, the scarcer the forest food became, often leaving them with no choice but to go to sleep hungry. Even Odorf's Hegervege potion was useless, as no wild rabbits lived in these parts.

Although still breathtaking, the scenery remained unchanging. It didn't help that with each new summit they reached, the view revealed many more awaiting them. The only noticeable variation in their surroundings was the sky, which had turned a threatening, cloudy grey.

'Put it away, Ralph,' Naldy said sternly. They had reached the top of another mountain, and she caught Ralph turning the emerald earring over in his fingers. His growing obsession with the trinket caused her irritation to flare. 'If you keep fixating on that thing, I'll take it from you!'

'It brings me joy, so why would you confiscate it?'

'You said it hasn't made any sounds since you've possessed it, so stop wasting your time fawning over the darned thing.'

'There's nothing else to fawn over, is there!' Ralph retorted, looking out over the endless mountains.

'We must be nearly there,' said Naldy, turning to Odorf, who was busy breaking a stale slice of pumpernickel bread into three pieces. She'd found it at the bottom of her rucksack.

'We still have some way to go yet,' replied Odorf, passing them each a portion of the unappetising bread. 'But we've made good progress, with little trouble.'

They finished their dry bread, their stomachs grumbling in protest at the meagre portion. A few hours later, the rain came, pelting so forcefully that they had to shout to be heard over the downpour.

Without the luxury of time, they couldn't afford to wait for the rain to pass. So, they pressed on, trudging over the slippery slopes despite the miserable weather.

'What's the point of it!' shouted Ralph as they struggled up a muddy path.

'Keep going, Ralph,' encouraged Naldy.

'It's probably useless anyhow,' he muttered. 'Maverick and Getergrin have probably already found the Devante.'

'The Devante are still on the list, Ralph. Look, you can see for yourself. We just have to keep going.'

'It's hopeless! Maverick already has a Devante! They've probably breezed effortlessly through these dreaded mountains. They're probably waiting there for us, like they were when we stole the Aurantiaco! I bet they didn't even have to ride the piglinns!'

Naldy gave up arguing with him.

'We don't have time to waste,' said Odorf firmly. 'We must keep up the pace.'

'I'm out of energy,' said Ralph stroppily. 'You seem to find this much easier, Odorf, and you must be at least three times our age.'

Odorf stopped walking. She reached into her rucksack, pulled out the tent, and unfolded it.

'Get inside. Get dry.'

'But you said we don't have time,' said Ralph, baffled.

'I said to get inside.'

Naldy and Ralph were both perplexed but obeyed her request, climbing gladly into the warmth and dryness of the tent. Odorf came in after them.

'It's surely not dinnertime,' said Naldy, her hair dripping wet as the rain pattered against the tent outside. 'We shouldn't be stopping.'

'I am two hundred and fifteen years old. Do you know what that means?'

'That you're too old to be trekking through Edengar.'

'Ralph,' Naldy scolded.

'It means I am old enough to remember The Great Witch Hunt. And the time that existed before then, when witches were respected.'

'The time of the Devante,' said Naldy.

'Hannah Hale was one of the most intelligent witches to have lived,' continued Odorf. 'She dedicated her life to developing and protecting new spells. When the Establishment banned the invention of new magic, she created the Devante to safeguard the art of spell creation.'

'We know all of this,' remarked Naldy, squeezing the rainwater from her clothes.

'The village,' Odorf said calmly, 'the one above ground, is where my people used to live. Like Hannah's team, we dedicated our lives to protecting the art of magic, but our focus was not on the craft of spells.'

'We really should get moving,' insisted Naldy, not wanting to waste any more time.

'What was your focus?' asked Ralph curiously.

'Potion brewing,' Odorf replied, pausing briefly as her eyes glistened with tears. 'When the burnings began, my people fled underground. We built the tunnel stretching to the Edengar Mountains and continued our work. Cowardice, you might think it, to hide underground, but those were frightening times.'

The rain continued to patter on the tent's roof. Ralph and Naldy waited for Odorf to speak again.

'How much do both of you know about brewing potions?'

'Very little,' said Naldy and Ralph in unison.

Ralph seemed surprised by Naldy's response. Potion-making was an ancient art, and most witches who still practised it did so only as a hobby.

'A dying artform,' said Odorf sadly. 'But you both probably know the essential requirements: a method, ingredients, and time.'

'Yes, yes,' said Naldy impatiently. 'Sitting over a cauldron for days on end just to create the simplest of potions, and years for anything slightly complex. I don't know why any witch still bothers with them —there are far easier ways to achieve the same results. It's called a spell.'

'You need to utter a spell to make the potion work, don't you?' asked Ralph.

'Some will tell you a potion also requires a spell, yes,' said Odorf, sharpening her gaze on them.

'Is that why you're on this quest with us?' Naldy asked, brushing her wet hair from her face. 'You want to secure the Devante for your silly potion-making?'

'We've known about the Devante for a long time,'

said Odorf gently. 'This might surprise both of you, but the Devante is not desirable to us. Our witch commune is not concerned with the quick-fix magic that the Devante promises.'

'But the Devante would improve your potion-making, wouldn't it?' accused Naldy, struggling to control her outrage. 'You're only helping us so you can keep the books for your silly potions!'

'You are not listening, girl,' said Odorf, fiddling with her potion satchel. 'I am not on this quest with you to save the Devante. I've never claimed I was. My people care nothing for quick creations. If we wanted the Devante for ourselves, we would have taken them many years ago. We know where they are and which cave they lie in.'

'Then why are you helping us?' asked Ralph.

'The truth is,' said Odorf, 'a pure potion does not require a spell. A true potion involves the correct ingredients, method, and time. Nothing more. Tinctures that require spells uttered over them are not natural potions, as the spell does all the heavy lifting.'

'But if you're not helping us save the Devante,' Ralph demanded, just as a clap of thunder broke overhead, 'then why are you helping us at all?'

'I am coming with you to protect the dragons.'

'The dragons?'

'Dragon ingredients are amongst the most invaluable in potion-making, and their magical quality is second to none.'

Naldy had foolishly believed that when they

reached the dragon caves, Odorf, being the eldest and wisest, would be the one to stop Maverick and Getergrin. But it was now clear that Odorf didn't care about the spellbooks. She was accompanying them to protect the dragons from harm.

'But don't you care about the Devante?' asked Ralph, his voice cracking. 'If Maverick and Getergrin destroy them all, there mightn't be any way left to create new magic!'

'Spells are not our concern,' replied Odorf, with a softness in her voice. 'Potions are.'

'Then why take us with you?'

'Because we share the same mission—to stop Maverick. Let's take the afternoon to relax and rest. We all look exhausted, so how about we take a nap before dinner?'

The rain outside showed no sign of letting up. They climbed into their hammocks. Naldy felt anxious, having heard Odorf state her mission was to prioritise the dragons' safety over the survival of the books.

'Are you really two hundred years old?' asked Ralph.

'Two hundred and fifteen.'

'But how?'

'Dragon blood,' said Odorf from her hammock, pointing to a thin red bottle in her potion satchel. 'Veserum. This potion requires just one spoonful of dragon blood per phial. It's a complicated potion and takes many months to stew. Regular consumption prevents ageing.'

'Only one spoonful?' asked Ralph. 'But if you killed the dragon, you could take gallions of dragon's blood and live forever.'

'The dragon from which the blood was taken must be alive when the potion is used.' Odorf shifted, making herself comfortable as the water drummed on the tent. 'Now you see why it is important for us to keep the dragons alive.'

'Imagine living forever,' remarked Ralph as a crack of thunder broke overhead.

'It prevents death from ageing,' said Odorf, 'but it doesn't protect against other causes of death. Let's get some rest. Tomorrow we have a lot more walking to do.'

'I never thought I'd say this,' said Ralph, rolling over in his hammock, 'but I wish we still had the piglinns with us. I'm tired of walking.'

The rain didn't ease overnight, if anything, it intensified. Their clothes were drenched as they lumbered up and down the rocky slopes. The storm showed no sign of letting up, with constant eruptions of forked lightning followed closely by reverberating thunder. Despite their low spirits, the three of them trudged on over slippery rocks and through muddy sludge.

Naldy knew Odorf was only accompanying them to ensure no harm came to the dragons, but she was still grateful for her guidance. Yet with each step, she began to feel the weight of saving magic resting solely on her shoulders. Even though Ralph was with them, his lack of magical abilities made her sometimes feel like she was the only one who could save the Devante.

'Naldy!'

Ralph had slipped on the wet rock and slid a few metres back along the mountain trail. Naldy carefully made her way downhill to help him up, steadying herself on the wet stones. Odorf stopped to wait for them.

'You're lucky,' said Naldy. 'You could have slipped right off the edge.'

'I was looking at the earring.'

'Ralph, it's a hexed piece of junk!'

'I dropped it somewhere when I—'

But before Ralph could finish his sentence, Naldy dived to pick up the glittering green earring from the mud and threw it as far as she could off the edge of the mountain.

'Why would you do that!' cried Ralph, horrified. 'Naldy! No!'

'Because you keep obsessing over it! It's driving you crazy. You wouldn't have slipped if you'd been watching your steps.'

'You think I'm the crazy one,' said Ralph bitterly. 'We're in the middle of nowhere, trekking to caves filled with dragons, and for what!? We don't have any hope of saving those books. We're walking to our deaths, Naldy, and you know it!'

Odorf had slowly approached them from higher up the slope. They were already so drenched that Ralph being covered in mud barely mattered.

'All she's given us,' said Ralph, pointing at the

wrinkled woman, 'is stale pumpernickel bread! She's meant to be a great potion-maker, so she claims, but she hasn't given us anything to improve our situation or our spirits. She carries around those glass phials, but what use are they to us?'

'Are you ready to continue?' asked Odorf calmly. 'We still have some distance to go before we stop for the night.'

Odorf turned her back and continued up the mountain.

Naldy didn't share her own doubts about Odorf's motives with Ralph. If Odorf was truly the grand potion-maker she claimed to be, then Ralph had a point. Shouldn't the old woman be able to offer them something to ease their pain and hunger?

Ralph barely spoke to either of them over the ensuing days, and Naldy was quietly grateful. She found herself becoming irritable with the others for no particular reason, and her patience was wearing thin.

The weather showed no signs of improving, and Naldy had long since lost track of the days they'd been hiking.

When Naldy couldn't access her magic during the daytime, she revisited her repertoire of hexes in her mind, carefully considering which ones she might use on her travel companions if they annoyed her once night fell.

Naldy felt little joy the day she awoke to find the rainclouds had dispersed. The change in weather made her realise that it hadn't been the relentless storm making her so miserable. Her misery stemmed from the fact that with each step, they were getting closer to the dragon caves, and she had no clear plan for what to do once they arrived.

Odorf and Ralph seemed quite pleased to see the sun, and Naldy managed a weak smile as they both bounded up the mountainside with newfound optimism.

She didn't believe Odorf when she stopped before a large boulder and proclaimed, 'This is it.'

'What is it?' asked Naldy.

'This is the entrance to the dragon cave.'

Naldy cautiously glanced at the enormous rock they were standing in front of. A large fissure ran through it, just big enough for a person to slide between.

'Are we meant to climb through there?' asked Ralph unhappily.

'Drink this,' said Odorf, passing them both a small glass phial filled with a violet liquid.

'What is it?' asked Ralph mistrustfully. 'We have a habit of eating and drinking things that get us into trouble.'

'You can't go merrily waltzing into a dragon cave without protection,' replied Odorf. 'This is a Gerlhend potion. It takes four years to brew and contains a quarter cup of dried dragon's blood.'

'You want us to drink dragon's blood?' said Ralph, affronted.

'Most other potions interfere with it working properly,' said Odorf, smiling. 'Your system must be uncontaminated, which is why I haven't given you any other potions. Now, drink up.'

'You could have told us that earlier,' said Naldy, rolling her eyes.

'But what does it do?' asked Ralph, squinting at the violet liquid with suspicion.

'It makes you invisible. It is how we collect the dragon eggs and other useful dragon ingredients.'

Together, they drank their phials of the bitter-tasting potion.

'It'll last an hour, tops,' said Odorf. 'Best to be quick. I need to collect some dragon blood and scales, and check they're in good health. We will meet back here in one hour.'

'But you're not coming with us?' asked Naldy uneasily.

Before Odorf could answer, Ralph interrupted. 'I can still see you both,' he declared nervously.

'Yes,' said Odorf, smiling calmly. 'You're right, Ralph. We can still see each other. The Gerlhend potion will only make you invisible to beasts, so if you catch sight of Maverick, it won't protect you. We best be quick now.'

Odorf continued up the mountain before Naldy or Ralph could ask any more questions.

'Do you want to go first?' suggested Ralph, eyeing the dark fissure in the rock.

Naldy reluctantly squeezed through the small gap in the boulder, hearing Ralph close behind her.

'I don't like that Odorf isn't coming into the cave with us,' grumbled Ralph.

'Tread quietly,' whispered Naldy tensely. 'The potion might make us invisible to the dragons, but she didn't say it'd mask the sound of us coming.'

It was pitch-black inside the cave, and they couldn't see a thing. The place had a strong, woody scent.

'We need light, Ralph, but I can't do magic.'

'The matches,' whispered Ralph, his voice clearly proud that he'd suggested she pack them.

Naldy leant down and, as silently as she could, rummaged through her rucksack. She found the matches at the bottom of her bag.

'Are you sure this is a good idea?' asked Naldy.

'We need to see what we're looking at,' said Ralph. 'How else do we search for the books? I don't think any dragons are in this cave right now.'

She lit a match and was relieved to see that Ralph was correct—no dragons were currently inside the gloomy cave.

The cavern was larger than Naldy had expected. The rocky walls were charred black, yet the cave had a damp feel. They began searching for signs of books.

The match burned Naldy's fingers as the flame reached its end, and she dropped it just as the light flickered out. She fumbled for another and struck it.

'Here,' said Ralph, passing her a large stick he'd found on the cave floor.

Naldy struggled to light the end of the stick, and it took nearly half the box of matches before it caught fire.

'Why is it so damp in here?' asked Naldy, frustrated. Even though she couldn't perform magic at the moment, she was thankful to be a witch. The struggle with fire reminded her how crucial it was to find the Devante—she didn't want to rely on silly matches for the rest of her life.

'Remember, we're invisible,' said Ralph. 'But we need to be quiet as we walk. Let's find these books and get out of here.'

'We might be invisible, Ralph, but I'm not sure the flame will be.'

Naldy and Ralph slowly wandered through the cave, but there were no books—only blackened rock. They eventually came to a corner flooded with light.

'The entrance is up here,' said Naldy, extinguishing the burning stick as sufficient light streamed in from the enormous rocky opening.

They made their way to the edge of the cave. The view was daunting. They were midway up an immense rockface, and across the ravine, on the opposite side, they could see three more shadowy caves in the parallel wall of stone. Naldy glanced down to gauge their height—far below, a stream wound its way through the ravine.

'Well, no dragons,' said Ralph thankfully, breathing in the mountain air and stepping away from the edge as a precaution.

'No books either,' said Naldy. 'We should look around to make sure we haven't missed anything. Then we can check the other caves.'

'How are we getting across to those other caves?'

'I don't know,' said Naldy uneasily. She stared across the ravine. It would surely take them half a day to descend, cross the gorge, and then scale the opposite rock wall. The Gerlhend potion wouldn't last that long.

'NALDY!'

Ralph's panic-stricken voice echoed off the cave walls. Naldy spun around to see what had frightened him. Sprawled over one of the blackened rocks was a charcoal-coloured magic carpet.

'Is that...'

'It's my carpet,' said Ralph, picking it up from the large rock. 'It's turned the colour of Maverick's eyes. They must have been here already.'

'Do you think they've slain the dragons?'

'Nope,' replied Ralph feebly, lifting his head in horror as he fixed his gaze on something in the sky behind Naldy. She heard something large land at the cave entrance. Ralph's face turned pale.

Before Naldy could turn around, she felt a surge of humid, warm breath and caught the scent of rotting fish.

'Don't move,' whispered Ralph. 'We're invisible, so it can't see us.'

But Naldy ignored Ralph and slowly swivelled around. An enormous dragon stood at the entrance of the cave. Its scales were a magnificent golden-brown, shiny and reflective. Its neck was elegantly elongated, and its sharp claws gripped the rock. The dragon's bat-like wings were folded sleekly behind its back. But its slanted golden eyes were the most striking feature—so captivating that Naldy couldn't look away.

'I think it can see us,' whispered Naldy.

Sure enough, its gaze was fixed on the exact spot where she stood.

'Quiet,' Ralph whispered as softly as he could.

Naldy slowly edged further into the cave, careful not to make a sound with each step. But as she retreated, the dragon's eyes remained locked on her.

'Ralph?'

'Quiet, Naldy.'

'I don't think we're invisible.'

Grey smoke rose from the dragon's nostrils, and it started—in an almost regal fashion—to march its clawed feet into the cave.

'Run,' whispered Naldy.

They both jumped out of the way as red-hot fire billowed from the dragon's open mouth, scorching the cave's wall.

Ralph instinctively leapt onto his magic carpet, grabbing Naldy and pulling her on behind him.

The carpet narrowly missed another jet of flame as they darted past the narrow gap between the cave roof and the dragon's scaled back, shooting out into the open air above the vast ravine.

Naldy's heart was steadying now that they were out of the cave and in the sun's rays. But her pulse soon quickened again when she turned and was reminded—dragons could fly.

'Can you go any faster, Ralph!'

The dragon's immense wings were outstretched,

and its pointed tail extended. The beast was an expert flier, effortlessly gliding closer to them. Just as Naldy thought things couldn't get any worse, she saw a second dragon appear at the entrance of one of the other caves.

'Ralph?'

'I'm trying to concentrate, Naldy!'

'I think the dragon chasing us is only a youngling.'

The dragon perched by the entrance of the cave was twice the size of the one chasing them.

'Ralph!'

Ralph's carpet swerved as another breath of fire narrowly missed them.

By the cave's entrance, the adult dragon pushed off the rock and spread its monstrously large wings, coming to aid the younger beast in its chase.

'Do you think Odorf wanted us killed?' shouted Ralph as he struggled to keep hold of the carpet's corners.

Naldy thought it a fair assumption that their travel companion had betrayed them. As the adult dragon approached, she could hear the flapping of enormous wings pounding the air.

Peering over the side of the carpet, Naldy spotted the river below and realised they might be able to seek sanctuary there.

'The water, Ralph!'

He understood and immediately steered the carpet downward at a neck-breaking pace. They were flying so fast that Naldy nearly toppled from the magic carpet. The two beasts showed no sign of letting up. Smoke billowed eagerly from the young dragon's nostrils as it stretched its wings and craned its neck. The larger dragon was close behind, and Naldy had the impression that the adult was teaching the younger dragon to hunt.

Naldy and Ralph plunged headfirst into the cold river. They were fortunate it was deep, as the force of the impact sent them far beneath the surface. Above, a yellow mass of fire struck the water, followed by the blurred outline of the dragons' undersides skimming across the river. The current carried them downstream, and they held their breaths for as long as they could before surfacing.

They gasped for air, relieved to see the dragons had given up the chase and were no longer in sight. The river swept them along, and they swam towards the edge. Naldy was about to climb out of the water.

'Wait!' shouted Ralph warningly.

Across the other side of the bank, an enormous reddish-brown dragon lay on the stones. But it wasn't moving.

'Is it sleeping?' asked Ralph.

'I think it's dead,' said Naldy softly, cautiously lifting herself out of the water.

The dragon wasn't breathing. Naldy noticed a brutal wound near its stomach, oozing reddish-blue blood that trickled into the river.

'I thought we were meant to be invisible!' said Ralph, climbing out of the river with his magic carpet and slumping onto the wet stones. 'That one over there is definitely dead.'

The dragon's eyes unsettled Naldy the most. They were slightly open and strangely black, as if all the colour had drained from them.

'I think Odorf may have used us as bait,' said Naldy sadly.

'But why?'

'Think about it, Ralph. Why did she take us with her so readily? Why not take one of the witches from her commune? She told us that she didn't care about the survival of the Devante.'

'You think it was her intention to kill us then?' asked Ralph, squeezing out the water from his magic carpet, which had changed back to its brilliant blue hue.

'I don't know,' said Naldy, her wet black hair sticking to her face. 'All I know is she gave us a potion that didn't work, and then she sent us walking right into a cave to be eaten.'

'Do you think Maverick and Getergrin were eaten by dragons?' asked Ralph hopefully. He shook the remainder of the water from his soaked magic carpet before laying it over a rock to dry.

'By the looks of that'—Naldy cast a sad glance at the dead dragon on the opposite bank—'it appears they've come and gone.'

'It's horrible,' said Ralph, his voice cracking. 'To kill something on the verge of extinction, and so heartlessly. Even if the things did try to eat us.'

'I would take a guess and bet the Devante were in that poor dragon's cave. Maverick probably killed the dragon to get the books.'

'Right you are,' said a familiar voice from behind them.

A blue light collided with Ralph, paralysing him and sending him dropping to the ground. Naldy spun around, searching for the source of the spell, but it was too late. A second blue light struck her, and she fell.

'Naldy, I can't move,' said Ralph, alarmed.

'You are right,' said Maverick coldly. 'We did have to kill the filthy beast to collect the books.'

—Chapter Eighteen—

THE HONEST LIE

Maverick's polished black shoes stopped beside Naldy's motionless body. Using the tip of his cane, he rolled her onto her back, forcing her to stare up into his smirking face. Getergrin stood proudly behind him, outlined by the cloudless blue sky.

'You got what you came for,' said Naldy bitterly. 'Now let us go.'

Maverick clicked his tongue as he strode towards Ralph, prodding him with the cane.

'Sit them up,' Maverick commanded. 'I want them to see this.'

The smile on Getergrin's face waned as he struggled to prop their bodies in a sitting position. Maverick's spell had caused their heads to loll comically onto their chests, forcing Getergrin to sit behind them and take a firm hold of their hair to keep them upright.

'What do you want with us?' asked Ralph.

Maverick reached a spindly hand into his black cloak pocket, retrieving a small, unremarkable, faded pink book.

'Rosea,' Naldy remarked, instantly recognising

the tattered book as a Devante. It was the entire reason they had spent weeks journeying through Edengar.

'Quite right,' said Maverick. 'The lowest-ranking Devante in existence. It's a pity we had to kill the father to take it.'

Maverick cast a mock sympathetic glance towards the dead dragon on the opposite riverbank, then threw the book at their feet. Naldy wished she could break free from the spell to swoop down and protect it.

'You'll tell us where we can find the Corium,' said Maverick, pointing his cane at the pink book, 'or we will destroy little Rosea, like we destroyed Rubrum, Aurantiaco, and that poor daddy dragon.'

'We don't know where any of the others are,' said Naldy.

Ralph remained silent beside her, but when Naldy looked in his direction, she saw tears streaming across his cheeks. He had given up. Like Naldy, he knew it was hopeless, and their journey through Edengar had been for nothing.

A fireball shot mercilessly from the end of Maverick's cane—Rosea burst into flames.

'No! Please!' cried Naldy—but her pleading did no good, for the pink book was already beyond repair.

'Getergrin,' Maverick commanded.

The round man let Ralph and Naldy's heads flop to their chests. They could hear Getergrin rummaging through his cloak pocket before he carelessly tossed a deep blue book over their heads.

It landed beside the smouldering fire with a thud. Getergrin raised their heads again, forcing them to helplessly watch.

'Let us give it another go,' said Maverick, running a hand through his greasy black hair before tapping the blue book with the tip of his cane. Beside it, the small pink book was already nothing but embers and ashes. 'So far, you've managed to know the location of every Devante on the list. Yet... you expect me to believe you don't know the location of the Corium?'

'We don't,' said Ralph, his voice cracking.

'Come now, there's no need for tears,' said Maverick, eyeing Ralph with disgust. 'I give you my word that if you tell us the location, we will let you walk away with the Caeruleum. What a pretty blue book it is.'

Maverick pointed his cane threateningly at the Caeruleum, which lay between them.

'We don't know,' said Naldy desperately. 'Please, we really don't know. Don't ruin another.'

Maverick slowly pushed the Caeruleum into the cinders with his cane, and the book caught fire. Naldy's heart pounded heavily. They had now lost two more Devante, and the list was rapidly shrinking. Naldy felt overwhelmingly foolish for ever believing she could be the one to save the Devante. A guilty lump formed in her throat as she couldn't shake the feeling that she was letting down every witch and wizard in the world.

'You want us to use force, do you?' asked

Maverick, pulling a metal book from his cloak and carelessly tossing it to the ground. It landed with a clink beside the dwindling fire.

Getergrin chuckled from behind them. Naldy wished the other dragons would come to chase Maverick and Getergrin away. She wondered if they feared approaching the wizard because he had slain the dragon on the opposite riverbank.

'This could be yours. Beautiful, isn't it,' said Maverick, as the sun reflected dazzlingly off the book's sleek metal cover. 'Imagine the things you could achieve with a Devante. It's already helped fix your broken bones, Naldy. All you have to do—'

'Alright, we'll tell you!' blurted Ralph.

'I'm glad to hear it,' Maverick sneered. 'It would have been a shame to see Metallum perish too.'

'But you must give us your word,' said Ralph confidently, 'that if we tell you, you'll let us have the Devante. And you'll let us go unharmed.'

'Unharmed. Yes, of course.'

Ralph's delivery was so convincing that Naldy wondered if he really did know the Corium's location.

'The Corium,' Ralph said boldly, 'is hidden deep in the Mortous Woods.'

Maverick's smile faded. He tapped his cane hard on the ground, and a white ball of smoke floated out of its tip, hovering between them.

'Again, boy,' demanded Maverick.

Ralph hesitated, staring apprehensively at the floating ball of white smoke.

'I said the Corium is deep within the heart of the Mortous Woods.'

The orb of wispy smoke shifted from white to a deep shade of blood red. Judging by the expression on Maverick's face, this colour wasn't what he'd wanted. He waved the smoke away with his cane and pointed it threateningly at the metal book.

'You think I'm playing games? I've had enough of your tiresome antics.'

A black flame shot powerfully from the end of Maverick's cane, and the metal book slowly melted under the intense heat of the spell.

Naldy's throat felt dry as she anxiously watched Metallum liquefy into a messy silver puddle. She was too shocked to speak, and it felt as though all her hope were melting along with the metal book. The silver turned to black ash, and Maverick lifted his cane, stopping the jet of black fire. The book had been destroyed.

'You think you can simply lie to me?' asked Maverick, retrieving another book from his inner cloak pocket. Although Naldy had never seen this spellbook before, she instantly knew what it was from its rich golden cover. Maverick had possession of the Aurum.

'Please,' said Ralph. 'Just let us go. You've got what you came for.'

Maverick didn't throw the golden book to the floor. Instead, he held onto it tightly with his long fingers.

'Oh, you recognise this, do you?' Maverick asked,

noticing them gazing in wonder at the golden Devante. 'I've used Aurum to create a spell that tells me if you lie. Come now, don't waste any more of my time. I am a very busy man.'

Naldy was awed by the medium-sized book. It was by far the most beautiful Devante she had ever seen. Its thin, golden cover gleamed wondrously in the sunlight, and its pages were crafted from delicate gold parchment. A coat of arms featuring two mule deer was embossed on its glossy cover.

Maverick placed the Aurum back inside his cloak, and Naldy felt a pang of sadness as it vanished from their sight.

'Let us try again, shall we? Where is the Corium?'

Naldy felt beaten. They didn't possess any of the Devante and had been unable to prevent the destruction of five of them. They had failed at every turn and had no clue where to find the remaining Devante.

Maverick tapped his cane hard on the ground, and another ball of white smoke rose between them.

'Do not consider lying, or there will be dire consequences. Where is the Corium?'

Ralph swallowed, then in a small voice, responded, 'I don't know.'

The white ball of smoke turned a deep blue.

'He's telling the truth,' muttered Getergrin from behind, still clutching their heads.

Maverick waved the smoke away.

'He is, yes. How interesting... hmm... so, the girl hasn't told you? Of course not—the information is too precious to share with you.'

Naldy knew it was all over. The moment Maverick asked her the question, the white smoke would confirm she had no clue where the Corium was.

'Your turn, girl,' he whispered, glaring icily at her.

The wizard tapped his cane, and another white ball of smoke drifted from it. Naldy knew she had no choice but to refuse to answer him. As long as Maverick believed she knew where the Corium was, they would be safe. She just had to keep silent.

'Where is the Corium located?'

'She doesn't know!' shouted Ralph.

'I wasn't asking you. You're both determined to make this difficult for me. Oh, dear, dear, dear.'

Maverick clicked his tongue as he walked through the white smoke, which instantly dispersed. He grabbed the collar of Ralph's shirt as Getergrin promptly let go. Maverick dragged Ralph a few metres away and shoved him violently to the ground. There was nothing Naldy could do.

'Make her watch this,' instructed Maverick, lifting his cane and pointing it recklessly at Ralph.

Getergrin already had his chubby hands clasped around Naldy's hair, but he tightened his grip for good measure.

'Please,' said Naldy. 'Please, I don't know. I really don't know.'

'We will see about that,' said Maverick, tapping his cane on the ground. White smoke floated between them, forming a translucent orb as

Maverick aimed his cane at Ralph.

'Do you know the location of the Corium?'

Naldy hesitated, knowing it was useless and that she had no choice but to answer him. If she didn't, Ralph would be harmed.

'No,' she said softly, 'I don't know where the Corium is.'

The white smoke did nothing for a moment, but then, to Naldy's surprise, it turned scarlet red.

'She's lying,' said Getergrin from behind her.

'I'm not. I don't know where it is!'

The smoke pulsed red again.

Naldy was dumbfounded. She honestly didn't know where to find the Corium, but the glowing smoke clearly thought otherwise. A greedy, malicious smile spread across Maverick's pale face.

'My dear girl, have you not had enough of playing games?' he asked, his tone oddly calm. 'You do know where the Corium is, and you will tell me, or he dies. Slowly and painfully.'

'But...'

'Let me ask you again, Naldy...'

'I don't know!'

'Where is the Corium located?'

'Please, I really don't know.'

A crimson light blasted from the end of Maverick's cane and collided with Ralph's chest. Ralph howled in pain, twisting uncontrollably.

'No! Please!' shouted Naldy. It was hopeless. She couldn't move.

The crimson light ceased, and Ralph's body

became motionless, apart from his shallow breathing.

'Tell me, or I'll make it worse for him.'

Tears poured down Naldy's face as she frantically searched her thoughts for a way out of the terrible situation. She couldn't understand why Maverick's smoky orb suggested she knew where the Corium was.

'Okay,' she said slowly, trying to buy herself some time. 'I'll tell you the truth.'

Naldy decided she had no option but to lie. She hoped the orb between them would deceive Maverick into believing her. However, she doubted Maverick would spare them once he thought he'd discovered the top Devante's location.

'Time is up, girl! Where is the Corium?'

'The Corium... it's... well... it is in the middle of the Kirkwood Forest.'

The white smoke pulsed momentarily, with everyone's eyes transfixed on it, awaiting its truth. Then, it turned scarlet red.

'You liar,' said Maverick, flicking his cane and shooting another fierce crimson light from its end. Ralph's body twisted unnaturally, his teeth clenched in an effort to endure the pain.

Naldy shouted, but there was nothing more she could do. As if sensing her desire to break free from Maverick's immobilising spell, Getergrin placed his free hand on her head.

Naldy didn't want to show Maverick how much she cared about Ralph, knowing it would only encourage him, but she couldn't stop the tears.

'Now, Naldy,' said Maverick, lifting his cane and giving Ralph a brief respite from the wicked spell. 'Oh, no need for your tears, my dear girl. It's obvious how much you care for this young man, but let's not waste tears when there's a simple solution.'

Ralph's body continued to squirm involuntarily, even without the command of Maverick's vicious magic. His eyes rolled back into his head, and his mouth hung limply open.

'The end to all this terrible pain is quite simple,' said Maverick. 'All you need to do is tell me, truthfully, where the Corium is.'

Then Naldy saw the blood. Fresh red blood dampened the chest of Ralph's cloak, soaking his clothes from a wound on his chest. Naldy knew he wouldn't survive another of Maverick's spells.

'Tell me the truth, girl. Because he will die if you don't.'

'Alright,' replied Naldy meekly. 'I do know the location of the Corium.'

The ball of white smoke flashed a brilliant blue. Maverick gripped his cane eagerly.

'Yes, girl, go on... where is it located?'

But Naldy hesitated. She didn't know what to say. She honestly had no clue where the highest-ranking Devante was. She knew that if she gave the wrong location, the smoke would pulse red, and Maverick would surely finish Ralph off.

Crack! A brilliant white spark knocked the wizard off his feet, sending his cane flying. Another spark whooshed past Naldy's head, narrowly missing her, and collided with Getergrin's bald, round face. Naldy dropped limply to the ground as Getergrin had unwillingly released his grip on her. Now lying sideways, she witnessed another tremendous white spark narrowly miss Maverick's leg as he scrambled to retrieve his cane. Although she couldn't see the conjurer of the white sparks, she had a clear view of Maverick desperately grabbing his cane and turning to face his opponent.

'You killed a dragon!' Naldy heard Odorf shout, enraged. 'You murderer!'

Maverick shot red spells in the direction of Odorf's voice, but more white sparks furiously flew back at him. It was clear that Odorf was a more skilled witch than Maverick was a wizard. Before Maverick could reach into his cloak pocket to summon the Aurum's magic, Odorf unleashed flashes like shooting stars, knocking Maverick off his feet again.

Getergrin cowered low, attempting to use Naldy's paralysed body as a shield. Odorf's spells forced Maverick to decide it was best to flee. The wizard dodged an oncoming white spark, ducking his head and using Ralph's limp body for protection. Ralph was still twitching slightly, his clothes saturated with blood. Maverick spotted the magic carpet on the rock beside Ralph and snatched it up.

'Wait for me!' cried Getergrin, scrambling over Naldy's body towards him.

Spells whizzed wildly, continuing their relentless

onslaught. Naldy was surprised Odorf could produce such impressive magic.

Getergrin awkwardly clambered onto the carpet behind Maverick, struggling to lift his stocky legs. More spells flew over Naldy's head as she watched the magic carpet glide upwards and disappear from sight.

A green light struck her body, and Naldy felt a sudden release within herself—she had regained movement, realising Odorf had somehow reversed the spell that had bound her. Another green light collided with Ralph, and he lifted his arms to his bloody chest. She didn't waste any time and rushed over to him.

'Ralph!'

'Naldy,' called Odorf from behind her. 'Come here, quickly, now.'

Odorf was lying on the ground, her cloak a blood-stained mess. Maverick's spells had done more damage than Naldy had initially realised.

'Odorf!' Naldy exclaimed as she hurried over to the woman.

'I thought the Gerlhend potion would work,' said Odorf, breathing heavily. 'The blood used to make it was taken from that poor dragon lying dead over there. If the—'

'Dragon's dead,' interrupted Naldy, trying to save Odorf the effort of explaining, 'the potion will be ineffective.'

'Yes, it's why you weren't invisible. I'm so sorry, Naldy. I didn't know they'd slain the dragon.'

'I need to bandage your wounds,' said Naldy, staring at her blood-soaked cloak. 'Ralph's too, but I can't do much more because it's daylight.'

'In my satchel,' said Odorf, pointing to the pouch tied around her waist. 'The blue bottle. I only have the one. You need to put it on Ralph's wounds. It will stop the bleeding.'

'But what about you?'

'My wounds are too severe,' replied Odorf as Naldy unlatched the potion satchel and took out the blue phial. 'There is just one, and you'll need to use the whole mixture for his wounds to heal properly. Now listen carefully—Maverick doesn't only want the Devante destroyed; he wants the dragons killed too. You must stop him. You must protect them.'

Odorf stopped talking. Her breathing became raspy, as if liquid had entered her lungs.

'Tell my people the dragons are in danger... their lives'—she took a rattling breath—'they cannot live without the dragons.'

Odorf stopped breathing. Her eyes glazed over, and she became still. She was gone.

Tears streamed down Naldy's cheeks as she lifted her body from the ground and rushed over to where Ralph lay. Her vision was blurred from crying. She knelt beside him. He was breathing steadily but was clearly in bad shape.

'Ralph?'

'Naldy,' he said weakly. 'Is Odorf alright?'

'I've got something to help you, Ralph.'

'I don't think I'm going to make it home.'

'I won't let you talk like that,' said Naldy, as she struggled to pull the cork from the blue phial. 'Odorf gave me this potion to stop the bleeding. If I can just remove this cork...'

'I thought you said potions were silly,' he replied with a faint smile. He had a faraway look.

Naldy frantically tried to remove the stopper from the potion bottle, but her hands trembled so much that she couldn't get the cork to budge.

'Take your time,' said Ralph weakly. 'I'm not going anywhere.'

Naldy gave a hard tug, and the fragile blue phial slipped from her fingers—smashing on the stony ground.

'No!' Naldy cried, desperately trying to scoop up the spilt liquid. It was no use. The blue potion quickly evaporated from the rocky surface.

'Naldy?'

'No, Ralph, no, I... I...' but she couldn't bear to say more.

'Naldy, it's alright.'

'It's not alright,' said Naldy. Her eyes were so wet and burning with emotion that nothing was in focus. 'How could I have been so clumsy? I let it slip from my grip, Ralph. There's none left. It's all gone. It's evaporated.'

'What about the spell?' asked Ralph weakly.

'There's no spell to heal wounds, Ralph,' said Naldy sadly. 'The magic doesn't exist.'

'Yes, it does,' Ralph whispered. 'Maverick invented it with the Devante, remember? When he healed your broken leg in Kirkwood Forest.'

'The sun is still up,' said Naldy. 'I could try, but even if my curse has broken, it could still go terribly wrong. It could make things worse.'

Ralph coughed, expelling a phlegmy blood clot from his mouth. Naldy wiped the blood from his face and glanced at the sky. The sun was still far from setting. She knew she had no choice but to attempt the spell Maverick had invented with the Aurantiaco. Ralph wouldn't make it if she didn't try.

'What were the words?' asked Naldy frantically. '*Sanitatem* something…'

'*Restituere*,' Ralph replied feebly.

'*Sanitatem Restituere*,' she said, holding her shaking hands over Ralph's chest.

But nothing happened. The blood continued to ooze slowly.

'*Sanitatem Restituere*,' she repeated, her voice filled with desperation. Still, nothing. 'The sun is in the sky, Ralph… I'm cursed.'

He didn't have the energy to respond. Naldy held her hands closer to his chest.

'Please work, please… *Sanitatem Restituere*.'

Nothing happened.

'I'm so sorry, Ralph. It's not working… It's not… I'm so very sorry.'

Naldy took Ralph's hand in hers and held it gently. The sun shone mockingly, the river gurgling peacefully, and there was nothing more Naldy could do but stay by his side, waiting for him to die.

'Ralph?'

He didn't reply. He couldn't. He could only breathe unsteadily in and out.

'I'm sorry I dragged you on this foolish quest... I really am...'

She lay beside him, wanting to be with him during his last moments.

Ralph let out an agonising shriek, startling her. His hands gripped hers tightly, and his face twisted in pain.

'Ralph!' said Naldy, sitting up in alarm. 'I knew it was too dangerous! I knew I shouldn't have attempted the spell.'

Ralph's body suddenly relaxed, and he stopped howling. His breathing became steady.

'Do you actually know where the Corium is?' he mumbled as the blood on his chest ceased flowing.

'Ralph? I think it's working! My spell is working!'

And it was. The blood on Ralph's chest was slowly drying up, and his wounds were healing.

'You're squeezing my hand a little tight,' he said.

'Sorry,' said Naldy, not letting go of his hand. 'Ralph! You're alive! You're still alive!'

'I don't feel alive,' he replied softly. 'I feel horrible.'

'But you are alive!' said Naldy, joy swelling inside her. 'You are, Ralph! You're going to be alright.'

'Does this mean you've finally learnt the importance of selflessness?'

Ralph tried to sit up but was still too frail.

'You shouldn't move, Ralph.'

'I'm happy your curse has broken, Naldy.'

'I don't care about my curse breaking,' she said,

tenderly pushing him back to the ground. 'I care about you getting better. Don't move. I've stopped the bleeding, but it's a spell I've never used before, and it looks like your chest hasn't fully healed. Your body will have to do the rest of the mending on its own. I'll set the tent up.'

Naldy stood and began approaching Odorf's rucksack to fetch the tent. But when she saw Odorf lying motionless, a wave of grief tightened her chest. She could hear Ralph sobbing behind her, but she couldn't bear to face him. Drained of all energy, Naldy wished she had never sought out the Devante.

—Chapter Nineteen—

THE BURNING AND THE BURIAL

Naldy had set up the tent beside the river. Using her newly restored magic, she had carefully carried Ralph inside and laid him gently in his hammock. She then spent the afternoon hollowing out a small grave with a digging spell.

'Are you sure about this?' Ralph asked weakly, climbing out of the tent and slowly making his way to Naldy.

'You should be resting,' she replied with a reprimanding glare. 'You're going to need your strength for the journey back.'

'I'm not certain we should be camping this close to the caves.'

'We don't have a choice,' said Naldy, glancing up at the expansive rock walls flanking both sides of the river. The dragon caves were visible from their position. 'I think if they wanted to attack us, they'd have done so by now.'

'They did attack us, Naldy.'

'It'll be dark soon, and we can't travel with you in this state. I may have stopped the bleeding, Ralph, but your body still needs time to fully recover.'

The sky glowed with a brilliant reddish hue, and the light was slowly fading. Naldy gently levitated Odorf into the hole she had dug.

'None of this feels real,' said Ralph sadly.

'*Terra,*' Naldy uttered, and the mound of soil beside the grave lifted and delicately covered Odorf's body.

Naldy lowered her head. She felt their quest to save the Devante had been both selfish and foolish. It hadn't been worth all the pain, suffering, and death it had caused. She was plagued with guilt, believing that Odorf would still be alive if they hadn't sought her help at the commune.

'What are we doing with the dragon?' asked Ralph, casting a pitying glance at the dead beast across the river.

Naldy would have liked to dig a hole for the dragon too, but it was enormous. She knew she wouldn't have the energy to complete it, even with her newly restored magic.

'It'll have to be cremated. *Comburite.*'

A small fireball shot from Naldy's palm, engulfing the dragon's body. She felt frail and light-headed as the flames consumed the dragon's flesh.

'Naldy, look!'

Ralph's pale face was turned towards the wall of rock, where three adult and two adolescent dragons stood at the entrances to their caves. Their necks were craned high as they let out a series of echoing roars. Naldy knew it wasn't an angry call. They had come to grieve and pay their respects. The dragons began to breathe magnificent jets of orange and blue fire high into the sky.

'They are beautiful creatures,' said Naldy softly to herself.

'Are you still certain you want to camp here tonight?'

'I feel a strange sense of security,' Naldy replied, 'with the dragons watching over us.'

They stood in silence for some time, watching the flames slowly consume the dead dragon. At Naldy's insistence, Ralph finally retired to the tent to continue his rest.

Naldy lingered outside alone, watching the sun dip behind the great rock wall as darkness settled around her. The warmth of the fire comforted her, and she breathed in the fresh mountain air as ash and smoke drifted away.

When the fire burned low, Naldy returned to the tent to find Ralph fast asleep. She climbed into her own hammock, her body aching. Glancing sadly at Odorf's empty hammock, she cried softly, hoping not to wake Ralph.

The following day, Naldy woke early, her eyes sore from grief. She made her way to the river and, using magic, caught two river trout.

When she re-entered the tent with the freshly cooked fish, she found Ralph awake. He was still unhealthily pale, but he had a little more energy after resting through the night.

'See, Ralph, we didn't get eaten by dragons in our sleep.'

'Naldy, look here. I found a map in Odorf's rucksack. Where did you get the fish from?'

'The river, of course. Now that my magic has returned permanently, I can do a few more things to help us.'

'Smells delicious, thank you,' said Ralph, taking the hot river trout from her and hungrily stuffing his mouth.

'I imagine the dragons snack on them,' said Naldy, examining the map. 'I'm not sure how helpful this will be, Ralph. It's just a mass of mountains.'

'When are we going home?' he asked with his mouth full of trout. 'I think we should leave today. I don't want to be anywhere near those dragons.'

'I'd quite like to stay here forever,' said Naldy. She had little desire to travel home and didn't want to think about continuing the search for the remaining Devante.

'I can pack up the tent,' Ralph offered.

'No,' said Naldy, eyeing his pale complexion. 'You need to rest and regain your strength before we go anywhere. We should spend some time here to rejuvenate—at least a week. I think we both need rest.'

'A week! Naldy, we need to catch up to Maverick.'

'Forget the Devante, Ralph! You look ghastly, and your chest needs to heal fully. Don't argue with me, or I'll hex you.'

To Ralph's dismay, the dragons occasionally visited the river for water and fish. They kept their distance, and neither party disturbed the other.

Naldy believed the dragons avoided them because they sensed no threat. Ralph, however, thought the dragons stayed away because Maverick had frightened them off by killing the father.

The weather remained sunny and warm for the rest of the week. Naldy spent much of her time by the riverside, lost in thoughts about Odorf. She felt a heavy sense of responsibility for Odorf's death and for the destruction of the Devante.

Ralph, meanwhile, spent most of his time sleeping, with no energy for anything else. This suited Naldy, as she welcomed the solitude and the chance to be alone with her thoughts. Hours would pass in quiet reflection by the water, and she found solace in watching the river flow.

On their tenth day by the river, Ralph's condition improved considerably.

'Can we leave tomorrow then? I'm much better, and you can't deny that.'

'I suppose so,' said Naldy as they strolled lazily along the riverbank, searching for edible mushrooms. 'If I'm honest, I'd like never to leave.'

'I don't know how much more fish I can stomach,' said Ralph. 'When we return, you'll have to make us one of your scrumptious butternut pumpkin pies.'

He bent to pick up a small mushroom—the first they'd found. 'I've wanted to ask you something, actually. I've been meaning to for some time now.'

'What is it, Ralph?'

'The Devante—'

'I don't want to talk about the Devante, Ralph,'

said Naldy bitterly. 'Just leave it alone, okay.'

She marched away from him. Ralph didn't bring up the Devante again that day, and Naldy was glad of this.

At first light, Ralph packed up the tent while Naldy gathered wildflowers. Ralph seemed relieved to be leaving the ravine, but Naldy felt a pang of sadness to be departing. Together, they laid the colourful flowers Naldy had collected on the dragon's ashes and over Odorf's grave.

'I don't know how we'll do this without you,' said Ralph, kneeling beside the dirt covering Odorf. 'You will be missed.'

After their tearful goodbyes, they made their way downstream along the river. They soon encountered a rocky stairwell leading precariously up to the ravine's top. Naldy kept glancing across the valley, hoping for one last glimpse of the magnificent dragons, but they were nowhere in sight.

As suspected, the map proved useless. After the first day of walking, neither Naldy nor Ralph could pinpoint their location on it.

'I don't remember seeing those boulders,' said Ralph as they slowly ambled down the rocky mountain.

'We saw plenty of boulders on the way here,' Naldy pointed out.

'Yes, though none looked quite like that.'

Naldy ignored him and pressed on, though she feared Ralph might be right. They had both assumed Odorf would lead the way back, and after just one day without her guidance, they found themselves lost.

'See, Ralph!' said Naldy, stopping to sit on a nearby rock. 'We should have stayed in the ravine. We're going to die trying to find our way home.'

Each rock and tree they passed seemed unfamiliar.

'Let's camp here tonight and continue tomorrow,' Ralph suggested.

'Ralph, see if you can find the Hegervege potion in Odorf's satchel, and I'll try to catch us some wild rabbit for dinner.'

Odorf's satchel held several potion bottles, none of which were labelled. Ralph recognised the Hegervege potion by its distinctive hexagonal phial and pungent smell. Naldy delicately uncorked it, and the herby scent wafted strongly through the air.

'What do you think the rest of them do?' asked Ralph, rummaging through the collection of coloured glass bottles.

'I don't know, and I'm not sure it's worth the risk testing them out.'

Sadly, no wild rabbits appeared, and they went to bed hungry. They woke up ravenous the following day.

Despite Odorf's rucksack containing more items than Naldy's, it was surprisingly lighter, so Ralph had been tasked with carrying it.

They walked slowly, not only because Ralph was still regaining his strength but also out of fear of missing a recognisable landmark. They were lost and worried that moving too quickly might cause them to overlook a familiar snow-capped summit or a rocky slope.

On their fifth day, as they trekked up a particularly steep incline, Ralph stubbornly brought up the Devante.

'I said I don't want to talk about it, Ralph.'

'The smoke said you know the location of the Corium, Naldy. You can't ignore that fact.'

'I don't know,' said Naldy, clenching her fists in frustration.

'Maverick's truth detector spell was invented by one of the Devante. So, you *must* know. You're just refusing to tell me for some reason. Don't you trust me? After all we've been through.'

'Ralph,' said Naldy, stopping to face him, 'if I knew where the Corium was, do you think I'd have wasted our time marching us through these dreaded mountains?'

'Maybe you do know, but you've somehow forgotten.'

'The truth is,' said Naldy firmly, 'I don't know, so let's leave it at that, can we?'

They continued in silence, not speaking again for a couple of days.

Their breaths were heavy as they trudged up and down Edengar's treacherous slopes.

Food was scarce; they found the occasional patch of wild mushrooms and some meagre raspberries, but for the most part, they were left hungry.

'It's hardly a map when it's just a page covered

with mountains,' said Naldy, irritated. She had restrained herself from tearing the map up on more than one occasion. 'These dribbly bits of text don't help at all. Listen to this: *Mount Stugg—unsafe, covered in toxic moss.*'

'Look,' said Ralph, inspecting the map over her shoulder, 'we at least know we are somewhere around here, between the ravine and the tunnel.'

'Yes,' snapped Naldy, 'but for all we know, we're currently standing on Mount Stugg and will die in our sleep from toxic moss!'

'At least then we would know where we are.'

Naldy had resigned herself to the belief they'd likely die from some horrible mountain mishap. Her rumbling stomach was a frequent reminder that if they didn't meet their end through a mishap, they would eventually pass out from hunger due to the lack of available food.

'I don't want vultures to eat us,' said Naldy. 'We need to find something edible soon, or I won't be able to go on.'

'Do you hear that?' asked Ralph, stopping abruptly.

'Hear what, Ralph? You're scaring me.'

He held up a hand to silence her, and Naldy listened intently. She couldn't hear anything except the soft breeze.

'What is it, Ralph?'

Without answering, he took off down the mountain. Naldy struggled to keep up, her heart pounding frantically.

'Ralph?'

He came to an unexpected halt, and Naldy nearly toppled over him. Ralph knelt and picked something up from the ground.

'Naldy, look! We're going the right way!'

'That blooming earring.'

'I could hear it calling to me,' said Ralph, turning over the green emerald in his hands.

'I suppose at least we know we're heading in the right direction now.'

For the rest of the day, Ralph kept glancing at the piece of jewellery and smiling happily. Naldy refrained from scolding him, and though she didn't want to admit it, finding the earring had lifted her spirits.

'You're jealous because it doesn't call to you,' said Ralph, throwing the earring up and proudly catching it.

'You're right,' said Naldy mockingly. 'If only Aunt Geraldine's trinket fancied me as much as it fancies you.'

'You can't confiscate it from me again because it has saved us,' said Ralph. 'We owe it our gratitude.'

'We're not saved from Edengar yet,' said Naldy. 'We've still a long way to go.'

Their luck didn't stop at finding the earring. That night, Naldy uncorked the Hegervege potion, and several rabbits appeared. Using a *Prosterno* spell, she caught one and prepared a warm, hearty meal for them. After dinner, Naldy's thoughts churned over Maverick's ball of smoke and its insistence that she knew the location of the Corium. As she stared into the crackling fire, her unease grew, and her mind drifted to the image of the dragon Maverick had slain.

'Ralph,' she said finally, breaking the silence, 'I think she might have been right.'

'Who?'

'Odorf. She believed Maverick wanted the dragons dead. I don't think he just wants the Devante destroyed. I think he might want to destroy everything magical.'

'Why would he want to do that?' he asked in disbelief. 'He's a wizard himself.'

'I don't know,' said Naldy, lifting another small log onto the fire. 'But think about it: Maverick ruined Harmony's dragon eggs by turning the yolks into scrolls, he's destroying the Devante, and he killed the dragon.'

'Why didn't he kill the other dragons?' Ralph wondered aloud.

'I'm not sure,' said Naldy, frowning. 'Maybe he intended to. I think Odorf might have scared him off.'

Naldy regretted leaving the dragons and wondered if Maverick would return to slay the others.

'We need to stop him, Naldy. We have to find the Corium before he does.'

'I've told you, Ralph,' said Naldy, exasperated, 'I don't know where it is. And I'm not sure we should continue searching for it anyway.'

'Not continue?'

'Looking for these books hasn't done us any good.'

'Naldy, if what you're saying is true, if Maverick is preparing to destroy all magic, then—'

'I'm tired,' said Naldy dismissively. 'I'm going to bed. Put the fire out before you come in.'

The next day, their luck ran out. Grey clouds gathered intimidatingly overhead, and it only took a few hours of walking for them to feel utterly lost again.

'I don't recognise any of these trees. Naldy, recheck the map.'

'The map doesn't help,' she replied sourly. 'Your beloved earring doesn't help. Nothing helps. We'll die in these mountains.'

They carried on walking in strained silence. The grey clouds didn't bring an onslaught of rain —instead, they showered snow. Wrapping their cloaks tightly around their cold bodies, they trekked miserably on, breathing in the icy air. The trees stood glum and frostbitten.

That night, Ralph dropped the Hegervege potion while struggling to uncork the phial. His hands shook from the chill, and the glass bottle emptied onto his cloak before falling and smashing on the icy rock. To add to their troubles, no rabbits appeared, and Ralph was left smelling of pungent herbs.

They lost track of how much time had passed, and both agreed they should at least have arrived at the place where they'd ridden the piglinns.

One icy morning, Ralph reached into Odorf's rucksack, rummaging around for the tent, and his mouth fell open as he pulled out an old metal compass. Naldy refused to speak to him for three whole days.

The snow soon stopped falling, and the sun returned, but this left the rocks slippery from the melting snow and ice.

'I'm not sure how we'll navigate the maze of snow gums,' said Naldy, rubbing her aching legs.

'If we make it that far. I'm more concerned about the piglinns.'

They were so famished that the leaves on the mountain trees were beginning to look appetising.

'We can't eat the trees, Ralph,' said Naldy, catching him staring hungrily at a low-hanging branch.

'But there are little red fruits.'

'They could be poisonous. We mustn't eat anything we don't recognise.'

Even after all these days, Ralph still smelt strongly of the herby Hegervege potion, but no rabbits seemed attracted to the blend of herbs and body odour.

'We should go back the way we came, Naldy. I don't recognise any of this.'

'Everything looks the same to me,' said Naldy, holding the compass in one hand.

They found themselves at the bottom of a rocky chasm. A large crack in the ground was wide enough to fall through. The rocky walls stretched higher as they moved along.

'There!' said Ralph, pointing ahead. Midway up the rock face was the tunnel they had first ventured through. Naldy stared at Odorf's map in disbelief.

'We haven't even passed through the maze of snow gums,' said Naldy, blinking to make sure it wasn't a mirage.

'But it is there! It must be! And there's the gap I wanted to throw a stone down, and Odorf told me off, remember.'

They shared a sombre look at the mention of Odorf before climbing the exposed rocky stairs, which felt more manageable than when they had first descended them. Edengar had made them fitter.

Upon reaching the tunnel's entrance, they were relieved to find it was real and not a mirage.

'Why didn't we take that route to the ravine?' asked Ralph. 'It felt much easier without needing to ride piglinns.'

Naldy stared at the map, trying to figure out where they'd just come from. Scribbled next to it in tiny, messy handwriting were the words: *Avoid this route at all costs. It's perilous. Riddled with pickernups.*

'What is a pickernup?' asked Ralph, reading the map over Naldy's shoulder.

'I don't know. It seems a miracle we didn't find out.'

'I think my lovely green earring protected us,' said Ralph, tossing and catching the jewellery piece. 'It's been my lucky charm.'

'I'm not sure I'd call our journey through Edengar

lucky,' she replied as a ray of sunshine emerged
from behind a fluffy white cloud. 'Some say Edengar
drives people mad, but I think that earring has done
that for you.'

He smiled as the sun reflected from his emerald
stone. Naldy clamped her forefinger and thumb
around Ralph's right earlobe.

'*Perforabit.*'

'Ouch!' cried Ralph, gasping with pain. 'What did
you do that for?'

Ralph reached his own hand up to his earlobe.
There was a tiny hole.

'Give me the earring,' said Naldy, taking it from
him and placing it carefully into his newly pierced
ear. 'Now you can stop staring at it all day long. Keep
it in your ear.'

'That really hurt.'

'If only Aunt Geraldine could see you in it. She'd
turn in her grave. She despised townspeople.'

'Maybe we can find the pair when we get back,'
said Ralph, hopefully. 'You could wear the other one
for luck?'

'We'll never find the pair in the Witch House,' she
said, laughing.

The thought of returning to her cluttered but
comfortable home soothed her.

'Come on,' said Ralph as the brief ray of sunlight
retreated behind the fluffy clouds again. 'We've got
Lignum and the Corium to save. And we'll need to
recover Aurum from Maverick, too.'

Naldy watched as Ralph made his way through

the dark tunnel. In truth, she didn't feel like continuing the quest to find the remaining Devante —it seemed impossible—though something within her told her she mustn't give up. She looked towards the sky and, through the clouds, saw the silhouette of a dragon with its large wings outstretched. It vanished, and Naldy wasn't sure if she'd truly seen it or if it was only her imagination.

'Naldy, are you coming? I can't see a thing. You need to light the torches. Use your magic, now you have it back, or toss me the matches, would you?'

She reached the first torch resting in its ornate bracket on the tunnel's interior wall.

'*Comburite.*'

The torches along the walls burst into flame, casting a soft, flickering glow. Naldy spotted Ralph a little further ahead, eagerly making his way back through the tunnel.

'It is good to have magic.'